BLUE SWORDS

BOOK ONE OF THE CRIMES & CRESTS SAGA

JAMES HORTON

Michael Terence

First published in paperback by
Michael Terence Publishing in 2020
www.mtp.agency

ISBN 9781800940079

I dedicate this book to my children
Jack, Ivy and Joseph,
for you to enjoy in years to come.

CONTENTS

PROLOGUE

The square was full, the mob were angry, and the guards knew the potential outcome of this act of terror that was unfolding before them. The baron laughed, "You call this whore your princess? Watch me spill her blood." Baron Asher pulled a large knife from his belt. The blade was smeared with dried blood from his day of hunting. He placed the blade against his wife's throat and released a chilling laugh.

I was wounded; beaten to the ground like a whipped pup. I was helpless to this serpent demon, who was standing over me. My destiny had been forced into his hands. I couldn't save her, poor Ivy, she was helpless and I was her only hope. I had failed her. I managed to lean my head upright to see her soft skin, marked with swelling and bruising. She was naked from the waist down, belittled and frightened. Her eyes were filled with despair. My mind raced, telling me to get up but I was paralysed, trapped within my body.

The blood of a local man leaked from his corpse, as his lifeless body lay next to mine. I started to think of another, someone I had recently lost, someone I thought I loved, and yet another person I was helpless to save. I was ready to meet her, to join her in the afterlife.

But then a figure appeared - was it my saviour? He walked with presence as he entered the market square. He shouted to my enemy, ordering them to take the fight to him. My faith had been tested but this time, faith had answered my call. He had arrived. His uniform carried the same colours as my own. It was fair to say my inexperience and brash actions had left me fallen and vulnerable, but he would not fall. He was an expert in his trade, fearless and skilful. Just like me he was a blue sword, and he had come to save us.

I

THE SIGN

It was the year 1411 and who I am now is neither here nor there. How I got there, that is the interesting part. For I have loved, lost and bled. Yet still I stand, proud and loyal. All in the name of the Blue Swords.

It was late Spring and the sun was slowly fading away in the distance. I had travelled far across the land of Thear. For days I had trekked over green fields and stone roads. I felt tired, hungry, but enthusiastic as I approach the main gate of Stanford. I had finally arrived. Stanford was a town known for its character and charm. Unlike most towns and villages within the land of Thear, it was extremely diverse. If you were rich, the town enabled you to live a charmed and extravagant lifestyle; if you were poor, the town was a place that would kick you in the gut, whilst you rolled around in the mud on the ground. To some it was bliss, but to others it was a rusty cage, that sliced away at you, the more you tried to escape.

The great stone wall acted as a boundary around the whole town. The stone gave off the message that the town was well prepared and organised for any unwanted attention. At the north side of the town was a well maintained, thick wooden gate which separated the wall. It was a sturdy entrance, wide enough to allow carts used by local traders to enter.

As I stepped off the road and approached the gate, I met my first local. The man was a similar age to me; he couldn't have been much older than eighteen years. He was short but well built. The closer I got the more territorial he appeared. He arched his back, in order to stand taller. He then slowly raised his chest looking rather uncomfortable. His hair was wavy and swept across his head. He was well groomed and clearly took much pride in his appearance. His robes were clean and in place, with a small knife on display, hanging from his leather belt.

He started to assess me as his eyes looked me up and down. I was very conscious of my appearance; my clothes were nothing but old rags and covered in dirt. I hadn't washed in days and even my own stench was becoming unbearable. The man looked at me in disgust,

"Oh dear, you do seem a sorry state, there will be no handouts here. I suggest you be on your way."

I replied, ignoring the insult. "Good day, I come asking for no handouts, only the chance to earn my keep."

He glared me up and down, sniggering. "Do you have dirt in your ears? You will find no welcome behind these walls."

I refused to acknowledge his instant refusal and continued forcing my voice upon him. "I was born and raised in a village north west of the great river. The village is called Somerby, do you know it?"

The gate keeper smirked upon learning my home. "The only thing to come north of the river are mutations from far too much inbreeding for my liking. I refused to go beyond the river, very uncivilised."

Breaking out in laughter, my will to amuse the man was clearly the right reaction. He lowered the arch in his back, and it seemed the initial chest beating had come to an end. Forgetting his previous rejection, he demanded my name.

Sharply and wittingly I replied, "My name is Jep. I am pleased to say, I have all the right number of fingers and toes."

The gatekeeper smirked, pausing as if he was contemplating options.

"Well, call me Hota. I am the watchman of Stanford. However, soon I am to move onto greater opportunities. You will need to speak with the Baron Asher; he is the ruler here, or so he believes anyway. Fortunately for you, Jep, Baron Asher employs my father. My father is one of the greatest and noblest guards tasked to protect the Baron."

Hota then opened the gate and invited me to step into the town. I felt nerves start to fill my body, as my head twisted and turned attempting to take in my newly found surroundings. Hota stopped, turning his body to face me.

"If I take you to the Baron's great hall, you will need to prove yourself willing. There is a slim chance he will grant you refuge. If by chance he does let you stay, you will need to work and stay out of bother. If you have come here expecting riches, you are very much mistaken. Truth is, you will most likely spend your days shovelling pig muck, and if you're lucky, you might get to bed a disease riddled whore. So, welcome to Stanford."

I excitedly responded to his remark, taking little note of his mention of the baron. Getting past the gate was a grand achievement and I felt relief to be off the roads.

The evening was creeping in as the sun had almost completely disappeared. The northern path leading into the town from the gate was nothing more than a mud trail, churned up from wagons coming and going from town. The slush crept through the holes in my dilapidated leather boots, until the mud thickened, and I stepped onto a solid stone pathway. The church had been erected perfectly at the front of the town, clearly to boast of the town's perfections. Each stone had been finally crafted, creating a spectacular building. The gravestones surrounding the church, covered the yard. They all looked pristine, still glimmering as if brand new. It was obvious to me that those stones were the memorial for the rich and privileged. But even then, aged just shy of twenty I thought about my gravestone and how it would appear to other travellers one day.

Hota noticed me pause, staring down the hill from the church. He called for me to wait, whilst he locked the gate. I nodded, refusing to look away from the breath-taking sight the town offered. The hill gave me a vantage point, allowing me to see the whole town. The market square appeared to be the centre point. East of the square I noticed a cluster of homes. Some were small and made from wood, others were much more elegant and made from stone. Smoke filtered from the roofs, delivering the smell of lentils and herbs all being cooked on fire pits; my stomach rumbled from hunger. Further east, I could see a large building. It stood out as it appeared secluded from the town, a small stone wall surrounding the structure. I squinted, to focus more on the building, until Hota reappeared, observing my curiosity.

"That, Jep, is the lock up."

I turned back to him and asked, "What is the lock up?"

Glancing back at me, he smiled, but never answered my question. He changed the subject by pointing to the south of the square and said, "That is where we are heading, the home of Baron Asher and his delightful wife, Lady Ivy."

The grounds to the Baron's home were as widespread as the town itself. The Baron's residency had been separated from the rest of the people, by water. The river stretched right across the south leading out of the town. I turned my head looking over at the western side of the town and noticed more homes and farming land. Hota led the way, heading down the hill towards the centre of the town. The sound of hustle and bustle oozed from the market square. The ground was cobblestone, something I had never seen before. The market was very well maintained and delivered a sociable atmosphere. Traders were packing up their stalls for the day, calling over to other traders, mocking each other with light-hearted humour. I followed Hota across the square, taking in the vibrant air. We entered Main Street; either side of me were rows of permanent stores. The butchers hung pig carcasses bigger than the average child. Sounds of clattering came from the local blacksmith crashing his hammer into metal. Further down the street, sounds of drums being struck drew my attention. I stepped away from Hota, following the sounds of cheers and laughter. It came from the local tavern. Outside the weathered sign swung as it dangled from matted rope. The sign displayed: Viking Invader Tavern. Hota caught me attempting to glance inside, "You got any coin?" He called.

I looked back at him with raised eyebrows.

He smirked, already knowing the answer. "No luck juice for you then, Jep. Shame though, the Invader houses some of most luscious girls in Stanford."

Hota stepped away, fixating his attention to a sign nailed to the wall. Squinting at its content, he double tapped his finger onto the sign.

"This is to be my fate Jep."

He moved aside allowing me to see the dishevelled scroll on the wall. The ink had run, making it difficult to read.

"Can you read Jep?"

"Just," I replied, attempting to make out its words.

Hota's tone changed, as he spoke with purpose. "It's an advert, for the Stanford BLUE SWORDS. Rumour has it they're recruiting at least four new swords to join them, and I plan to be one of them. They are holding trials in the Square, tomorrow at noon."

My father had told me stories of the Blue Swords as a child; however, I was yet to meet one. They had never been seen passing in my village. But their reputation was greatly respected. My father would refer to them as knights, guardsmen that would rescue you in your time of need.

I felt Hota watching me read the scroll, ensuring I was taking note. I was keen not to offend my new friend and risk being thrown back onto the roads.

"Do they get good coin?" I called.

Brashly he responded. "Coin? Who cares for coin when you are one of the most feared warriors in the land? They are guardians, protectors. They are the voice of the people, upholding justice in our land. They refuse to allow people like Baron Asher to do as he pleases. There are six of them here in Stanford; well there were six of them. Last winter, one of them got taken off guard."

Curious, I asked what happened.

"Some playhouse dwarf was being abused by some drunken locals. The sword intervened and, well, one of them struck him from behind, the coward. Poor chap hasn't been able to speak since."

I stood engrossed in his description of the Blue Swords. Hota picked up on my keenness to learn more and continued.

"If you do wrong, you best hope they don't catch up. Look around you, Jep. No one has a weapon strapped to their belt; not without permission. The only carriers of arms are the Baron's guards and the Baron himself. They allow me to carry this pathetic knife, as I'm employed by the Baron. But hear my words, Jep, if you ever mess up and you find yourself before a Blue Sword, always run, don't fight, the only outcome will be your own death."

Continuing along Main Street, my mind began to wander. What if I, Jep, were to become a Blue Sword, a protector? But what was I thinking; I was nothing more than a village peasant, so the idea was to remain a thought, nothing more than hot air.

2

IVY

Walking away from Main Street, the cobbled streets ended, the ground went back into mud and slush. Hota turned to look at me with a serious expression on his face.

"I warn you now, Jep, Baron Asher does not suffer fools lightly. He is a stubborn and arrogant man, filled with his own self-importance."

I replied nervously, "I will not offer him any insult."

Hota sniggered, "If you did, you would be sure to lose them pretty looks. A word of warning, the baron's most prized possession is his wife, Lady Ivy. Do not overlook, she has enough problems dealing with his foul temper."

Approaching the Baron's estate, I felt jittery after Hota's warning. His grand hall was glorious; the track had been levelled with gravel, with thick iron gates securing the entrance. Behind the gates was a courtyard, followed by stairs, leading to the entrance to the grand hall. Tall trees and luscious green hedges surrounded the building. Hota pointed to some out houses to the side of the grounds.

"That's where I stay. It's the guard quarters, all of Asher's guards sleep there with their families."

We approached the gate to be greeted by one of the tallest men strutting towards us from the courtyard. He wore a fine, tight fitted, claret tunic, which emphasised his muscular build. He made up for his lack of head hair with a long bushy brown beard. He was a true mountain of a man and not someone you would want to make an enemy of. He called over to Hota in a deep and slow tone.

"Hota, you sad excuse of a man, I have already told you not to bring your lovers home."

Hota laughed, "Open the door Chenchi, you big tree. He is here seeking residency."

Chenchi's tunic displayed embroidery on the right side of his chest. He glared at me; it was as if he was contemplating whether to allow me into the yard or tear my head from my shoulders. Chenchi smirked, opening the gate allowing me to follow Hota into the courtyard. He stood facing me and to my relief, he held out his hand, greeting me. Sternly he demanded my name.

"Jep," I replied.

"Well, Jep, I suggest you tread carefully. Baron Asher is in an awkward mood."

Chenchi led us through the courtyard and opened the front door to the grand hall. He instructed Hota and I to wait as he left us in the hallway. Scanning the room, it took me back to something my father always told me; that you could tell a lot about a person by how they decorated their home. The walls were filled with hunting trophies of animals that had been caught and killed. They were all stuffed with their teeth displayed, intentionally posed to create a dangerous and fearful entrance to this grand home. I heard heavy footsteps, along with deep male voices laughing to one another.

From the other end of the hallway two men appeared. They didn't give me a second glance as they both continued to humour one another, purposely disregarding my presence. Hota coughed nervously in order to draw their attention, before announcing himself.

"My Lord Baron, may I speak with you?"

One of the men answered. He was a well-built man, wearing a white doublet that clung to his rounded belly. I couldn't help but notice the wine stains that covered his thick, dark beard. He spoke with a deep, bellowing tone.

"Hota, have you decided to follow in your father's footsteps?"

Hota appeared awkward, instantly deflecting the attention to me.

"My lord, this man seeks to earn coin in your town."

The Baron replied. "Do I not have enough mouths to feed?"

Baron Asher then glared over to me. His smile had turned into a frown as he eyed me up and down. The other man with him was dressed in a black tunic, which carried the same crest as the one Chenchi wore. He was shorter than the baron, but stockier. His hair was thin on top, and he must have been of similar age to the baron, nothing more than thirty years old. His fierce eyes were fixed on me and his mouth gave off a permanent snarl. He muttered, speaking on behalf of the baron.

"You stink, boy, not even my dogs would eat you."

The Baron let out an almighty laugh and slapped the snarling man on his back, impressed with his mockery. Then he encouraged him further.

"You're right, Gil, he is repulsive."

The Baron looked over to Hota, "Why do you bring me these peasants? Take him back to the gate."

Gil interrupted, turning his glare to Hota. "If he tries to get back in, cut his throat."

I glanced at Hota. My eyes wide, displaying the need for us to leave and quickly. I was keen to get out of there, still intact. Before we had chance to go, I heard footsteps coming from the hallway. It was then that I saw the most angelic sight of my life. Her light brown hair flowed over her shoulders, resting on her chest. Her eyes were as green as freshly cut summer grass. Ivy's silk dress hugged her hourglass figure. She was truly beatific; she glanced over to me, giving me a welcoming smile. Her smile was infectious, forcing me to smile back. Requesting to know my name, her soft voice made my stomach flutter.

I stuttered, feeling even more unnerved by her presence. "Jep, my Lady."

The moment of purity was shortly lived by Gil's interruption. "Don't get too close, my Lady; Heaven knows where he's been."

I glared at the ground visualising it swallowing me whole. My emotions were mixed, I had never felt so timid in my life. Any confidence I had was being drained away by Lady Ivy's husband and the snake that stood beside him.

Ivy was quick to notice my awkwardness: taking pity on me she began to question me on my reasons for seeking an audience with the

Baron. Placing her hands on her husband's arm, she began to plead my case.

"My love, you were only saying the other day that the West farm was struggling."

The baron looked back at his wife and appeared hypnotised by her stare, before glaring back to me. "Hota, take him to Carre's farm, he has been whining all winter about needing more hands."

Hota sharply acknowledged the baron's orders. "Yes, my Lord."

The Baron stepped towards me. He leaned forward and placed his face closer to mine. The stench from the stale wine nearly made me retch.

"She is a beauty, isn't she boy?"

He stood upright and stepped back, closer to Ivy. His hand smacked her firmly on the buttocks, making her lightly shriek.

"I'm having your flower later," he muttered to her.

Ivy glanced back at her husband, with what appeared a nervous smile. Hota, now wide eyed, glared at me; this time it was him nodding for us to leave with haste. Before we could reach the door, Baron Asher shouted out to me.

"Boy, where did you say you were from?"

I turned, feeling enthused by his sudden interest. Excitably I replied, "I have travelled from the north my Lord; I was born and raised in a village known as Somerby."

He glanced over to Gil, sniggering, before cupping his mouth with his hand, looking up at the ceiling. I looked at him with eagerness, awaiting his reply.

"Somerby? Hang on, yes! Gil, haven't you mounted a lot of whores from the north? I knew it. Boy, Gil is your father, say hello to papa!"

The Baron and Gil burst into fits of laughter. As for Ivy, she gave me a sympathetic look. I could feel the blood rushing through my veins. He had wound me up tight. Hota gripped my arm, reminding me of my place. For sure I had always been hot headed, but not foolish. Their bullyish laughter echoed down the hallway as we made our way to the courtyard.

Once well away from the Asher's grounds, Hota sensed my tension.

"He gets under your skin, doesn't he?"

"How did that pig manage to get Lady Ivy into his bed?" I fumed.

Hota chuckled. "He wasn't always like that with her. Ivy couldn't have been more than ten years old when she arrived with her father, Isaak. They moved here from the north after her mother died of plague. The baron had only just taken over the title from his father. He wasn't much older than twenty and he groomed that poor girl. He made sure she was provided with a good education and by the age of twelve she was socialising with the high and mighty of Stanford. When she turned fourteen, he married her."

"What about her father? Where is he now?" I asked, curious.

"Isaak, he disappeared two years back. I'm sure the baron was behind it. He was always jealous of their relationship. The baron put Isaak in charge of North farm. Everyone knew this was to keep him out of the way, to stop Isaak having any influence over Lady Ivy."

"Is he dead?" I interrupted.

"No one knows. The Blue Swords are leading the investigation now," replied Hota.

The streets were still bustling as the night sky covered Stanford. Bright flames lit Main Street. People were sat beneath them begging for coin, as others staggered their way out of the local taverns. At the market square, Hota came to a standstill insisting that we were to part ways. He directed me to Western farm, ensuring that I would be welcomed by the farm owner, who was named Carre. Before departing Hota held out his arm for me to shake. I couldn't help but raise one final question.

"So, why not follow in your father's footsteps?"

Hota grinned. "I wouldn't be able to keep my hands off Asher's wife."

His comment left me amused walking from the market square. The cobbled streets transformed to sludge as I struggled to see through the estate of wooden huts. This was the type of place I was used to, damp huts for homes made from thick branches and mud. The stench was familiar, human waste lining the pathways, only made bearable by the smell of meat and vegetables boiling. Some of the more fortunate peasants were lucky enough to have the odd goat or pig, all skin and bone and undernourished. Smoke blackened the air, filtering out from the straw roofs.

The light faded and fewer flames now lit my path. I could see my destination in the distance, three large crop fields surrounded two stone buildings; both the buildings needed repair; cracked stone and rotten wood made up the farmhouses. The path leading to the front door of the house was nothing but slush. The door was missing its upper half. I glanced through the gap but couldn't see anyone; I called through and heard a reply from a loud and jolly voice. A large, stocky man appeared from inside. He wore baggy, woollen clothes that were covered in dirt, his long ginger beard was scruffy and unkept. The large man looked me up and down:

"Can I help you, big man?"

I replied, "I'm looking for Carre."

"You're looking at him." His voice was loud and brash, but jolly.

"Sir, my name is Jep, Baron Asher has sent me to assist with duties on the farm."

He pulled the door open, scratching at his beard. He paused for a moment, before giving me an approving grin.

"Don't call me 'sir' again, and then you may come in."

The smell of mead lingered from his breath. I decided not to reply, in case he changed his mind. Carre called me out on my lack of speech.

"Are you deaf, big man? You don't say much."

Before I had chance to reply, Carre said, "Meat - that's what you need. Luckily for you, I butchered a swine earlier and he is all stewed."

My eyes lit up and my stomach rumbled. It had been over a day since I last ate, my gut ached from hunger. Carre led me into his home. I noticed a large cooking pot with stock boiling over the side. The food smelt rich and meaty. Next to the fire pit was an old bench with a wooden table. Two young boys, eagerly awaiting their evening meal. They were no more than five years old, looked and dressed identical. They paid me little attention, as if strangers were a common presence in their home. Carre's eyes filled with pride as he greeted them.

"My boys, he beamed.

Carre excitedly approached the children from behind, lightly tapping their heads with the palm of his hand. They smiled up at him; you could see they were besotted with their father. Carre ordered me to join them at the table. I wanted to ravish whatever food was put in front in of me; however, I was keen to not appear ill mannered.

As I took my place next to Carre, a woman appeared. She was short, with pale skin. Her face was covered in freckles. The lady wore a neat dress, with a laced bodice. At first, she didn't make anything of me; like the children, it was clear she was used to having new guests in their home. She approached the boiling pot and began filling bowls with the stew. Carre handed me a beaker filled with mead. The stew was still bubbling as the woman placed my bowl down in front of me. It reminded me of home, and my mother's cooking. I felt welcome, their company was easy. Carre led the conversation talking of his sons and how one day they would run his farm; he was proud to have two identical boys. He laughed about how it was down to his superior breeding abilities. The lady serving the food rolled her eyes as if she had heard his boast several times before. The conversation then changed to the baron. I felt my mood instantly change, as my blood started to boil like the stew in the pot. I was eager to hear Carre's thoughts on Baron Asher. I hadn't quite been able to gauge his opinion, so I listened with interest. Almost as if he'd read my mind, Carre bluntly made his statement.

"The man is a turd."

The woman nodded towards her sons as she reprimanded him.

"Language, Carre!"

Carre rolled his eyes, "Oh Dam, we all know that he ordered Isaak's death."

Dam bit her lip as she tilted her head to the side and raised her brows. "There is no evidence that he had Isaak murdered. That poor girl Ivy, she must be going out of her mind pondering on her father's fate."

Carre grunted. "Isaak is buried in the woods somewhere, feeding the worms; those Blue Swords are next to useless; for two years the man has been missing."

I listened, whilst Carre and his wife Dam bickered over the baron, Ivy and her father Isaak. The hot stew had scalded the inside of my mouth, but it hadn't taken me long to empty the bowl. There was a pause in the conversation at the table, so I felt it was fit to speak.

"I hear they're holding trials in the morning."

Carre paused for a moment, dipped his head and laughed into his fist. "You have only been here an hour big man; You are planning on leaving us already?"

I stuttered, feeling embarrassed that Carre thought of me ungrateful at his hospitality. "No, not me. They would never let me in."

Dam stepped in with her voice raised. "You have as much chance as any man; if you want it, go get it. That's what my father used to say."

Carre continued to chuckle. "Hey, big man, you're not sworn to me, but I do like you. Go to the trials, if they laugh you away, you have a bed here. I'm telling you; those Blue Swords are a waste of honest taxpayers' coin."

I felt shocked, that someone as confident and boisterous as Carre didn't mock the idea of me, a wandering peasant going to try-out for the Blue Swords. For a few seconds, I even went silent and began to think about arriving at the trials, writing my name down on the scrolls. But the daydream was short lived, I soon remembered exactly what I was, and I wasn't a Blue Sword.

Carre drank more mead; he continued to rant about the Blue Swords. He said they were led by corruption and secret handshakes. I didn't engage, I knew little about the politics behind the Blue Swords. To me they were childhood heroes, knights that protected and saved people. Another man entered the room. Dam welcomed him by rubbing his upper arm.

"You must be freezing Rye, you have been out there hours."

She turned to Carre, with a frown on her face. In a stern tone, she said, "You're working this boy too hard."

Carre glanced up to the straw roof, rolling his eyes. She began serving Rye her stew. Rye was similar age to me, just shy of twenty. His duties on the farm left him athletically chiselled. Carre began to question him, ensuring all the chores around the farm had been completed. I understood from their conversation that Rye was a farm hand who lived with Carre and Dam and was of no relation.

Carre stood, "Rye, take the big man here to the Invader for some real ale. Maybe you can convince him to forget about the Blue Swords."

Rye grinned and looked over to me, "You have no chance, they only allow noblemen in the Swords."

Dam then shouted over to Rye, "My dear husband has rubbed off on you, boy. Jep, you prove these farm boys wrong."

She scurried over and cupped my chin, as she gave me an encouraging pat on my shoulder.

"The path you wish to follow young man is your own choice. Any man is as capable as the other."

Dam was a breath of fresh air, just like my mother. She glimmered, like an angel. The most endearing thing about her was that she didn't even know the positivity she fed to others around her. As Rye and I headed towards the door, Carre shouted over to us.

"Watch them local girls; they are full of all sorts. Mark my words, it will drop off," he jested as he pointed at my crotch.

I nervously laughed, more embarrassed that Dam was in earshot. I wasn't as naive as I looked; I liked a local girl as much as the next man.

Dam playfully slapped Carre around the back of his head, but the loving smile she permanently reserved for him remained on her freckled face.

I left the farm with Rye and we made our way to the Viking Invader tavern.

3

THE SWORD

Rye was keen to disclose his past, including how he came to work on Western farm. We had a lot in common; like me Rye was born a peasant and lost his father at a young age. He spoke of Carre like a father figure, ever since he caught him stealing his crops when he was a child. Carre's forgiving nature landed Rye a job, rather than face the baron's justice.

The noise from the Viking Invader was deafening. Sounds of drums and spurts of cheers vibrated the ground. I couldn't help but notice the chipped stones, clearly caused by steel, a result of previous quarrels. I pushed open the heavy wooden door, entering the crowded room. Tables and stools had been dotted around the outside of the room, allowing space for dancing and merriment. Locals crashed their beakers together, egging each other to drink more and cause mischief. The leather of my boot squelched from the ale soaking the floor, as Rye led the way to the serving table. Dim lighting generated from candles was just enough to make out faces inside the tavern. The smell of body odour and stale mead became bearable after taking a few sips of ale from my beaker, which Rye had purchased from the irritable old man behind the serving table.

"Move away. No loitering unless you're buying."

The old man serving ordered us away as he continued to take coin from drunken men who were stumbling around each other to be served.

We sat at one of the unoccupied tables allowing me to sit and observe the locals, gauging the mood, along with the type of people I was to live amongst. Some local girl was having to endure having her buttocks groped by some heavily intoxicated men. Rye struck up conversation, leading once again with Carre.

"He will look after you, Jep. He has worked that farm for years and treats all his workers like family. What you see is what you get, the man has lived here all his life. Rumour has it, he has been known to have quite a temper back in the day. He was always having run ins with the Blue Swords and spent many a night in the lock up. Well that was before Dam came along; she squared him up good and proper."

I was able to make out snippets of what was being said, however Rye was being drowned out by the noise inside the tavern. Hearing him mention the Blue Swords prompted me to lose concentration; my mind drifted to thinking about the trials. Rye was able to draw back my attention, mentioning the name Gil. Leaning closer to Rye I raised my voice for him to hear me clearly.

"I met Gil earlier, he didn't like me. The man looked at me like something he had just stepped in."

Rye shook his head, "You don't want to get on the wrong side of Gil, he is one of the most feared men in the town, and Baron Asher's right-hand man. I wouldn't be surprised if the baron himself feared Gil."

I felt tense just hearing the name 'Asher'. I thought of the way he mocked and belittled me in front of his wife Ivy. Keen to learn more about Baron Asher and Ivy's relationship, I discreetly orchestrated the conversation towards Lady Ivy.

"It was the Baron's wife who secured my fate."

Rye smiled at me, as if he had caught me out thinking lustful thoughts. "You're talking about Ivy; now isn't she a sight. Baron Asher is a lucky man."

Mindful of not appearing too eager to hear more, I carefully picked my next words, ensuring it would lead Rye's answer. "He must treat her well."

Rye shook his head and began to slowly look around, certifying no one was listening in on our conversation.

In a lowered voice, he said. "The baron is wicked; he is always accusing that poor woman of adultery. No man dares even speak to her because they'll be accused of bedding her, or at least attempting to! I'm sure he beats her, especially when he's drunk. The ironic thing is, Jep, she is the most loyal girl you could ever meet."

I gave a sympathetic smirk, keen not to give away my thoughts on the matter. All I could think was why she would be with such a tyrant of a man or was she satisfied with riches and status.

It wasn't long before Rye was distracted by some old friends. I decided to call it a night and left the tavern. The air had turned cold and the streets were empty. I took in a deep breath and stared up at the night sky. I felt a moment of loneliness and began to think of my mother and sister, back home. My brief reflection was interrupted by the sounds of whimpering coming from the passageway at the side of the tavern. It sounded like the whine of an injured animal. I didn't think much of it at first, until it was accompanied by male voices, laughing. Standing at the entrance of the passage, I squinted trying to adjust my eyes to see. The lane was too dark to make out the source of the disturbing sound with only the flames from Main Street aiding my vision.

My instincts warned me to walk away; however, curiosity took over. I headed down the passage, taking short steps, filled with apprehension. Stone walls either side enclosed the pathway, it was dark and the light from Main Street was fading. The stars gave me enough illumination to guide my steps. The further I walked down the passage, the clearer the whimpering became, until I witnessed the disturbing sight. A peasant woman was being held against the wall. Her haunting cries forced shivers down my arms. The woman's dress was wrapped around her waist. She was skinny, with her long matted hair pressed up against the cold, stone wall. I couldn't make out if her slender legs were covered in bruises or dirt. She made eye contact with me, silencing her whines.

Two men, one either side, held her upright with both legs apart. A third man had her pinned to the wall, his hand cupping her collar bone, whilst he thrusted into her waist. With each thrust, he groaned, leaving the other two men sniggering. I was stood only yards away, whilst the man continued to roughly penetrate what appeared to be a helpless woman. One of the men holding her leg called for him to hurry up. The other man was glaring down the opposite side of the passage to where I stood.

For several seconds I paused, frightened to intervene. The woman gave me another glance. I could see her tears and look of distress. My blood boiled, I felt my body struck by rage. Any fear I had was being consumed by anger. I clenched my fist and lunged towards the man nearest to me holding the woman's leg. He turned to face me looking flabbergasted by my presence. He was a scruffy looking man missing most of his teeth. I struck my fist into his face hitting his chin, forcing the back of his head to hit the wall from the impact of my punch. He fell to the floor gripping his jaw, squealing with pain. The second man holding her other leg had a frail appearance; he was barely able to hold the woman's leg up. He dropped her in a panic and pinned himself to the wall, like a frightened child.

The stocky man in the middle was scrambling to pull his trousers up. He was going to be more of a problem, his large height and solid build made him much more dominant than the other two. With gritted teeth he lunged forward towards me. The stocky man landed his head into my face forcing me to stumble backwards; I heard the bone in my nose crack from the headbutt. He drove his shoulder into my hip as he tackled me, pushing me to the ground. Climbing on top of me, he delivered one punch after another. His fists thumped into my face; I was helpless to move. Each strike felt like I was being hit by a hammer, forcing my brain to rattle around my skull. One of the other men called over, advising they all leave. It fell on deaf ears; my attacker continued to hit me with one hit after another. Fortunately for me we were not alone.

I heard metal hit the ground. It was slowly timed, one thud after another; each strike vibrated the ground floor. The noise had distracted the stocky man; he lifted his body from mine. His attention was drawn to the sound coming towards us from the other end of the passage. I took advantage of the distraction and got up off the ground. I glared in the same direction, examining what was responsible for the clanging sounds. Then I saw the front two hoofs, stomping onto the ground. It was the biggest horse I had ever seen; its coat was as black as the night sky. The horse looked aged but experienced. Glancing up to the rider, he was dressed in a dark navy brigandine, with white under linens. His helmet was silver with grooves around the outside of his nose, displaying his mouth and chiselled jaw line, his clean-shaven face snarling as he slowly rode towards us. All of us froze still, apart from the peasant woman, who scarpered down the opposite side the passage.

The toothless man was the first to step forwards, raising his arms in the air, submitting. He pleaded with the rider, as if he knew what fate had in store.

"No sir, please."

The rider pulled at his horse's reins, forcing the animal's head to snap to the side. This knocked the submissive man against the wall. He then redirected his horse and positioned himself alongside the stocky man. Neither the rider nor the man said a word; they just glared at each other in a stand-off. I waited in anticipation of who was going to back down first. The rider raised his leather boot and kicked his heel into the stocky man's face, striking his nose. The man yelped out in pain and fell to the ground, clutching at his face. Blood spilled from his nose whilst his loose teeth hit the ground.

The rider dismounted his horse, glaring between me and my attacker, who was clutching at his injured nose. I anxious awaited for my turn, however the stranger just paused. The stocky man leaned upright, the blood still flowing from his face. He growled angrily like a wild animal towards his punisher. Storming forward, he brushed past me.

"Watch him!" I yelled to my saviour.

The rider was as fast as a lightning bolt; he reacted swiftly, meeting the stocky thug with his steel gauntlets. He penetrated his chest, forcing the now toothless man to crash to the ground. My attacker gasped for breath, whilst staring up at his opponent. The rider stood over him, still snarling, before slowly removing his sword from his scabbard. The stocky man begged for mercy and pleaded with the horseman. I squinted, not wanting to see the execution.

The armed knight called over to me, his voice gruff and rugged. "Boy, what is this man's crime?"

I hesitated, not wanting to cause the death of my attacker, but I was afraid. This fierce warrior appeared merciless and I didn't want to be next.

Stuttering, I replied, "A woman, sir; he was taking a woman. She seemed distressed."

My now floored attacker bellowed to the knight, "The whore had been paid."

I turned around, anticipating the protest from the other two men, but they had both fled. The rider placed his sword back in his scabbard, still eyeballing the stocky man beneath him. He raised his leg before striking his foot in the groin of my attacker, who was left squealing like a pig. My saviour leapt onto his horse, patting its mane. The passage was too tight for him to turn his horse around, so I stood upright against the stone wall to allow him past. The rider glanced down at me. I was mesmerised by his stature and couldn't help but notice the gold stitching in his brigandine; the letters read *BS*. That was when I knew it was the first time I had met a Blue Sword.

The following morning my face felt tender and bruised. I was pretty sure my nose was broken again; the feeling was all too familiar. It certainly was not the first time I had woken with my head ringing from the beating I had received from the night before. All too often a good night out in my local tavern would result in me scrapping with one of the village folks. Usually, it was due to my terrible attempt to toy with another man's wife. With a gut full of mead, my tongue had a habit of becoming that much looser. I had woken with a nervous stomach; it was slightly relaxed by the spring sun beaming through the barnyard at Western farm. I sat upright and stretched my throbbing back, unaware if the stiffness was caused from last night's fight or the haystack I now had for a bed. My movement disturbed the mice that scurried underneath the hay.

On leaving the barn, I dipped my head in a barrel of old murky water; it was the closest thing I had had to a wash-down in days.

A friendly voice called over to me. "Good luck big man."

Wiping the water from my eyes, I noticed Carre; he cupped my chin, turning my head, examining the bruises to my face.

Smirking he said, "I do hope the other man looks worse."

Pulling away I raised my eyebrows, "Why wish me good luck?"

"Why - is it not the day of your trials?" he said.

I sniggered, glancing to the ground. "I had no intention of going to the trials. Look at me. I have humiliated myself enough in this town."

Carre let out a sigh, "Listen, it's no secret: I have little respect for the Blue Swords, but I have less respect for a man who shies away from opportunity. You will go to the trials; you will be mocked. But, my boy, at least you will stand."

Listening to Carre, I couldn't help but feel motivated by his words. Remaining silent he allowed me to reflect on what he said. I glanced up to the sky, taking in a deep breath. Turning to face Carre, I felt my eyes well up, whilst nodding my head. Carre gripped the back of my head, smirking.

"Now go, unless you want to go and muck out those swine instead."

Approaching the market my stomach churned, with nerves ripping my belly. The Blue Sword trials were due to be held from sunrise, and after last night's encounter, I admired them even more. My enthusiasm was drowned by doubt; the pure presence and ability of the Blue Sword I had faced cast shadows on my excitement. How could I ever be that authoritative and powerful? Yet filled with all that self-doubt, I continued to walk towards the trials. Something inside me kept pushing me to go; I thought back to my father and what he would have done in my situation. His determination to never give up ran through my veins.

The usual sounds of hustle and bustle came from the market square, as did the smell of meat being cooked in garlic and herbs. The square was overfilled with market stalls, all selling foods, ranging from fish to fruits. Locals bartered with traders selling antiques and wool. Beggars wandered calling for coin, being ushered away from stall owners. The mood was vibrant, with each person scrambling for the next bargain. Children sprinted between the stalls, to the annoyance of the traders.

My attention was drawn to the man-mountain that swaggered across the square. It was Chenchi. His beard appeared well groomed and to my surprise he was not wearing the same tunic he wore the day before, when he guarded the Baron's gate. Instead, he was dressed in a fine red tunic and wore smart leather boots. He didn't notice me, so I decided to follow him in the hope he would lead me to Hota, a familiar face to help me settle my nerves. He marched onto Main Street and passed the Viking Invader tavern. I continued to remain close, glancing down the passage, where I had met the Blue Sword. My thoughts wandered to the previous night's events: if my saviour hadn't arrived would I have just been another peasant found dead, drenched in their own blood? Fate had brought me here, and it was fate that allowed me to meet the Blue Sword.

Chenchi stopped outside the town's playhouse; it was there that I noticed Hota stood, waiting. He was dressed in a fine dark green robe and his hair was brushed to the side. His face was clean shaven, and he almost resembled a nobleman.

I called out to Hota, who met me with a welcoming smile. Chenchi turned, noticed me and raised his eyebrows, seemingly both surprised and confused at my presence.

"You made it Jep; good for you," Hota exclaimed as he placed his shaking hand on my shoulder.

He was clearly more anxious than he wanted to let on. I told him how well he looked as he straightened his robe out and stretched his back nervously. He casually yawned and diverted the attention onto Chenchi.

Chenchi scanned me up and down, clearly unimpressed at the condition of the rags I wore.

"Do not tell me you are going to the trials," he said gruffly.

He scrunched his face, keeping eye contact with me, spitting on the ground. Shamefully I glanced to the ground, nodding my head. I was well of aware of my appearance and if Chenchi was shocked by my brass, what would the Blue Swords think? Instantly regretting my decision to come, I felt a fool. I had merely been in town a day. Who was I, a northern peasant boy, to think I could become a prestigious Blue Sword. Before I could loath myself any further,

Hota interrupted, directing frustration at Chenchi. "Why not? All are welcome to try out for the Blue Swords. Half the men that stand are common folk."

Chenchi raised his arms in the air, chuckling. "Hey, it's nothing to do with me. I mean, a good bath and the man will look adequate, but you can't polish a turd. Have you even handled a blade, read a scroll or ridden a horse?"

My silence gave him his answer. I was ashamed to have even contemplated attending the trials. Hota tried his best to fight my corner.

"They will teach him."

Chenchi leaned into Hota and muttered, "It's man's basic skills, like walking."

He strutted off, reminding me of the arrogance the Baron had shown me the previous day. I was quick to forget my inabilities and bit back at his discourtesy.

"Are you not sworn to Baron Asher?"

He glanced back around, frowning, almost disgusted at my question. He spat, "I'm sworn to no one; the baron can kiss my hairy arse. He is a turd."

Hota and I smirked at each other. I got the bite I wanted. Hota decided to wind him up further, referring to him as a pet for the baron. Chenchi paid little notice; instead, he showcased his bicep and proceeded to shrug off Hota's comments. I apprehensively asked if the baron would be present at the trials.

Hota responded, "he goes to all Blue Sword events; he likes to interfere in their affairs. The man just can't accept that he has no authority over them. Despite his efforts to conceal it, the whole of Stanford knows that he despises them, and I'm fairly sure they don't think much of him either."

Chenchi nodded in agreement. "He hates it when Lady Ivy visits the Blue Swords to get updates on her father."

The mere mention of her name gave me goose bumps. As much as I didn't want to so much as set eyes on Asher, the thought of seeing his wife set off a flutter in my stomach.

"Why doesn't she just start digging the grounds of the Grand Hall? I'm sure she will find her father then."

I remarked in frustration - or jealousy. The lines were blurred even for me to differentiate between the two.

Chenchi's brow furrowed and he leaned towards me. "What do you know about it, boy? You best be careful, spouting off like that."

I stuttered, unable to respond to Chenchi's annoyance. Hota intervened once again, demanding we remained focussed on the task in hand. Chenchi sneered at me as Hota started to walk away. I couldn't help but have taken an immediate disliking to him; he oozed arrogance, relying on his brutish appearance to intimidate.

We made our way to the other side of the market square. My attention was drawn to two heavily armoured men, guarding a platform. The stage was occupied by Baron Asher and Gil, his head guard. Baron Asher sat upon a thick, wooden chair, with Gil standing alongside of him. Gil observed the square, displaying what appeared to be his natural scowl. The black tunic he wore fitted his harsh, weathered face. He leaned in and whispered into the Baron's ear. Whatever he had said amused the baron, most likely at the expense of another. The Baron was dressed in his finery with his enormous gut hanging over his black leather belt, his beard still covered in stained wine. I felt myself grow tense and gritted my teeth with disgust at the sight of him - until I saw her. Ivy's hair was perfectly platted as it fell down her slender back; she sat upright, poised, wearing a light pink dress matching her fresh and pale skin. Her infectious smile made my mouth mirror hers. As locals passed them, they bowed their heads out of respect. Lady Ivy acknowledged their greetings with a graceful nod; however, Asher ignored everyone except Gil. I couldn't help but wonder how someone so blissful could be matched with someone so vulgar.

My thoughts were swiftly interrupted by Chenchi nudging me in the back

"Best nod at the turd."

It was the first time Chenchi brought a smirk to my face, he was right - the man was a turd. I couldn't help but notice Baron Asher eyeballing Chenchi, whilst chewing on a chicken thigh. The juice from the meat dripped down into his beard. Ivy freshened the scenery; we met each other's eyes and I couldn't help but feel her smiled widened. She was infectious leaving me to involuntarily smile back. Hota hurried his pace to match mine; he leaned over firmly, muttering in my ear:

"Don't stare too hard."

Hota lowered his head to the baron in order to mark his respect. Asher just gave him a disapproving look, slowly shaking his head. His attention seemed to be fixated on Chenchi. I felt pleased to have gone unnoticed.

I heard Gil's gruff voice call over. "Chenchi, you're making a fool of yourself."

Glancing back at Chenchi, he ignored the remark and continued to stride pass them with his head held high. Gil stepped forward and appeared angered by Chenchi's brush off as he slammed his beaker down on the table in front of him, causing him to lose most of its contents.

"I own you, boy; you fail Chenchi and I will cut you down at the root," he growled.

Baron Asher laughed as he beckoned Gil back to his seat.

A few yards on from the baron, I noticed a ready-made arena, marked off by loose rope. A long trestle table was overlooking its centre. A flag was being displayed above the table. It bore the image of a sword on a dark navy background, with the marking 'BS' integrated within the blade. I took in the sight; I was in awe of this badge of honour before me and I inhaled deeply as I braced myself for what the trials would entail.

Examining the arena, I noticed a neatly formed line of around thirty men. Most of them were dressed in fine tunics and well presented with well-groomed hair and clean-shaven faces. I couldn't help but feel out of place. I scanned the line, wanting to see another man dressed like me. My clothes were mud stained and loose fitting. I rubbed my face, feeling the stubble on my chin. Running my fingers through my hair, I could feel thick specks of dirt. There was very little relief at the sight of a shorter, scrawny man than myself, ahead of me in the line. My build was nowhere the size of Chenchi, but I was still taller and stockier than most. Hota noticed me eyeing up the other contenders with an inferior expression. He leaned in and muttered with a smile on his face.

"Don't be alarmed; with those piercing blue eyes your looks alone will get you this."

My mother had always told me I relied far too much on my looks to get me out of trouble, but this time I knew my charm was going to have little effect.

I stared onto the arena, to get a glance at one of the Blue Swords. I could see three of them sitting at the table; two appeared to be wearing navy tunics and the one in the middle a smarter white doublet. I remembered Hota telling me there were at least five. I scanned the arena, looking to get a glimpse of the other two, and more so the one that had saved me the previous night.

The set-up had been staged perfectly to evince nerves and self-doubt. The grand table was dressed in an elaborate tablecloth and scrolls were laid out neatly before the Blue Swords ready to record any notes. I could see the townsfolk were beginning to gather at the side of the arena, making it even more terrifying. I expected most used the trials as an opportunity for entertainment.

A fourth man in a navy tunic, displaying the Blue Sword crest, appeared at the front of the line. He stood in front of the table, facing the queue of contenders. A single silver chain hung from the breast of his tunic. He was a tall, slender man, with sharp facial features and a pointed nose. His hair was blond and neatly combed forward. He began to smirk, looking back and forth, between the line and his fellow Blue Swords. Stepping closer to the line he shouted:

"Order and silence; oh dear, it gets worse every time. When I tell you, you will step before the governor."

The arena went silent at his command; everyone in the line listened intently.

I watched as one after another was called before the table. It was impossible to hear what was being said, from the position I was in the line. Some of the men were only up for a matter of seconds before they were ushered off again, seemingly dismissed at a mere glance. The odd one got longer at the table, leaving with neutral expression. Closer to the table, I was still unable to locate my saviour.

By midday Hota was next in line to approach the table. A large enough gap had been left to ensure we could not listen in on his trial. I felt my hand start to shake with nerves. I had not eaten since Dam fed me at the farm the day before, and the hunger was agitating my already knotted stomach. The blond-haired man was still stood facing the line, indicating when we should step forward. The sight of Hota being examined made my mouth dry. He was there for several minutes, before being dismissed. Hota stepped away from the table refusing to acknowledged me or Chenchi. As he left the arena, I was quick to forget him and became engrossed in my own fate.

Chenchi was next to go; he strutted up to the table casually and undeterred. He was there a similar time to Hota and again left the table refusing to glance back at me and give anything away. The Blue Sword with blond hair stepped closer to me; he rubbed his nose and winced.

"Ok, your turn. Some advice lad: after this, jump in the river - you bloody stink."

I walked towards the table; my skin was sweating, and my teeth started to chatter. I took a deep breath and thought of my father. He could never accept he was nothing more than a farm hand, always attempting to better himself, coming up with one idea after another. He may have failed, but he tried and now I was going to try for him.

Behind the table sat three Blue Swords. The man furthest to my left was wearing a navy tunic, although he displayed two silver chains. He appeared shorter than the other two men. His hair was dark and brushed forward. He was older than me, about forty years of age, perhaps. He appeared wearied as he inhaled deeply and sighed.

"Name and birthplace, boy?"

"Jep sir, I'm from the village of Somerby," I replied sharply.

The man then smirked, which caused me alarm.

"Don't be calling me 'sir' boy. The big one in the middle wearing white is the only governor at this table; he is the only one you call sir, understood?"

I nodded and began to stutter as I started to apologize to both the older man and the seated governor. He was quick to stop me rambling. He muttered, fluttering his hand in my direction.

"Let us begin."

I glanced at the governor sat between the other two Blue Swords. He was a muscular man, with fierce brown eyes that were emphasised by his dark complexion. His stubbled face and shaved head made him appear even more intimidating. His crisp, white doublet displayed three silver chains hanging across his chest. I assumed they were a mark of rank or authority. He did not speak or make a sound and left the interrogation to the wearied Blue Sword who referred to himself as Sergeant Hock.

Abruptly he said, "So, tell me young Jep, what is it you think us Blue Swords do?"

My dry tongue stuck to the roof of my mouth. I took a deep breath and tried to compose myself.

"Protect the townsfolk sir - I mean, Sergeant."

Sergeant Hock glared at me and let out a sarcastic snigger. "And I'm guessing you want to serve the people and you work well under pressure?"

"I want to protect the townsfolk," I mumbled.

I was unsure whether this was the answer he was after. Hearing his cynical response made me feel it was not the right answer.

"Why, isn't that noble of you, young man."

He was quick to dismiss me, calling over the Blue Sword at the front of the line to collect me. He referred to the blond-haired Blue Sword as Lev and demanded he bring up the next candidate. Sergeant Hock lifted his hand, waving me to leave. I was deflated, flattened by the instant rejection. I heard a deep voice call out from the table. I turned, flabbergasted that it was the governor.

"Boy, so say you were a Blue Sword. Your mother is caught stealing fruit from the market. Tell me; do you bring her to my dungeon so I can remove her hand? Or do you let her walk free?"

I lifted my head, startled, endeavouring to think of the right answer. Pausing, I panicked and blurted out the answer I thought he wanted to hear.

"In truth, sir, my mother would have to face judgement like any other."

His depleted reaction to my answer gave away his disapproval. Rolling his eyes and nodding his head he advised me I was better placed with the baron's guards. I tried to vent my frustration and rectify my answer; however, I was met with a stern demand to leave. Sergeant Hock advised me not to make a pest of myself and once again dismissed me from his arena.

The third Blue Sword, who had remained silent, stood from his chair. He glanced at the governor, requesting permission to intervene. The governor gave no objections:

"Go ahead Fulten."

Fulten straightened his tunic over his rounded belly, "What happened to your face, boy?"

I quickly replied, "Last night, I came across three men attacking a woman in the passage by the Viking Invader tavern."

Fulten raised his hands, indicating for me to be silent. "I was reliably informed that the lady had been paid, she was under no attack. However, I was told you showed courage, even pre warned Sword Fawkes of an attack."

Deflated I replied, "I was hoping to meet him here today, to thank him."

Fulten, sniggered, "He needs no thanks; he did what was necessary."

Sergeant Hock interrupted, agitated. "This has no point whatsoever, Fulten; look at the state of the lad: he is not Blue Sword material."

Fulten debated, "I beg to differ, Sergeant. Not all Blue Swords are of noble blood, born into silver and finery. I mean, just look at Lev."

Lev, who had been greeting the contenders, turned to face the table. "I have to agree with Fulten, Sergeant, we all suckled our mothers' breast once."

Sergeant Hock grew irritated and began pleading with the governor to end the dispute. A gruff, familiar voice called from behind me:

"Let him face me at sundown; put the boy through."

It was the Blue Sword who had come to my aid the previous night, his face now on display, his eyes squinting, beyond the battle scars on his skin. He eyeballed the governor, pressing his request further. There was an uneasy silence as I awaited the governor's reaction. He eventually bellowed over to me:

"So be it, come back before sundown."

Sergeant Hock rolled his eyes in disbelief. I stepped towards Fawkes to express my gratitude, but the scowl on his face was an indication of my time to leave.

Walking through the market I embraced an extra spring in my step. As I passed the Baron and Lady Ivy, I looked for her reaction. Had she just watched my triumph? I felt a sense of pride and stature, passing their podium. My thoughts began to run away with themselves; surely Lady Ivy would take more note of me should I wear the crest of a Blue Sword. My muse was short lived. I was pained to see that she had lost her smile; she was staring at the floor, expressionless. The grand spark that illuminated her presence appeared defused. Baron Asher was still focusing all his attention on Gil as they appeared deep in conversation. Ivy glared at the ground, with one hand cupping her forehead, as if she was pained. The locals continued to express their respects to the Baron and Baroness; however surprisingly this was going unnoticed by Ivy. The description I had been given of Lady Ivy's relationship with the common folk was not evident in her presentation that noon.

Keen to locate Hota, I spent most of my afternoon searching Main Street and the square for him, without luck. I decided to give in and headed to the Viking Invader for some refreshments. The tavern was filled with locals, harmlessly quarrelling and drinking mead. My feet squelched over spilt ale as I approached the serving table. With my last coin I purchased myself a beaker of mead. It was the same man that served me and Rye from the previous night; he was still as belligerent.

Taking my first sip of ale, I scanned the room, to find an empty table. I noticed Chenchi seated in the far corner of the tavern, and he wasn't alone. Gil, the baron's head guard had left the Baron and now sat alongside Chenchi. They appeared deep in conversation and seemed oblivious to anyone around them. I sat on an unoccupied bench only a few yards from their table. I ensured I was facing the tavern entrance with my back to them, keen to go unnoticed. I was determined to listen in on their conversation, eager to learn more of their relationship. Gil's voice sounded irritable.

"Chenchi, I saved you from your miserable existence, I gave you a taste of the high life, women, weapons, silver. Now you screw me. Why?"

Chenchi replied brashly. "I'm done Gil, no more. You know I still see them; their faces disturb my dreams. I refuse to be this person. I have repaid my debt to you a thousand times over."

Gil raised his voice and crashed his fist onto the table. His actions brought a brief silence to the room. I couldn't help but focus on

Chenchi's remark of faces, disturbing his dreams. Clearly, he was as dirty as Gil.

"Damn you, Chenchi, I own you, boy."

Unable to turn around I pictured Gil's face scrunched up and angered.

I heard another thud and like the rest of the tavern couldn't resist but glance to their table. Gil launched himself from his seat, knocking the stool to the ground. He stomped towards the tavern door, muttering curses. The locals faced away, clearly concerned that their curiosity would be noticed by Gil's wrath. He slammed the tavern door against the wall before leaving.

It wasn't long before Chenchi left the tavern. I wanted to question Chenchi on his quarrel with Gil, however I thought it wise to keep my nose out for now. After finishing my beverage, I headed back to the square. My mind was going over their spat and I was keen to remained focused on my trail. Wandering the town, I was still unable to locate Hota and with the sun beginning to lower on the horizon, I made my way back to the arena.

Walking through the square my legs felt as if they were detached from my body; the nerves had started to kick in again. The chairs where Baron Asher and Lady Ivy sat were now unoccupied. I counted nine men lined up within the arena, whom I assumed were awaiting their second trial. I noticed Hota stood at the front of the line, which instantly lifted my spirits. Chenchi was in the middle of the line towering over all the other contenders. No one seemed to notice me as I joined the back of the queue. I noticed the blond-haired officer, Lev, in his navy tunic walking up and down the line. He had a cunning smirk on his face as if he was amused by our anxieties. As he approached me his smirk became more of a chuckle, clearly at my own expense.

"Still no bath then?"

His smile indicated no offense was meant from his remark. He nodded his head, which made me feel I had his approval.

Lev ordered us to stand in a horizontal line and present ourselves to the governor. Hota was on the left of the line, with Chenchi still in the middle. I was on the far right. I glanced across, attempting to make eye contact with Hota; however, he glared straight ahead, facing the Blue Swords. I was unaware whether he had even noticed my return to the arena. I tried not to overthink his coldness, assuming he was keen to remain focused on completing his trials. Sergeant Hock stood from his chair, peering back and forth, across the line. He applauded us on trials so far; however, whilst glancing at me reminded us that some were more fortunate than others. Lifting a thick, wooden baton, he gripped its handle tight.

"You will take the baton and attempt to disarm the handsome looking man behind you. As many of you may know, Sword Fawkes has quite the reputation. So, I wish you the best of luck. You will need it."

We all turned to face Fawkes. He stood glaring towards us; his face showed no emotion as his eyes scanned across our line in an intimidating manner. I would have recognised that jaw line anywhere; it was the same Blue Sword that had come to my aid the previous night. He had a permanent squint in his eyes. He stood poised and straight, displaying his muscular physique. His baton was casually pointing to the floor, gripped firmly in his hand. He wore the same navy tunic, with a single silver chain. The chain took my eye, making me more curious about their meaning. He glanced to Sergeant Hock and nodded his head, prepared and ready for combat.

4

THE LOCK UP

Sergeant Hock glanced at his list and yelled out the first name. Fawkes's first opponent stepped forward from the line. He was middle aged; his finery indicated he was from wealth. Leaning over to grip the baton, his hand jittered. He raised his chin and began to eye up Fawkes. Without warning he lunged towards Fawkes, teeth gritted and his fist firmly gripping the baton's handle. His attempt to deliver a finishing strike was floored by a skilful Fawkes who stepped to the side, allowing the man to hit nothing but air. Fawkes took his opportunity, swinging his baton directly into the rear of his opponent's knee. The accuracy and the power of the attack forced the candidate's leg to buckle, putting him on the ground.

Each one of us began to glance down the line at each other wincing at the thought of who was next to face this mighty warrior. Hock ordered the fallen man to leave the arena. He pulled himself to his feet, clutching at his back, before leaving the trial. The next name was called, forcing hairs to rise on my arm. Hota was next to challenge Fawkes.

Hota knelt and picked up the peace baton, left by the previous candidate. He refused to lose eye contact with Fawkes. He was clearly focused and composed. They stood only a few yards apart and it was Hota who made the first move, attempting to strike Fawkes on the arm. Fawkes repeated his previous move, stepping to his side, before attempting a counter-attack, aiming to take Hota's legs away from him. Fawkes was unsuccessful as Hota was just as quick to move, stepping back, this time forcing Fawkes to hit nothing but air. Fawkes then went on the attack, raising his baton parallel to his shoulder and swinging it towards Hota's side. Hota reacted quickly and blocked the attack, causing both their batons to clash. Hota quickly offered a counter strike, jabbing his baton towards Fawkes's chest, however Fawkes was able to defend his attack. Undeterred, Hota swung his baton outward, yet still Fawkes was too fast, dodging the second attack. With two hands on his peace baton, Fawkes drove his weapon upwards hitting Hota on the chin. Hota stumbled back, cupped his jaw with his free hand and let out an unsettling growl. Hota was livid as he tensed his body. His lack of composure made him predictable in his next move. Fawkes eyeballed him, calmly awaiting Hota's wrath. Hota began to rush Fawkes, but before they collided, Sergeant Hock bellowed across the arena, demanding it come to an end.

Hock glanced over to Fulten and the governor, letting out a sigh of relief. The governor gave him a nod, indicating Hota's fate.

"Hota, you have passed the initial trial, report to the lock up at sunrise."

Hota glanced over to me, smirking, finally acknowledging my presence at the trial. Watching him fight filled me with adrenaline. However, there was no way I had any chance of disarming Fawkes. I knew how to fight with my fists but my experience with weapons was very limited. More contenders stepped forward, each being floored by Fawkes and dismissed by Sergeant Hock. It was clear the governor was making the final decision as he indicated his conclusion to Hock, who delivered each verdict. All men so far, bar Hota, had failed; most leaving with injuries and their pride in tatters.

Next up was Chenchi, as Sergeant Hock ordered him forward. Chenchi rested his baton casually on his shoulder as if he didn't have a care in the world. Fawkes eyed Chenchi up and down as the pair stood and faced each other. Sergeant Hock called out to Fawkes with a grin on his face, referring to Chenchi's stature.

"Good luck with this one Fawkes. He is clearly well bred."

Fawkes appeared undeterred at the sight of the man mountain that stood before him. This time it was Fawkes who delivered the first attack. He lunged forward jabbing the tip of his baton into Chenchi's stomach, aiming to finish the giant with haste. The baton connected with Chenchi, however, it made little impact. Any other man would have been gripping at their stomach; however, Chenchi just glared back at Fawkes, giving him a chilling smile.

Fawkes didn't hesitate in delivering a second blow, this time slicing his peace baton down on to Chenchi's collarbone. Fawkes stepped back to assess the outcome of his attack; however, Chenchi didn't even flinch. Most would have given up, but Fawkes refused, still keen on defeating his challenger; he repeated his move and swung his weapon, aiming for Chenchi's collarbone. This time Chenchi had predicted his attack, catching Fawkes' baton mid-air. Chenchi gritted his teeth, grunting, whilst pulling Fawkes closer into him. I glanced at the Blue Swords who sat behind the table; they all clung on to the edge of their seats, curious to know the outcome. Struggling to pull back against Chenchi's brute strength, Fawkes jumped forward, crashing his forehead directly into Chenchi's face. Chenchi stumbled, releasing Fawkes' baton. Finally, he appeared dazed, shaking his head from side to side. His eyes were squinting as he attempted to regain focus on Fawkes. Fawkes stepped back, crouching and assessing what if anything was next to come. He eyed Chenchi up and down, composed, as if he was considering a finishing blow. I waited in anticipation of Fawkes's next move and couldn't help but stare over in admiration; he was truly a magnificent warrior.

Sergeant Hock glanced to the governor, smirking, clearly impressed by the magnitude of Chenchi. He called over, applauding them both for the spectacular fight. Sarcastically he asked if Fawkes needed a rest before his next challenger. Fawkes grunted at the insult. Chenchi was awarded passage and invited to attend the lock up with Hota the following day.

With only three of us left, Fawkes made easy pickings of the other two called before me. My legs went numb at the thought it was my turn to face Fawkes. Hock sniggered at having to call out my name. Dismissively he requested that Fawkes make our encounter quick. I crouched down, gripping the handle of the baton tightly. My hand shivered, drawing the attention of Fawkes. He discreetly nodded his head and pursed his lips. I felt as if he was showing me slight pity, seeing me standing before him like a whipped, cowardly child.

My breathing became erratic, as nerves began to take over my body. Fawkes held back, allowing me to gain composure. The pause gave me the opportunity to assess the situation. I convinced myself that all I needed to do was stay on my feet to impress observing Blue Swords. I knew I had little chance of disarming this finely crafted combatant, so I considered my options. I decided on a different approach, something simple that was passed on by my own mother: persuasion. Inhaling a deep breath, I ordered Fawkes to put his baton down. Fawkes frowned at the three assessing Blue Swords, who all glanced between each other, clearly confused.

Fawkes paused, refusing to react to my command. He remained still, which baffled me even more. There was an eery silence throughout the area; even the crowd were hushed by my lack of action. I couldn't understand why Fawkes was refusing to ground me. Committing myself to this strategy, I threw my baton to the ground. This may have appeared madness to some, but I was inexperienced at fighting with weapons and I hoped that Fawkes would drop his baton, allowing the odds to even.

Unfortunately for me Fawkes was growing impatient. He shook his head, clearly disappointed with my approach. Now I began to panic. Before I could react, Fawkes had driven his body forward and with the back of his fist, struck me to the face. My head jolted; the impact was like being hit by a hammer. Still on my feet I was able to pull myself upright. But just as I recovered, Fawkes delivered a second punch, making me stumble back. Before I could regain my footing, Fawkes stood directly in front of me. He raised his leg and struck the sole of his boot into my abdomen. I leaned forward, clutching my stomach. As I glanced up Fawkes hovered over me, disgusted at my lack of fight.

Rage began to fill my blood stream. For that split second, I forgot my disadvantage and my temper flared. Standing upright I leapt forwards towards Fawkes. He was not anticipating my reaction and was unable to dodge my temper fuelled attack. Lunging my shoulder into his waist, I lifted Fawkes off the ground. We both crashed into the sludge, this leaving me with the advantage. A voice bellowed from the Blue Swords' table.

"Enough," called the governor.

Stepping up, I offered Fawkes my arm. He refused it getting up onto his feet unaided. He glared at me, initially looking as if he wanted to tear out my throat. Glancing to the table, he nodded before walking away and leaving the arena. I glanced to the floor and noticed his baton lodged into the mud. I looked back to the table awaiting their verdict. Hock was muttering into the governor's ear, whilst Fulten gave me an approving smirk. The governor then delivered his decision.

"Your performance was pitiful, yet I can't help but admire your attempt. The question is what do we do with you, boy?"

Sergeant Hock interrupted. "Sir, with all due respect, the boy is not what we are looking for."

The governor was quick to cut him down, demanding his silence,

"You will report to Sword Fulton at sunrise. The real trial starts tomorrow, and I have no doubt, you will fail."

Before I was able to return my gratitude, I noticed Fulten dramatically waving his hand at me. This was clearly my direction to leave, before any decision was changed. I hurried out of the arena, refusing to look back at the table of judges. I remained composed, attempting to hide the sheer joy which I felt.

The feeling was euphoric; my head thumped from the thoughts that expanded in my mind. This was like no feeling I had ever had before. I had passed the trials and was a step closer to becoming a Blue Sword.

Hota and Chenchi were stood outside the blacksmith's, the other side of the square. They appeared enlightened, laughing and patting each other's back. I caught Chenchi's eye; he made little fuss and continued to engage with Hota. I called to Hota, who appeared pleased to see me. He was unaware of my achievement and removed his smile, attempting to gauge my mood. I struggled to contain my involuntary grin as I approached him. Hota met me with a firm grip of my hand.

"Did you triumph?" He said, gauging the poor attempt I made to hide my joy.

"That I did, that I did," I replied.

I glanced to Chenchi, who rewarded me by slightly nodding his head. Hota on the other hand yelled out my name in delight.

"Jep of Somerby, a Blue Sword. Yesterday you were nothing more than an underprivileged traveller. Now you have great opportunity staring you in the face. I love this bloody town."

We continued to speak of the trial, laughing and mocking each other's struggles against Fawkes. As the night sky darkened the town, we went our separate ways. I headed back to Western Farm to plead with Carre for the mouse-ridden bed and some of Dam's piping hot stew.

The morning was dark and gloomy; however, the weather had no effect on my mood. Carre had been kind enough to let me sleep another night under his roof. Unaware it was his encouragement that got me to the trials, Carre spoke little of my achievement. His wife Dam, on the other hand, congratulated me with ale and cheese. They were gracious people whom I hoped would never become strangers.

As I set off towards the market square, my own stench filled my nostrils. As soon as I was to earn my first coin, I promised myself a bath. The stalls were already set up for the morning and the traders stood eagerly awaiting their customers. I took the eastern path from the square. The stone cobbles transformed into sludge as I followed the track. I walked between rows of old wooden built houses. The smell was more potent than the rags I wore. The homes were similar of those of the Western Estate; The houses clearly belonged to the poor living within the town. I noticed a broken wooden sign on the ground at the side of the track; the sign read 'Burn Oak' which I assumed was the name of the slum.

The track eventually transformed back into stone, not as neatly built as the square but still it was much more pleasant to walk on. Once out of the slum of the Eastern Estate, the homes were well built and in good order; most were made from stone and only a small handful had been crafted from logs. These were clearly the homes that belonged to more privileged townsfolk. Fresh green grass separated the houses with each home marking its boundary with wooden fencing.

At the end of the path I arrived at my potential new home. The stone-built structure had an upper floor. No gates or barriers protected the building, but then I couldn't imagine there were too many folks out there brave enough to trespass into a building housing the Blue Swords. My stomach began to knot as I stepped closer to the two wooden doors, posing as an entrance. I was about to knock on the door until I heard a familiar voice call over to me in a mocking tone.

"Wait, do not make fools of us." It was Hota, joined by Chenchi.

My face lit up and my nerves eased. Hota shook my hand, greeting me excitedly.

To my surprise Chenchi raised his hand in order to receive me. "As it stands, we will be embracing the same crest. For that reason and that reason alone, I offer you my hand." Chenchi was a complicated fellow;

it was clear he was attempting to treat me as his equal, but there was an undertone in his words. He had taken a disliking to me and in truth his arrogance was repulsive. Hota on the other hand had showed no prejudice towards me; he had accepted me from the day we met, disregarding any past variance.

I knocked at the door eagerly, waiting for it to open, when Hota spoke.

"I hear Fulten is tutoring you, Jep?"

I looked back at him, confused. "Tutoring? I don't understand."

Hota replied. "Fulten is to be your mentor. He will decide if you are good enough to become a Sword. Don't worry, he is a nice fellow, you're sure to learn a lot from him. He has been a Blue Sword for many years."

The door opened, halting my reply. It was Lev, the Sword who met us at the trials. He displayed what I can only describe as a cunning grin on his face, but still he was welcoming. Lev caught me eying the single silver chain, dangling from his tunic.

"You make it, you get one, you become Sergeant, you get two and if you really set the world alight, you get three of the things. Don't get excited though, they're worth piss. Let's get you lot inside; if any of you have any sense you will leave now and forget this place."

We all remained silent, none of us sure how to reply.

Lev chuckled, "No? Well you had best come in."

Through the door, the room was cold and felt damp. The walls were covered in cobwebs and dust. The only item inside was an old, cracked wooden table. Lev proceeded to talk:

"This, my friends, is the greeting room. It's open to the locals so trust me when I say they will come in and whine like weary children. The common folk expect you to solve all their problems. Get used to this table, you will spend most your time in here."

Behind the table was an iron gate that led into another room. Lev accessed the gate with a key; once we were through, Lev turned back to us.

"Combat, this is where Fawkes will beat you, make you real men."

The room was filled with hay and wooden training blocks. There were sacks filled with sand hanging from the walls, with heavy pig bladders dotted around the floor. I wondered what the purpose of the bladders were. I leaned down gripping one in my hand.

Hota whispered, "They're to improve your strength. They're heavier than they look, aren't they?"

In one corner, I noticed wooden shaped swords lined up, used to improve combat skills. Lev closed the iron gate and turned his key, locking us in.

"This remains locked; we don't want any curious peasants wandering around."

A staircase was situated at the back of the room. The passage was narrow. Lev led the way before turning to Chenchi,

"Watch that Swede of yours."

We followed Lev to the top of the stairs. The passage contained shelves either side filled with stain-ridden scrolls. Most of the scrolls were damaged and torn. The light was restricted, peering through cracks in the walls.

Lev pointed to the scrolls; "Forgotten investigations."

The room at the end was barely visible from dust and cobwebs. You could hear rodents scurrying, disturbed by our footsteps.

Lev pushed open the creaking door. "This was the detector room. If you decide that the armour is getting too heavy and your knees are weary, you can come here to the detector room. Some say to become a detector you must be very skilled and competent. Me? I think detectors are lazy Swords who dismiss real work."

Chenchi looked puzzled. "Detectors, what are they?"

Lev became animated in his tone, hinting sarcasm. "Why, they are of the utmost prestige; very few Blue Swords show the character of a detector. Some say it is promotion, I say they are nothing more than stuck up, modest men, focused only on how they appear. Hota, you appear a man impressed by well-groomed presentation. Maybe this will be your path."

Hota did not react. Lev was a tease and still hadn't explained the role of a detector. Neither one of us asked any more, keen not to encourage his cynicism any further.

Lev guided us back down the stairs and through an archway at the rear of the combat room. This room was different; it was cluttered, empty ale beakers and chicken bones covered the tables and there were pieces of armoury dotted around the floor. Less than impressive, it was obvious the room was well used.

Lev smirked, clearly familiar with room. "It doesn't look much, but this is your haven, we call this the parade room. Here you will receive your duties."

Lev pointed to a thick wooden door at the back of the room. "See that door there; if the governor ever walks through it, you rise to your feet. Right- follow me and I will show you the dungeon."

We walked through the back door of the parade room. The yard was gravelled and led all the way around to the front of the lock up. Opposite the doorway was a grassed area surrounded by trees and thorn bushes. Scattered around the grass were small wooden huts; some were slightly bigger than the others.

Lev stood in front of us. "They are your quarters. Hope you three play nice, you will stay together for now. We are required to reside on the grounds; that way if you're needed, we know where you are. You can only stay away at night if the Sergeant or governor has authorised your absence."

Lev stayed close by, allowing us to familiarise ourselves with our new surroundings and talking us through each area.

I looked around with a sense of pride. There were six barns, each filled with the finest thoroughbred stallions. Following on from there was a storage room filled with armour and weapons. As we entered, I noticed my saviour Fawkes stood separating swords and neatly lining them up. He glanced over to us, making no fuss and didn't say anything, before continuing to sort through the weapons.

Outside the armoury, we were joined by Fulten. His presence was warming. Unlike the other Swords, he was slightly overweight and his tone of voice much softer and less oppressive. His uniform was well pressed and his leather boots polished. His single, silver chain glimmered and hung neatly. I felt nervous to meet him after hearing he was to be my tutor. I arched my back, standing straight.

Fulten cupped his hand onto his beard and grinned. "Don't listen to a word this man says, he is a menace."

Lev shook his head, dismissing his colleague's humour. "Fulten, would you be so kind and take these wide-eyed pups to the dungeon? I am required elsewhere."

Fulten rolled his eyes; "You always have somewhere you need to be, you waste of a man."

Lev broadened his shoulders and raised his chin, leaving us, walking through the rear door of the parade room.

Fulten laughed. "Don't mind him; how that man gets himself dressed of a morning is beyond me."

Fulten's pleasantness made me feel more at ease. We followed him to the far side of the rear yard. There was a stone building detached from the main lock up. The stone was covered in algae and the iron door that posed as an entrance was coated in rust. Fulten began to turn a key unlocking the iron door; he looked back at us with a stern expression.

"This gate always remains locked. Always."

Stepping through the gate, the stench was unbearable. It smelt like bodily fluid which had coagulated over time. It was a gruesome place; the roof leaked as rainwater dripped onto the floor. There was stained blood covering the walls and the sound of rats scratching at the stone.

We walked down a short, dark alleyway which led to an open room with a table against the far wall. The room was barely lit as one torch burned next to the table where Sergeant Hock was seated. When he noticed us, he stood from his chair. His eyebrows raised as he surprisingly appeared satisfied to see us; my guess was he was just pleased to have some company.

"Now then folks, welcome to my inn. As you can see there are eight dungeons here. Solid and sturdy - not one man or woman has ever escaped these cages and I plan to keep it that way. You will each be issued a key for the main door but only I have the key for the dungeons. If any of you lot lose a prisoner, then I will rip you a new arse. Got it pups?"

We all nodded sharply in agreement, making it clear we understood his instructions.

The cage doors were solid, the space in each one sparse. The floors were littered with spoilt hay left over from the horses. More dried blood stained the ground of the dungeons and some of the iron bars appeared to be smeared in human waste.

Fulten called over to Sergeant Hock. "Who is in the traps, Sergeant?"

Hock replied sarcastically: "We have two of life's winners on this fine morning, Sword Fulten. Pups, do come closer."

We stepped forward following Sergeant Hock to the first occupied cage. There, a stocky man stood with both hands gripped tightly on the iron bars. He snarled, glaring directly into my eyes, his face purple from bruising. The prisoner's nose was bent out of shape and both his eyes were bloodshot red. Then it clicked: I had met this man before. It was the same man from the passage: he was my attacker, the brute Fawkes saved me from. It was obvious he recognised me. I couldn't understand why he was here; as far as I knew, Fulten said the peasant woman he was mounting had been paid. He had clearly taken a disliking to me. He remined focused on me, eye balling my every move, leaving my bones chilled.

Sergeant Hock leaned onto the cage door and shouted to the prisoner.

"Step back or I'll come in there and kick your balls into your tiny brain."

The prisoner didn't even flinch. He casually stepped to the back of his cage; his eyes still locked onto mine.

Hock laughed, "There's a good dog! This fine specimen is here because he was found wandering around the market square armed with an offensive item. Not something we allow in Stanford, unless authorised of course."

He walked back to the desk and picked up a short wooden stick. Its shaft was thick and solid, with several spikes fixed onto it.

Holding it up on display, he said. "This mace belongs to our good friend here, Linc. Rumour has it he was going to open someone's skull with it, isn't that right, Linc?"

Linc sneered. "Aye, it was just taking me time to find him, Sergeant."

Linc fixed his gaze back on me with a haunting smirk.

My spine tingled; whether he had meant to or not, Linc had made it clear the mace he was caught carrying was meant for my head.

Hock interrupted my moment of alarm. "Anyway, Linc is enjoying my fine hospitality. He enjoys it so much he visits us most weeks."

Hock led us to another cage; this time the prisoner was a peasant girl. Her robe was ripped and dirty. She was bare footed, and I could hardly see her skin for the dirt on her legs. She was curled up in the corner with her head facing the floor; she appeared cold, her body shaking continuously.

Sergeant Hock's stringent demeanour suddenly changed. He appeared almost father-like to the young girl as he opened the cell door and calmly walked in.

Kneeling beside her, his gruff and short-tempered tone softened. "Sweetheart, you will be free by the end of the day, you have my word."

Hock proceeded to quietly explain that the girl had stolen vegetables from the market square; her punishment was to spend a night in the dungeon. I could sympathise with the girl; I was not unfamiliar to stealing food to keep my family alive. Whilst the rich threw their leftovers to the dogs, us common folk did what was needed to survive. Sergeant Hock's warmth towards the girl was comforting.

The Sergeant looked over to us, ordering us to leave the dungeon. He told Fulten to see us out. I turned to take another look at Linc, who was leaning back, gripping his cage door. He glared over, scowling at me. I looked away, unnerved by his expression.

Hota placed his hand on my shoulder, clearly aware of my concern. "Ignore him Jep, the man is full of piss and wind."

Hota spoke loud enough, so Linc could here. I glanced back around to see Linc's reaction. He had taken a step back, clearly backing down upon hearing Hota's words. I felt a sense that I would be meeting Linc again, and it was not going to be pleasant.

We followed Fulten across the rear yard; he looked back at us. "See, Sergeant Hock does possess a more elegant side."

Lev approached us, laughing. "The man is going soft in his older years. Is he still sulking over me bringing that vagrant whore in for stealing?"

Fulten frowned at Lev and glanced over to the rest of us; "Ignore my stale friend. Come, let's get you lot fitted up."

We followed Fulten and Lev to the armoury. Fawkes was still inside, sifting through various pieces of armour. He was certainly the most fearsome looking of the Blue Swords; he didn't say much, and his face never gave anything away. He must have noticed us inside the armoury but refused to be distracted from his chores. After a few minutes of waiting in an awkward silence, Lev managed to get his attention.

"Oi – are you doing this on purpose, or have you gone lame on us again?"

Fawkes slowly glared over to Lev and entertained him with the slightest of smirks.

I felt overwhelmed by all the different axes and crossbows. The armoury was filled with a range of weapons; the room was the best kept place I had seen so far. Armour filled the back wall; the left-hand side was stocked with long swords and arming swords. Shields and crossbows hung from the ceiling with axes covering the side right wall.

Fawkes finally broke silence, his voice firm and gruff. "You will be issued with an arming sword and short shield. The only other weapon you will carry will be your peace baton. You don't touch anything else, understood?"

Hota and I nodded instantly in agreement; however, Chenchi frowned and couldn't help himself but speak out:

"I have much experience with a long sword; an arming sword is nothing more than a child's toy!"

Fawkes replied in a stern tone. "You will carry what I tell you to carry; when I'm convinced you won't remove your own head, I will allow you to arm yourself with whatever weapon you choose."

Chenchi shook his head in disapproval, prompting Fulten to talk. "You are new Swords, which in turn makes you probationers in your craft. You will be required to patrol on foot. Each one of you will be issued with an arming sword which must always be carried. You will rest upon it come night and dine with it in the day. Never let it leave your side. If you're asked to remove it, you remove yourself."

Fawkes then handed me one of the arming swords. Gripping its hilt, I felt taller than Chenchi. I had only ever held my uncle's old blunt sword when I was a child; it was rare us peasants managed to obtain such weapons. Gripping the sword made me feel like a knight. The sword was light to carry, with a double-edged blade; the hilt was crossed with leather straps that stuck to my hand. The sword felt truly amazing. Fawkes looked at me with a raised eyebrow; my eyes lit up as I glared at the shiny steel glistening from the blade.

Fawkes was satisfied with my appreciation; "Later I will show you how to use it."

I beamed like a child who had found his father's old rusty knife. I noticed Chenchi looking unimpressed as he held his new sword. Chenchi was at least ten years older than me; he had been a Baron's guard for several years, so was used to armed combat. He was clearly underwhelmed by the weapon he had been issued, making no attempt to hide his annoyance.

Lev began to hand out our uniforms; navy tunics with white underlinings with dark brown boots made with the smoothest leather I had ever felt. Lev supplied us each with a nasal helmet. The steel grooves curved around our noses allowing us to breathe; he informed us that the helmet was optional to wear on daily patrols. We received a thick leather belt to attach our scabbards and peace batons to our waist.

The best additions were our common order armour, only to be worn in pre-planned battle or when ordered by our superiors. We were handed a great helmet which was bucket shaped with a horizontal gap allowing us to see. Fawkes gave us each a steel chest plate with *BS* engraved in the top left corner. We tried on gauntlets for our hands and chausses for our legs. Hota and I looked at each other, impressed with the armour we had been issued. I had seen knights covered head to toe in this type of armour and was not surprised by its heavy weight, restricting my movement. The most amusing part was witnessing Chenchi attempt to squeeze his body into the armour. Fawkes soon spoilt the fun and demanded we remove the common order armour and hand it back.

I left the armoury stumbling and dropping pieces of kit on the ground; this was clearly amusing Lev who was barely able to contain his snigger.

Fulten raised his eyebrows and sighed. "Lev will see you to your quarters, get your tunics on and return to the parade room immediately."

Passing the stables, Lev looked back at me still chuckling as I dropped my sword on the floor like a bumbling child. I avoided eye contact, feeling frustrated at myself.

"Can you all ride?" He asked.

Chenchi scoffed and flapped his hand at Lev; "I was a Baron's guard, of course I can ride."

Lev was unamused. He raised his chin and peered down his nose toward Chenchi, pursing his lips. "You're lucky the governor ever granted you permission to join us, he can't stand the baron and his band of whoreson guards."

Chenchi shook his head as he muttered something under his breath. In my mind, he wasn't making the best impression. I couldn't quite work out why he was even here; his arrogance and self-righteousness surely wouldn't do him any favours.

The green field behind the lock up was the grounding for the log-built huts. The largest of the quarters was surrounded in wooden fencing.

Lev pointed over to it. "That's the governor's hut."

He needn't have said, it stood out like a sore thumb against the others. It screamed 'superior' with its large plot. The oak was glimmering, unlike the others that appeared dilapidated.

Lev nodded his head in the direction of the smallest hut on the grass. It was in the worst condition with some of the wood rotting. However, for me it appeared as grand as a palace. My family home was much smaller and housed three of us after the death of my father.

Lev smirked; "Granted, it leaks a little. The mice are friendly though."

I let out a little chuckle at his remark which seemed to please Lev. I got the impression that he was quite fond of me; or rather, he tolerated me more than he could Chenchi and Hota. Regardless, I was just grateful to be given this opportunity, and I'd make damned sure I stayed onside.

5

SWORN

Chenchi snarled in disgust as he examined our new quarters. Three small wooden beds covered in cobwebs occupied part of our chambers. The pot covering the fire pit was rusted and covered in old food stains.

"It's a dump; they live better in Burn Oak," Chenchi muttered angrily.

Hota sharply replied; "It's home, so get used to it. Although I'm not sure you will get on that bed, it will be amusing seeing you try."

I chuckled along with Hota, laughing at Chenchi's expense. I playfully nudged his shoulder in unspoken agreement. We began to get dressed in our new navy tunics, which appeared to distract Chenchi's grievance with our quarters.

Walking across the rear yard I felt a sense of pride, gripping the hilt of my sword, which hung down my thigh. My mind wandered to Lady Ivy. I was curious to see her reaction to me, now wearing the uniform of a Blue Sword. Would my new-found honour make me more appealing to her? The beatific thought was short lived, by remembering her status as baroness. I couldn't wait for Asher to set eyes on me, no longer having to endure his ignorance.

The parade room was full on our arrival; Fulten, Lev and Fawkes were all seated, waiting. I caught Fulten examining my uniform, ensuring I was well presented. He nodded in approval, before Lev began tormenting us.

"Fresh new puppies, now if only your mothers could set eyes upon you now. Would almost have made it worthwhile pushing you from their bellies."

Moments later, the rear door opened. It was him, the governor. He stomped into the room appearing fiercer than I remembered. He glared over to the three of us scanning up and down, observing our new attire. I arched my back upright in order to stand up straighter, glancing towards Hota, mirroring his greeting. Even Chenchi seemed inferior towards the governor. His three chains hung neatly, dangling from his broad chest. He stepped to the front of the room, before addressing us.

"You may wear the tunic of a Blue Sword, but be assured, this does not make you worthy of its crest. The real trial begins here and now. I have no doubt that one if not all of you shall fail. I do not care for opinion, emotion or expertise. From here on you are to be impartial, detached and integral. You only justify yourself to me, no baron nor judge. Do you all understand?"

We all dropped our strong personas as our eyes flittered between each other and the rather standoffish man before us – I could only assume the previous recruits were just as perplexed as I was at his statement. I expected to give my everything to the Blue Swords, but I almost felt as though he was asking us to sell our souls in this opening statement.

Fulten stood abruptly and frowned. "The words you are looking for are 'Yes, sir.'

We all instantly responded, swiftly repeating Fulten's words.

It seemed none of us valued our souls too much after all. The governor glared at us with intense eyes and continued his speech. He glanced down to a scroll in his hand;

"You will be paired with a tutor. Jep, you will be with Sword Fulten, Hota will join Sword Lev and Chenchi, you will be tutored by Sword Fawkes. You have been given the privilege of working with some of the most capable Swords in Thear. I urge you to embrace their wisdom and do exactly as they ask and don't get yourself killed, for neither I nor any other in this room will mourn you."

My attention was drawn to the archway detaching the parade room from the combat room. A man wearing a long black robe gracefully entered, followed by Sergeant Hock. He was probably around forty years old but looked older with his unkempt hair. Sergeant Hock proudly introduced him, before indicating for us to stand.

"This is Father Arrend. You will listen to his guidance."

Father Arrend gave us all a beaming grin as he looked around the room, greeting us individually with his kind eyes. His warmth was refreshing after receiving the governor's speech.

"Welcome to the Blue Swords; what a blessing you are. Please protect us and be patient with us. May the Lord guide you through and keep you safe on your journey."

I noticed Fulten bow his head, muttering the word Amen. Like me he was a man of faith, even though my past behaviour had tested that at times.

Father Arrend invited us to attend Sunday service, offering us his council should ever we need it. He held out his hands, requesting that we repeated him in taking our oaths.

"I do solemnly swear and declare that I will serve the people as a Sword; I will be fair and do my best to keep the peace. I will protect the people and uphold the law."

We repeated the vow in a shallow chorus of mumbles as Father Arrend bowed his head slowly in gratitude. Offering us peace, he stepped back and made way for the governor.

The governor showed his appreciation to Father Arrend, before addressing the rest of us.

"You are now officially probationary Swords. You will begin your journey with continuous training and mentoring to become independent Blue Swords. You will abide by our values and uphold our laws. We expect commitment, dedication and passion. If I sense at any time that any of you are not capable, you are gone."

The governor turned on his heels and left the room without a second glance. My stomach grumbled loudly; Hota who was sat nearby turned to look at the source of the roar. At times I had gone hungry for days; I looked forward to having regular meals as a Blue Sword; it was as much about the security they offered of being fed, watered and having a roof over my head as much as it was about the status.

Father Arrend left with Sergeant Hock. The room became a lot more relaxed with Fulten taking over, giving direction on our training to come. Fawkes was to deliver our combat application, Sword Lev in charge of our stable duties and Fulten deliver our Blue Sword etiquette. Fulten insisted that we begin, ordering us to the combat room.

Once there Fawkes took over instructing us to grip the handles of our swords with our strongest hand. Fawkes taught that whichever arm was our strongest, we were to place the sword on the other side of our belts; this way we could draw the sword accurately and swiftly. We were shown the most basic of strikes and blocks, but I was so eager to learn it all. It was the first time I had ever handled a sword and it felt good. After a few hours, the sword became a part of my dominant arm and felt natural to swing. I wished I could spend the whole day training with my new weapon as I felt myself improving with every lashing of the blade.

Occasionally, Fawkes would call over to me and give me slight praise for my efforts. Hota and Chenchi were much more competent with a blade; it was clear their previous experience training around the Baron's guards had given them much combat experience. As much as their abilities were inspiring, it made me more driven to practice so I could one day match their capabilities.

As the combat room darkened from the evening sky, Fawkes dismissed us for the day, inviting us to attend the parade room for food and ale. Tables and chairs had been pushed together forming a makeshift banquet table. My eyes widened at the sight of the spread that had been placed before us. Cheese, bread and meat filled the table, all causing my mouth to water. To my standard, the meal was fit for royalty, but from Chenchi's grunt I could only assume he was accustomed to much better. Lev was already seated with Fulten to his right and Hock to his left. Sergeant Hock wasted no time and had already began to scoff on a chicken leg, so much that its juices ran down his chin. Three empty stools lined the opposite side of the table, on which Fulten invited us to sit. Fawkes entered behind us and took the seat at the head of the table. I noticed there was no other chair;

I muttered quietly to Lev sat opposite me. "Will the governor not be needing a seat?"

Lev began to chuckle only to be interrupted by Fulten, "He dines with his family in their quarters."

"He wouldn't want to eat with this ugly lot, enough to put a man off his food," bellowed Hock across the table, spitting out the food he chewed.

Fulten asked Fawkes to comment on our time combat training; however, Fawkes did not appear talkative, grunting and giving one-word answers. He offered no praise for either one of us seeming rather unkeen to socialise with the rest of the table. The rear doors opened to the parade room, catching Fawkes's attention. He slowed his chewing down and discreetly wiped the crumbs from his mouth.

Lev cheered; "Finally, more ale!"

Turning around to see the cause of Lev's excitement, I noticed a woman enter the parade room, holding a wooden tray. Her luscious long blonde hair disguised her tattered dress; she was pale with flush red cheeks.

On entering, she yelled back to the open door in a stern tone: "Come on girl, the men are waiting."

A young girl burst into the doorway, brash and excitable. Her hair was also golden blonde like the woman who called for her. Her laced vest covered a dirty white shirt, whilst her oversized dress dragged across the floor. She answered back to the woman, calling her mother; the girl's accent southern and high pitched. Her cheerfulness was infectious, making me smile. The woman was much more tense and stressed; she called to her daughter, demanding her to behave and fill the beakers with ale.

Fulten attempted to calm her; "No one will go hungry or thirsty at this fine table. Men, I want you to meet the young lady who keeps this place running: Isa."

A cough came from the little girl, who stood, arms folded, frowning at Fulten. Fulten smirked and sat back in his chair.

"Oh - and not forgetting her fine warrior of a daughter, Blair."

Blair shouted; "One day, I will be a Sword, won't I, Fulten?"

Fulten giggled. "That you will, little one, that you will."

Chenchi leaned forward cupping his beard, letting out a sigh.

Fulten glanced over, noticing his impatience. "Do I irritate you Chenchi?"

Chenchi looked over, shocked at Fulten's challenge. He stuttered, questioning the Blue Swords' rules on male only Swords. Fulten remained collected and allowed Chenchi to continue digging his hole.

Blair cut the tension by mocking Chenchi; "I have cut down trees bigger than you."

Isa demanded her daughter's silence, requiring that she apologise to Chenchi for her manners, but the room filled with laughter, coming quickly to Chenchi's aid.

Blair was a curious little girl; she was not fazed by the company she kept and continued to engage in conversation, wanted or not. She was engrossed by Chenchi's mass, asking him question after question; he rolled his eyes, clearly growing annoyed at her pestering. Isa's instructions were ignored by her daughter; she was encouraged by Fulten's light humour. The more ale I drank the more I could not believe that I, Jep, a peasant boy, was being waited on, eating rich cheese and fresh meat.

Isa wandered between Fulten and Lev, leaning over the table, filling their beakers. Lev glared at her rear, eyeing her legs up and down. He sniggered, enjoying the view before raising his hand.

"Touch her and I will cut your fucking hand off."

"I think we should all retire for the night; the pups need their rest."

We left the lock up and headed for our quarters. My stomach was grateful and the growling I'd endured all day finally settled. Chenchi struggled to fit his large body into his bed, his limbs hanging over like a sloth on a tree branch. Hota nudged me and subtly nodded over at the great lump, laughing. I couldn't help but burst into a fit of hysterics, giving the game away. Before we knew it, Hota and I were in full fits of giggles at Chenchi's attempt to adjust himself in his bed. He bolted upright giving us an unimpressed glare as he finally settled in for the night.

Composing ourselves, conversation moved onto our day; it wasn't long before Chenchi's heavy snoring kicked in. Hota congratulated me on my first day. I reminded him that it was himself who allowed me to enter Stanford, at which he proudly placed his hands behind his head, before stretching out his bed.

Letting out a sigh, Hota said: "I get a good sense about people; something tells me we will be great friends."

As I climbed onto my bed and gazed up at the thatched roof, my thoughts drew back to Ivy; I drifted off to sleep, envisioning her infectious smile.

6

DAY ONE

Sleeping on a bed took some getting used to. It was strange waking feeling well rested; even Chenchi's snoring and groaning in his sleep gave me little interruption. The sun splintered through the cracked wall of the hut as birds sung from the surrounding trees. I was the first one awake in our quarters and after getting dressed in my new attire, I went outside and began to swing my arming sword just as Fawkes had shown us the previous day. The steel hissed as I thrashed it from side to side; it felt good. The hilt felt smooth and natural in my grip. Empowerment filled my body, sourced by this neatly crafted weapon. This feeling was unfamiliar, but it was bliss.

The creaking door to our quarters opened; I was joined by my new companions Hota and Chenchi. Chenchi appeared in a lighter mood; he greeted me with a half-hearted grin, whilst Hota patted me on the back, yawning as he spoke.

"See the big lump just needs his sleep; he is no different to a new-born."

Chenchi laughed, "Who doesn't miss sucking on their mother's breast?"

We were the first in the parade room that morning and refused to speak amongst each other, anticipating the arrival of the governor. The rear door opened and we all sat upright in our seats until we noticed it was only Lev. He started to wave, frantically upwards insisting we stand up. Behind Lev, followed the governor. He glanced over to each of us, ensuring we were all ready and prepared for the day ahead. Turning his attention to Lev, he demanded that we were briefed for duty.

Lev wasted no time, embracing the governor's authority. "Yes governor. News from the dungeon: Linc has been released without judgement, his time has been served. We have three travellers enjoying our hospitality after getting in a brawl with some locals at the Viking Invader. From the town we have had more reports of thefts from the Finch estate and lastly, Baron Asher has ordered we spend more time patrolling his grounds for poachers."

The governor appeared irritable, shaking his head, before interrupting Lev. "The Baron can kiss my arse if he thinks my Swords are assisting his guards."

His comments forced me to snigger, clearly unintended from the governor's firm expression. It was refreshing to learn that the governor shared my hatred for Asher as my mind began to wander back to our first meeting, where he humiliated and belittled me. Lev interrupted my thoughts to continue with the briefing.

"One more thing you pups will soon become familiar with are our two rival bands. Rumours are that the Western Peasants have taken the life of a local from the Burn Oak band. No one has claimed responsibility. With the Baron Hill festival around the corner tensions in the slums are running high."

The governor gave us the history surrounding the two bands that had declared unrest on each other within town. The peasants from the west side of Stanford had a long-standing feud with the peasants of Burn Oak. There appeared to be no logic around the clash, just two sets of people from different locations at loggerheads over nothing. It was hard to understand, and I could only imagine it was down to poverty and territorial human instinct. I was unaware of the Baron Hill festival and was too apprehensive to raise my arm to ask in front of the governor.

The door flung open and we were joined by Sergeant Hock who glared over to us. He clucked on seeing us sat tensely in our gleaming uniforms.

"Don't you pups look smart? Right - listen up; the postings are as follows: Jep, you and Fulten will be on daytime duties, Lev and Hota night hours, which leaves Chenchi and Fawkes doing station duties. Sir - am I right in thinking you will be making a rare appearance in the town today too?"

It was the first time I noticed the governor smirk as he replied, "I may show my face and endure a local or two. Right – come, let us get to work."

I felt a slight flutter hearing my name called out for daytime duties, even more so on knowing that the governor would also be present. My stomach settled on seeing Fulten arrive; however this was short lived. He appeared red faced and slightly agitated, as if he was in a rush to leave. He firmly waved for me to follow him into the rear yard; there was no welcome, only a stern order to check I had my sword and peace baton. Once on the yard he came to a halt and looked either side to check who was nearby.

Turning to face me he said, "I suspect you have heard that Linc was released from the dungeon. I am sure you understand the mace he carried was intended for you?"

I replied nervously, "Yes, I could sense his hatred towards me."

Fulten stepped closer, leaning down towards me, lowering his voice.

"Linc is a one of hell's greatest creations, he was once a Baron's guard and even they turned their backs on him. He comes with a reputation, so be mindful not to underestimate his capabilities. You have shattered his reputation and the man does not have the courage or honour to challenge the likes of Fawkes, so you my boy are easy prey."

I paused, not knowing how to respond. A shiver went up my spine as the name Linc haunted my mind for a few moments. Placing my hand on the hilt of my sword my thoughts began to settle.

Fulten had an edge about him, even though he came across jolly and friendly; he was clearly experienced and didn't suffer fools lightly. I was excited at the thought of being tutored by him and keen to learn from his wisdom. He was different from the other Swords, milder and more patient. His rounded belly and bushy beard made him appear more like a butcher than a warrior. He did however take great pride in his uniform: the tunic he wore was well pressed, without a speck of dirt in sight.

With a clear blue sky above me, the air felt fresh. Fulten led the way, walking at a steady pace. Not much was said walking through the

Finch Estate, my nerves blocked any thoughts of making conversation. The slight incline up towards the market square left Fulten red faced and out of breath.

He glanced over to me, clearing his throat; "Jep I'm not walking you boy, you're a Blue Sword so stop slouching and walk by my side."

I struggled to maintain my grin, risen from Fulten's frustration over his lack of mobility. Our presence drew attention, and this was something I was not used to. Most of the locals made a point of wishing us good day, whilst some lowered their heads at the sheer sight of us. I naturally lost my usual slouch and arched my back, standing tall. The feeling was grand, I was thriving from all the attention.

Fulten began to question me on my home. It was refreshing to hear that he had passed through my village of Somerby whilst on his travels. Unlike Hota, he made no sarcastic remark about me being from north of the river. He asked about my father, emotionless upon learning of his death to plague. Fulten began to interrogate me on my intentions and reasons for leaving home. He admired that I arrived with the intent of bettering my life and one day providing enough coin to return home to aid my mother and sister.

In the flow of my conversation, he rudely interrupted me. "Can you read and write boy?"

"I can read a little, my sister taught me. But no, I cannot write," I replied.

Fulten smiled, giving me a heavy, reassuring pat on the back. He pointed towards the square, enthused by what he saw. "I shall teach you to write, but first we need to eat."

At the square, the market was bustling. Fulten had a natural way with the locals, embracing them at every opportunity and greeting the warier folk. He comforted people in his surroundings by his jolly demeanour. Most made efforts to be noticed by him, as if he was someone of huge importance. I on the other hand appeared to go unnoticed, as if I was a warmup act rather than the main event. This suited me, for I couldn't help but feel apprehensive and out of place around the large crowd. Most my life was spent going unnoticed, so this sudden urge of attention was a lot to deal with. It was most certainly the crest Fulten and I displayed which created so much interest.

Rich odours of herbs and spices filled the air, all produced from local food traders. Fulten glanced over to the far side of the courtyard, his face illuminated like an excitable child. He marched away, forcing me to hasten to keep up with him. He came to a halt by a stand selling thick rustic bread and pots filled with loose meat cuts.

Waving his arm, he demanded I hurried. "See -that, my boy, is what I call food."

He pointed to the meat, inhaling its aroma. "They call it a slab. Look at that thick, crusty bread. Just bloody marvellous."

He was right; the bread looked divine; it was the freshest loaf I had ever seen. The man behind the stall was thin, with long, matted, greying hair. He was scruffy and like me well in need of a wash. His skin was wrinkled from age and I couldn't help but notice his lack of teeth when he grinned at the sight of Fulten.

"Sword Fulten, a pleasure to see you as always."

Fulten looked back at the old man, with an equal grin. "Pip, my old friend, how are you on this fine spring morning?"

Pip was much less upbeat in his reply. "I have been better. But you're far too busy to hear the grumbles of an old man."

Fulten arched his back, "Hey, on the contrary, what troubles, friend?"

Pip glanced around, to ensure no one else was listening in. "It's them damn Baron's guards. They come here demanding more tax. Gil, he is the worst, like an angry terrier, the man hasn't been made right, he has devils' blood. Anyhow who is this shiny new coin?"

Fulten glanced down at me, proudly introducing me as his new student Sword. Listening to him describe me as a Blue Sword gave me goose bumps. The feeling was surreal, to be somebody, not just a flea to smack away. Pip held out his hand and welcomed me to his stall; hearing him greet me as a Sword gave me a sense of honour and nobleness. Pip himself was easy to like, he had an air of warmth about him, which made it easy to be in his company.

Fulten requested two of Pip's finest pork slabs. Pip obliged, filling two slices of thick, crusty bread with hot fresh pork. Refusing to take any coin, Fulten demanded he take payment. There was no way he would have dined off Pips livelihood, after hearing his struggles with the Barons guards.

"You're a good man Fulten, may angels forever watch over you."

Fulten bit into his slab, spitting food, whilst wishing a Pip good day.

Fulten insisted that we remained in the centre of the town. Not many words were exchanged as we devoured our pork slabs. Each bite was perfection, the meat was tender and fell apart in my mouth. Fulten gave me a nudge in the ribs, nodding his head at a distraught peasant woman approaching us. She was pacing, getting closer to where we stood. She rubbed tears from her puffed eyes. It was hard to understand what she was asking; the lady stuttered with emotion.

Fulten brashly ordered her to be calm. "Speak clearly, woman, what troubles you?"

The peasant woman caught her breath, before blurting out the cause of her distress.

"They cut him; he is only a boy, why would they do that? Please come quick."

Fulten raised his voice demanding to know the location of the injured boy.

The woman gulped, "He is at the Baron's hall, please come quick, help my son."

She sprinted off in the direction of the Grand Hall. I was close behind her, my hand firmly gripping the hilt of my sword, in order to stop the scabbard catching my leg. Fulten panted like old dog on a hot day, whilst attempting to keep up. I noticed him lean over, clutching his hips, attempting to catch his breath. He waved me on, so I stayed close to the distraught peasant woman. The main gate to the hall was open. A trail of splattered blood led towards the front doors of the baron's residence. The woman began to bellow at me, indicating that her son was inside. I remained close, startled by the thick blood stains on the ground.

Once inside, we hurried into the bakehouse where I saw the horrific sight of a young boy flat on his back. He couldn't have been more than ten years old; his light blond hair was drenched in blood, as were the rags he wore. One of the servant girls was cleaning a deep gash above his eye. With each wipe the boy shuddered and yelped like a trapped animal. I glanced over him, examining the wound. It was deep and skin had been separated, showing bone. I glanced to the boy's mother, who was glaring back at me, awaiting my input.

Kneeling next to the boy, he looked at the crest on my tunic. He went silent just glaring between my face and the crest. I called up to his mother, demanding more cloth, to stop the bleeding. I smiled at the boy, offering him reassurance, before his mother returned.

"Do you have a name?"

"Caleb," muttered the boy.

Caleb's mother interrupted, demanding that he identified the person who had done him harm. Paying no attention, he remained engrossed with me, before divulging his desire to become a Blue Sword.

I smirked back down at the pale boy; "This will be your first battle scar."

The blood gushed from the wound relentlessly. I shouted for more rags as the cloth was not soaking up the volume of blood. I felt a gentle brush against my shoulder, followed by a soft voice;

"Here you are, I have called for water to be brought immediately."

I turned, looking over my shoulder to see Lady Ivy glancing down at me. My heart began to race as her angelic face looked at me giving me a heart-warming smile. Heavy panting came from the doorway as Fulten bundled into the room.

"How are we doing here Jep? Good day, my lady."

Whilst updating Fulten, I continued to hold the cloth over the boy's wound, applying pressure to stop the bleeding. Fulten began to question the boy's mother. I overheard her telling him that Caleb was making his way back from the market with a delivery of pheasants and before he reached the grounds, he was ambushed by an older man demanding his goods. It appeared that the boy refused, resulting in him being slashed above the eye. Loud footsteps came from behind me, followed by a sternly toned voice.

"That little bastard best not be bleeding on my floor."

It was the Baron Asher. Lady Ivy met him with sarcasm; "My dear, would you rather him bleed in the kitchen?"

He ignored Ivy's remarks and bellowed to Caleb's mother pointing his finger; "You had best clean your spawn's mess, woman."

The baron stomped forward, his gut close to my ear, whilst leaned over, glaring at Caleb. I refused to look up at him; my blood started to boil with frustration at his insensitive words.

Baron Asher called down to Caleb. "You, boy, will need to toughen up if you're ever to become one of my guardsmen. Now tell me you didn't lose my birds."

I snapped, standing up to face the baron. My teeth were gritted, attempting to contain my annoyance.

Fulten called over; "Easy Jep."

Baron Asher grinned, relishing my bite. He eyed me up and down, transforming his grin into a sneer.

"Do we have a quarrel?" He muttered.

Fulten ordered me to back away, leaving the baron sniggering at my submission. Lady Ivy broke the tension assuring the boy's mother that the physician had been summoned.

Fulten knelt to question the boy, but unfortunately Caleb was unable to name his attacker. He demanded that I attend the market square and look out for anyone selling pheasant.

"Do not engage them, observe only until I arrive," he ordered.

I nodded, glancing over to Lady Ivy before leaving; she smiled before looking away at the sound of her husband's voice.

"Make sure you get my birds, there's a good boy," he muttered to me.

Grunting, I left the room and headed out of the Baron's great hall. I had visions of hitting the stout pig right in the gullet, but I had far too much respect for Fulten's commands.

Arriving at the square, I made my way to a friendly face. Pip, who had been at the market all morning, confirmed that no one had been seen selling any game, so I decided to try the Viking Invader tavern. The tavern was empty, with just a red headed lady stood behind the serving table. She gave me a flirtatious smile, catching my eye. I strutted over, attempting to appear bold and confident. She gently stroked her fiery red hair, giving me the impression, she was enjoying my presence. Her skin was freckled and fair; she was a true rose. Her voice was poised and seductive.

"Am I in trouble? Must I be shackled?"

Unlike Ivy, this red headed beauty didn't make me shy and nervous. I was the opposite: I felt my old confidence and flirtatious wit come back to life.

She rolled her hair with her fingers, whilst maintaining a permanent smile. This girl was glamourous and fun. I asked her if anyone had been seen selling birds inside the tavern, however she ignored my questions and returned with mischievous wittiness. The tavern girl requested my name and instantly required my current situation. She bit down on her bottom lip once I revealed I was not promised to another. We continued to exchanged pleasantries, giggling back and forth at each other's loose tongues.

"My father always warned me of red heads."

"Your father was right too," she replied.

Leaning casually against the serving table, the tavern doors flung open and we were joined by a flustered and exhausted Fulten.

"Jep, stop drooling boy; the robber is outside."

The tavern girl smirked, whilst I felt my face burn up with humiliation and belittlement. I sprinted, following close to Fulten as he charged towards the market square. He pointed towards a man in the distance,

"It's bloody Soy: grab him."

The robber turned, hearing the commotion, spotting both me and Fulten. He was scrawny, his clothes in tatters. His attempt to flee from us proved his guilt even more. He dropped a wooden crate containing the stolen birds causing a minor obstacle for me and Fulten. Dashing through the market square, locals separated, clearing our path. I felt alive, charging through the streets, chasing down the wrongdoer. I gained distance on the man and then panicked at the thought of what to do if I caught him. Glancing back at Fulten I needed reassurance; sadly, he was running out of steam and falling behind.

The ground became boggy once the robber, Soy, had made it to the Burn Oak estate. I could feel my legs getting heavier, allowing Soy to increase the gap between us. With Fulten so far behind and my lack of familiarisation with the estate, it felt inevitable that Soy was going to get away. Out of nowhere Soy somersaulted in the air as he struck the arm of an onlooker. The impact of the strike caused Soy to collapse to the ground. The onlooker stood over Soy, his demeanour mighty and powerful. I was stunned to see it was the governor who stood over Soy. The governor didn't acknowledge my presence; he looked through me, smirking at an exhausted Fulten.

"You seem uncomfortable, Fulten; may I suggest you are more suited to horseback duties."

Before Fulten could respond our attention was drawn to Soy. He scrambled to his feet, pulling a small knife from his waist. The governor met Soy, gripping both his shoulders, and struck his knee directly into the robber's groin. Soy's feet left the ground from the impact of governor's blow; he let out an almighty cry as his body crashed to the ground, forcing the knife to drop from his grip.

Fulten ordered I detain Soy. Holding his arm, I pulled him up from the ground; his groans were a clear indication of his defeat.

Fulten chuckled; "Not bad for an old man, sir."

The governor snarled at Soy and then limped as he turned to Fulten. "I have buggered my damn knee again; get this scum to the lock up."

Fulten grabbed Soy's other arm and insisted the man was to be placed under arrest. Soy was unsteady on his feet, still in agony after meeting the wrath of the governor. He complained of loss of feeling in his legs, at which the governor threatened him with further loss of feeling if he wasn't silent.

Back at the lock up, my first arrest came of interest to the others. The most enthused was the young girl Blair, who came tearing up to us demanding to know what Soy had done. Fulten insisted she stand clear, that he was extremely dangerous; however, this did not faze her in the slightest, if anything it made her more intrigued with the prisoner.

Once in the dungeon, Sergeant Hock demanded we present the inmate to him. He glanced Soy up and down, noticing his grunts and whimpers.

"What happened to him?"

"He met the governor," replied Fulten,

Hock placed his head closer to the robber's.

"Cut a boy, what a man you must feel. Chuck this scum into a cage where he belongs. He will face judgment in the morning. The noose for you man, let's put you out your misery."

There was no denying that my first arrest was handed to me on a plate, but still it was my first and one that I would remember for the rest of my life. Fulten gave me little praise, not that I expected any. In truth I felt he was a little distant once we left the lock up. My only assumption was that he was feeling rather humiliated, knowing it was the governor who apprehended our robber. I returned to my chambers thrilled by the day's events, eager to boast to Hota about my arrest. One thing was for certain, my first day was one to remember and I was excited for my next.

7

MISSING

The noise from the church bells intensified the mood in the parade that morning, I sat eagerly awaiting briefing with my steel sword pressed against my thigh. Chenchi was seated next to me, with little to say, his posture remaining upright with his hand gripping the hilt of his sword. We both faced forward, glaring at the door, anticipating the arrival of our tutors. Hota remained at our quarters, sleeping off the previous evening's night patrol.

The rear door opened, and we stood to our feet, anticipating the governor's arrival. Sergeant Hock stomped to the front of room, muttering under his breath. The frown displayed on his face indicated he was in his usual foul mood. The rumour around the lock up was that Hock was a heavy mead drinker. It appeared that his moods were a consequence of his previous evening's indulgences.

He addressed us sharply, keen to hurry the briefing along. "Jep; you will join Fulten for lock up duties, once he has returned from morning prayer and Chenchi you are to join Fawkes in the armoury."

Both me and Chenchi glanced over to each other, assuming there was more to come. However, nothing more did come. Hock glared at us, growing irritated with our lack of response. I reluctantly raised my hand, well aware that my actions would cause him further annoyance.

He rolled his eyes and snapped. "What is it?"

"Sergeant, may I ask what became of Soy?"

"Soy has been handed over to the Baron's guardsmen; he stole the Baron's birds, so he will face the Baron's punishment. Now is that all boy?"

Without any opportunity to comment, Hock stomped out the room with no further word. I turned to Chenchi, confused.

"Why is Soy not facing public judgement?"

Chenchi stood up casually before answering. "If it's a crime against the Baron it's out of Sword jurisdiction. Which means Gil will decide his punishment, poor bastard."

"What will happen to him?" I replied.

"It all depends on what mood Gil wakes up in."

Chenchi then left the parade room to join Fawkes. I thought of Soy; the beast deserved everything he got, but for Chenchi to show him sympathy, knowing he was left at the mercy of Gil, had me curious about what Gil's real capabilities were. I was keen to make good use of my time before Fulten returned so I attended the combat room, in order to improve on my sword craft. My morning was spent slicing and swinging my arming sword at the wooden blocks. Stopping to wipe the sweat from my brow, Fulten entered the combat chambers.

"Good day, Jep. Get cleaned up, I need you looking presentable; we have an important guest in attendance today."

Before I had chance to reply Fulten went through the archway into the greeting chambers. I gathered my things and straightened my tunic before joining him.

The dark and dingy greeting room had been illuminated by the presence of Lady Ivy. She met me with a glowing smile from her angelic face. Her long brown hair flowed loosely, resting against her blue silk dress. My stomach grinded with nerves and I felt my back naturally arch to stand taller.

"Sword Jep, we meet again," she said in her soft, elegant tone.

I could feel the skin on my face burning as flutters filtered around my body. My attempt to reply resulted in a muffled stutter. Anxiously I greeted her as Ivy, which was corrected by Fulten in a harsh tone.

"You will address her ladyship as Lady Ivy, if you wish to remain representative of that crest."

I wanted the roof to fall in on me; the flutters turned to palpitations, squirming at my own error. Lady Ivy was quick to downplay the insult and brushed it off as nothing more than a slip of the tongue; she giggled, clearly entertained by my ineptitude. Fulten however did not see the humorous side and ordered me to the combat room, excusing us both from Lady Ivy.

After slamming the room door, Fulten stepped closer, red faced and irritated.

"What the bloody hell was that?" He muttered.

"Well, it was a mistake, a slip of the tongue."

"It was ghastly, flirtatious interaction, that's what it was," mumbled Fulten crossly.

"It was nothing of the sort, I assure you," I argued.

"Well may I remind you, young Sword, that Lady Ivy is a baron's wife and however glorious she is to the eye, she is married to one of the most powerful men in this town. So, I suggest you put your teeth back in and start acting like a bloody Blue Sword. Do we understand one another?"

I thought it foolish to even attempt to argue my mistake further, so agreeing with Fulten we made our way back into the greeting room to join Lady Ivy. Her grin was still pinned to her face as she welcomed us back. Fulten remained casual, acting as if nothing had happened, whereas I remained in the corner like a bashful child. Fulten insisted that he was merely briefing me and bringing me up to speed with her current grievance.

"Young Jep will be heading the investigation of your father; of course, I will be overseeing all progressions."

Ivy squinted, clearly sussing that something was amiss.

"Is your new Sword aware of my misfortune?"

It was Fulten's turn to look bashful; stutteringly he assured her that I was in fact up to date with her complaint. I saw the opportunity to return to Fulten's good side. Remembering the conversation, I had previously had with Hota and Carr, regarding Isaak, Lady Ivy's father, I interrupted.

"Yes, my lady, your father's disappearance. I give you my word that I will devote all my time and efforts to obtain the truth."

Fulten glanced over to me wide eyed, before anxiously looking back at Lady Ivy's reaction to my knowledge. She nodded her head in approval of what I had relayed to her. Fulten smiled, letting out a sigh upon seeing her satisfaction.

I requested that Lady Ivy gave me her own version of the facts to allow me to look at it, through fresh eyes. Fulten nodded in agreement.

"Splendid; then I shall leave you to brief young Jep, my lady."

Fulten gave me an approving nod, before leaving me and Ivy alone in the room. I felt superior and rather smug. Inside I couldn't have been more enthused to be leading the investigation into Isaak's disappearance. The thought of spending more time with Ivy thrilled me, quickly allowing me to forget that this angelic woman was promised to another.

We sat down at the greeting table and Lady Ivy began to open up about the circumstances surrounding her father. She became teary eyed, relaying that she had not seen her father for several years and that the last time she spoke with her father was the day she wed Baron Asher. Ivy claimed that her father leaving was out character for him, as he was devoted to her. I questioned Ivy about her father's demeanour on the day of her wedding. She began to tell me how much he had enjoyed the day's merriment and was full of love. Her memories of the day with her father brought her to a pause; she covered her mouth in attempt to hold back her emotions, before handing me over a dishevelled scroll. The ink was smudged but still legible.

"My father left me this note; it was handed to me by one of his workers at North farm. I take it you can read?"

I smiled back, glancing down at the scroll Ivy handed me.

"My dearest Ivy,

How you are every father's dream. When I look at you, your mother's beauty stares back at me. You have grown in many ways and I have kept my promise to guide you best I can. Please do not feel I have abandoned you, there are things I must do, and I have my own destiny to fulfil. I beg that you always follow your heart and I pray that one day I will walk with you again.

Your loving father

Isaak"

I looked up to Ivy after finishing reading the scroll; her eyes were filling with tears as I handed back the note.

Confidently I said, "I will learn your father's fate; you have my word."

"I have no doubt, the Blue Swords will uncover the truth," she replied.

My gut feeling was that Baron Asher was behind Isaak's disappearance. But I knew that this was led by my hatred of him. Foolishly I allowed this opinion to lead my next question, placing her husband as prime suspect. Ivy's expression transformed from sad to fractious. She jumped to his defence, insisting he was a kind and gracious man. I instantly began to back track, unnerved by her reaction.

"Please my Lady, I mean no offence. I just need to consider all possibilities."

Ivy sighed; "Well may I suggest you tread very carefully. As for my husband's involvement, he refused to allow his guards to rest for days after my father left."

Deflecting her frustration with me, I thought up another question, this time assuring there was no connection to her husband, Baron Asher. I was keen to know more about the farm hand that had delivered her the note from her father. Ivy informed that his name was Elis, the son her father never had. He had worked on the farm for several years, after Isaak took him under his wing.

"Is he still here my Lady?" I asked.

"No, I heard that he left two winters back."

I leaned back in my chair, evaluating the information Ivy had passed on. Ivy remained silent allowing me to concentrate. I was well out my depth; having no knowledge of interviewing I was desperately attempting to come up with a question. I tried to put myself in Isaak's situation, assuming he left out of choice. Where would I go? The answer was simple; home. Forgetting my company,

I blurted out, "Does your father have family in Thear?"

Ivy replied, swiftly. "Yes, he has a brother, my uncle. He is north of the river. But they haven't spoken in years. Besides my husband has already sent his men to speak with him; he hasn't seen my father since I was a child."

My suspicion was that Ivy's husband had done enough to appease his wife. Even with her defensive position around Asher, in my mind the baron was the cause of her grief. I had no choice to but to excuse myself from the greeting room, keen for guidance from my absent tutor. I relayed the information Lady Ivy had provided. Fulten paid little attention, insisting I was going over old ground.

"I would like permission to attend North farm, I want to learn more about this Elis."

Fulten scratched at his beard, considering his response. "I have exhausted all leads from North farm. Elis left because of his illustrious lifestyle as a womanizer. I can only imagine he is in another town, sowing more of his oats. But that aside, go; you may fare better with the investigation than I."

"Will you come?" I asked.

Fulten smirked. "No, you will go alone. Straight there and straight back, you hear me boy?"

Lady Ivy was satisfied with my returning to North farm. Leaving the lock up, I glanced up, noticing a man stood on the gravel outside. His tunic displayed the baron's crest.

Ivy approached her husband's guard. Dismissing him from duty, he disputed her request. Interrupting his debate, Ivy abruptly said: "I appreciate your concerns, however, are you blind to the company I keep?"

The guard glanced over to me, taking a second look at the sword I carried. He raised his concerns, reminding Ivy of his orders from Baron Asher.

Ivy lowered her voice. "Leave my husband to me."

The guard left the courtyard, leaving me alone with Ivy. She smiled at me, insisting we head to the farm. I was quick to forget the attire I wore and oblivious to my surroundings. We walked side by side, engrossed in conversation as if no one else existed. Like Fulten, Ivy questioned me, appearing intrigued to learn more about my past. We were interrupted several times by locals, insistent on passing on their blessing to Ivy. Passing the church north of the town, Ivy stopped to admire its spectacular sight. She made a reference to how remarkable she found father Arrend.

The path to North farm was overgrown with weeds and shrubs. The land surrounding the farm was much smaller than Carre's plot. I approached the farmhouse door, knocking loudly. The door flung open and we were met by a short chubby man, his clothes covered in soil. Clearly annoyed by my interruptions, he greeted me with a grunt. Clearing my throat, I insisted on speaking with the master of the farm. This frustrated him even further.

He bellowed, "You are looking at him!"

Gruffly I replied; "I have some questions about a farm hand that worked here."

Rolling his eyes. "You lot have already been sniffing around here. I will tell you the same as I told the other one. I don't know where Elis went. The lad has been nothing but a pain in my arse."

Ivy stepped forward, removing her hood. The chubby man was quick to recognised her, cowering in her presence. He gulped, pleading forgiveness for his foul tone that she was made to endure. Ivy met him with courtesy, requesting he answered my question. The farm master stuttered, offering us beverages and hospitality. His vulgar tone had left me wound up tight. I was unable to give him the gallantry Ivy had displayed. Abruptly I demanded to know more about Elis.

Bashfully he directed his replies to Lady Ivy. "My Lady, Elis was nothing short of useless when your father was no longer around to guide him. He spent his days chasing around a local tavern girl. Your gracious husband granted me permission to dismiss him."

Brashly I demanded the name of the tavern girl, only to learn she was not a stranger to me. It was the fiery, flirtatious red head, from the Viking Invader. The chubby man could not provide any more. He insisted that I spoke with the tavern girl, assuring me that she would provide me with further information. Ivy began to thank him for his time. He scurried past me insistent on flattering Lady Ivy.

"May your husband live a long prosperous life, my Lady."

Ivy glanced at me, cringingly rolling her eyes. She did remain composed, assuring the farm master that the Baron would learn of his cooperation.

Closing the gate to the farm, Lady Ivy insisted we attend the Viking Invader to speak with the tavern girl. I reluctantly declined, aware of Fulten's orders to return straight back to the lock up. Refusing her request made me feel inept, like a child being summoned home by their mother.

"Are you allowed to escort a Lady home, or do you need permission?" Ivy said mockingly.

I was certain that Fulten would criticise me leaving the Baroness to wander unaccompanied. I had no choice but to joyfully accept her request.

Ivy showed a hint of satisfaction with the new lead we had discovered. Seeing her mood lighten was refreshing, making her company easy. We slackened in pace, strolling away from the farm. The conversation flowed between us allowing me to soak up the time I had with her. Approaching the church, a handful of townsfolk stood in the grounds, gawking up at its tower. The horror on their faces indicated all was not well. A member of the group broke away on seeing me approach.

Calling to me the person insisted on my help; "Please, Father Arrend needs some help, you must come quickly."

Glancing up at the tower, I learned the cause of their panic. A man stood, clutching to one of the ghoul statues. Without hesitation or thought I sprinted inside the church. Running between the pews, I noticed the entrance to the tower staircase. Darting up the steps, I was unaware Lady Ivy had followed me inside. Voices echoed from the terrace at the top of the staircase. Father Arrend was stood under the archway calling out to the man responsible for all the commotion. He had wrapped his scrawny body around a statue at the edge of the walkway. Arrend looked at me awaiting my next move. I began to creep forward, slowly moving towards the man.

With each step my heart raced, conscious of the audience relying on my input.

Arrend recklessly blurted out; "This man is filled with demons, guide him away father."

I turned back with gritted teeth, displaying my annoyance to Father Arrend. Adding even more pressure to my actions, Lady Ivy was now stood alongside the priest. Now closer to the distressed male, I noticed one of his bare feet was dangling over the edge of the tower. My footsteps didn't seem to startle him; I gently called out requesting his name. Chillingly he turned his head slowly to face me. Drool foamed from the corners of his mouth, whilst his bloodshot eyes filled with tears.

His attention appeared drawn to my sword, hanging from my belt. Immediately I raised my arms to verify I was no threat.

Delicately I called out to him again. "Please; I am a friend, let me help you."

Giving no verbal reply, the man began to stare at the ground, appearing rather subdued. Allowing him to reflect, I thought it best to remain silent. Eventually he glanced back up at me giving me a sinister look.

"I have burnt them," he muttered, hauntingly.

Returning the conversation, I decided to appease him. "Who is burning?"

"The children, their flesh is burning." He chuckled.

Unbeknown to me Father Arrend had stepped out onto the terrace, closer to my position.

"See: the boy is riddled with the devil," said Arrend, abruptly.

This prompted the sick man to chant at the top of his voice, howling into the sky, like a possessed wolf. I turned, reprimanding Arrend, irritated by his interference. Aware of the steep drop from the tower, I pleaded with the man to join me back on the terrace. After his excitable shouting, he re engaged with me, still speaking gibberish of the burning children.

Lowering my stance, I offered him my hand. "Let me help you. I will stop them burning."

Father Arrend insisted I stopped encouraging the man, however his comments were ignored. I put out my other hand, hushing him.

The troubled man flickered his eyes, appearing to be weighing up my intentions. I paused, giving him time, ensuring he was not put under pressure. Repeating my offer of help, the man glanced at my open hand, reluctant to take it.

Now seemingly more attentive the man spoke back to me. "I fear you will burn too."

The tear fell loose from his eye, motivating me to offer him more reassurance. "We will stop the burning, protect one another."

Gently he placed his fingertips onto my own. Remaining still, he lowered himself from the ghoul and stepped closer towards me. His stare was now fixated on my eyes. Linking my arm, he glared at me, clearly desperate and afraid. I could feel the shivers from his arm, vibrating my body.

Father Arrend retreated with Ivy, giving us distance to walk together down the stairs. The trouble man sunk his nails in to my forearm, before hysterically sobbing. At the bottom of the tower Ivy let out a sigh of relief. I assisted him take a seat on a pew, whilst he continued to cry. For a moment I pitied the troubled man, curious to learn the cause of his distress and torment.

The doors to the church slammed open; Hota and Lev came charging towards me. The commotion startled the man, who leapt onto the bench, hissing like a cornered animal. I called out to him, reassuring him he would be ok, but it was too late. He eyed around the room, glancing between us as if we were all a threat. Leaping forward he jumped towards me and Lady Ivy, his teeth displayed like a wild dog. Stepping in front of Ivy to block his attack, I pulled my arm back and struck my fist into his mouth. The force from my punch knocked him to the floor, prompting Lev and Hota to sprint forward and detain the troubled man.

Gripping Ivy's arm I led her to the church doors, only to turn to the sounds of murmuring coming from the ill man. Lev removed his peace baton, striking the handle into his head, knocking him unconscious. I winced at the outcome. Father Arrend joined me and Ivy in the church yard, acknowledging my efforts. I had little to say, still feeling deflated about its conclusion. Lev appeared from the church, insisting I returned Lady Ivy home. Not many words were spoken on the way back to the grand hall; Ivy had sensed my reflective mood. Once we arrived at the gate, she turned to face me, gently touching my arm.

"Jep, I feel very blessed to have met you. Your actions today were sincere and noble."

I fluttered at her touch, stuttering in my over-formal response. "I will inform you of my findings when I speak with the tavern girl. Good day my Lady."

My eyes were fixated on her as she wandered across the courtyard. For a moment I had forgotten my place, staring at her as if she was like any other woman. Turning away, I was met by the harsh reality of my informal actions towards Ivy. Gil, Baron Asher's head guard, stood glaring, blocking my path. His initial snarl transformed into a chilling smirk, sending shivers through my body.

"Men are blinded by curiosity. Tread carefully; you wouldn't want to lose them wandering eyes," he muttered.

Reminding myself of the crest I wore, I refused to give in to my fear, created by the reputation of this man stood before me.

Bluffing, I replied; "My wandering eyes will be watching you, Gil."

Gil let out an almighty laugh, mocking my attempt of bravado. His laughter was forged, confirmed by his instant scowl before passing me by. That's when I knew I had gained another enemy.

8

FULLMOON

The dawn sky invigorated my thoughts. Standing outside my quarters, I glared across an empty courtyard. Most of the other Swords were out on patrol. Fulten had already retired for the evening, without consultation on my day's events. Ivy glimmered in my mind, only to be drowned by my thoughts of Gil. Aware of the enemies I had created in such little time, I felt unsettled that evening. The sounds of a child's laughter eased my mood. Blair was outside the armoury, waving around a wooden training sword. Her laughter was caused by Sword Fawkes's role play, entertaining the little girl. Unaware of my onlooking, Fawkes appeared relaxed and playful with the servant girl. It was a side of him I had not yet seen, a side that reminded me he was human. Whilst Fawkes and Blair joyfully played, Elsa, Blair's mother, called out for her to return home. Fawkes glanced over to Elsa, smiling, wishing her good night. Shyly Elsa waved back, grinning at what she saw.

Footsteps crunched across the gravel; Hota and Lev had returned. Lev headed straight for the lock up and Hota strolled towards our quarters.

"Your mind not allowing you to rest?" said Hota.

Conversation was easy with Hota and considering the amount of time we had known one another, I considered him one of my closest friends. I asked about the fate of the troubled man from church. Hota told me of his banishment;

"You act like a wild animal, your get released like one. There is no future for him in Stanford."

Alarming as it was to hear the man's fate, Gil was the true weight of my anxieties. Hota paused, attentive to my reflective mood.

"What troubles you, friend?" said Hota.

I was reluctant to disclose the true reason behind my sulk, but Hota was someone I had grown to trust. Muttering the name of my troubles, Hota instantly played down my concerns.

"Gil is nothing more than a tormenter, ignore this quarrel. Asher, now he is one to keep an eye on. Don't be fooled by the protection of your crest, Baron Asher is not one to play by the rules."

"Why does your father protect him?" I questioned.

Hota brashly replied, clearly unnerved by my response. "My father is sworn to an oath, an oath he gave to the Baron's father, at a time when being a guardsman stood for something. Values like the crest you and I currently uphold. My father has little interest in the spoils that form the current guardsman, but he does have his honour."

Nervously I replied, "I mean no offence, your father must be very proud of you becoming a Sword?"

Hota smirked, playing down the tension, "My father is stubborn, he wouldn't tell me if he was."

The following morning, I glanced over to Chenchi who was sleeping off a long evening on duty. I felt curious about his relationship with Gil, thinking back to their dispute in the tavern on the day of the trials. Hota was keen to make the briefing, insisting I was to get dressed immediately. Alarmingly the governor, along with Lev and Fulten, were awaiting our arrival. The governor paid us little attention, leaving Lev to belittle us before morning briefing.

"Good of you two to join, I do hope we didn't interrupt your sleep."

Hota glanced over to me, bewildered, assuming we had made morning parade in good time. Lev continued with the morning briefing, praising Fawkes and Chenchi's catch of two horse thieves in the town. Finalising, there was no mention of my efforts from the previous day.

Fulten requested I stay behind. Once the room emptied, he lifted his stool, placing it closer to mine. He passed on Father Arrend's appreciation of how I conducted myself at church. Noticing my puzzled expression, he challenged my lack of obligation.

I answered sharply, aware that my silence was beginning to cause offence.

"Why was the deranged man not treated? He has been banished?"

Fulten exhaled, glancing down at the ground, considering his words. "Rarely will you find a happy ending here, boy. However hard you beat your stick and exhaust your lungs, things are what they are. What you must decide is can you live to fight another day?"

Fulten stood from his stool. He clutched my shoulder and softly directed for me to continue with further combat training.

Before closing he turned back to face me; "You will find your way, Jep. Remember this is all a trial. Why do you think I entrusted you to one of the most controversial investigations this town has ever seen?"

His referral to Lady Ivy's investigation was the motivation I needed. Hota was already in the combat room awaiting my arrival. He smirked on learning we had been left to our own devices. Inviting me to collect a wooden sword, he insisted that we duelled. His intention to taunt me worked, waving the tip of his sword at the ground, grinning, awaiting my move. Gripping its hilt, I lunged forward, surprising Hota with the first attack. Hota was quick to react, showing his natural swordsmanship. Stepping to the side he clipped the edge of my sword, before humiliatingly spanking my backside with his wooden sword.

My next attack was as uncontrolled as the first. I charged forward, fuelled by frustration, allowing Hota to estimate my move. He repeated his manoeuvre, this time leaving his leg out, tripping me up. I crashed face down onto the ground, losing grip of my wooden sword. Turning around, Hota stood over me, offering out his hand.

Sternly he said: "Slow down; composure. Gil would have sliced you in two by now. Try again and this time think!"

Taking his hand, I brushed the dust from my tunic. Picking up my sword, I turned to face Hota. Taking his guidance, I inhaled, composing myself and preparing my attack.

Hota yelled across the combat room. "Again, strike me down, man."

Distracting Hota, I threw my sword in the air. I lunged forward, aware of his fixation with my sword. Once close enough, I wrapped my leg around his calf. Giving him no time to react, I struck my forearm into his chest, knocking him off balance. It was his turn to hit the ground; falling backwards, he lost grip of his own sword. I quickly acquired my own weapon, hovering its tip arounds Hota's throat.

He glanced up at me, grinning. "There you have it."

My victory was interrupted by commotion coming from the courtyard. Aiding Hota to his feet we both sprinted to learn its source. Chenchi came stomping towards us, his beard stained with blood. With one hand he dragged a peasant man who was yelling and objecting to his arrest. Chenchi stomped past, refusing to acknowledge me or Hota. Casually following behind was Fawkes, displaying little emotion to what was happening.

He glanced over to a wide eyed Hota; "That's how you do it, boy." Clearly, he was proud of his student's dominance.

Hota gave me a look; "I thought the big man was asleep."

I shrugged my shoulders, unaware of the circumstances surrounding the commotion. Seeing the brute strength of Chenchi made me all the more wary of him. Fulten came from outside the parade room, sniggering at the astonishment displayed by me and Hota. He ordered me to prepare for duty. This time it was I who was leaving the comfort of the lock up.

Strolling through the Finch estate, Fulten began to quiz me on my new lead. He appeared impressed with my interrogation at North farm, unaware it was in fact Lady Ivy who secured the progression of the investigation. By the time we reached the square, darkness had enveloped the town of Stanford. The streets were littered with drunks and folks out to get their fill of entertainment. Seeing it as a peacekeeper made it rather eerie and intimidating. I felt reassured having Fulten by my side. He reminisced past dramas that had unfolded whilst patrolling at night. I listened attentively whilst he spoke about unravelled plots and tavern fights. I was partly excited by what he said, along with apprehensive at the thought of my own involvement in future upheavals.

Wandering down main street we received a few uninvited heckles from some weary eyed men stood outside the Viking Invader tavern.

Fulten ignored their jeers. "Men have a habit of finding bravery at the bottom of a beaker."

It wasn't all that bad: a few local girls staggered over, insistent on being shackled. Fulten gave them little recognition; prudishly he marched on, calling me on like a stray dog. I was relishing the attention and the status.

A voice called from behind, chipper and merry. "Blessings to you."

Fulten was delighted to see Pip, his old friend from the market. Fulten blushed at Pip's compliments towards him.

"Come, come, let me buy you men a drink," said Pip joyfully.

Fulten sniggered; "The Viking Invader, no respectable man would drink there."

"Agreed, agreed. Come - let's head to the Dirty Duck tavern. Don't offend an old timer."

Fulten glanced at me, deciding whether to take Pip up on his offer. "Ok, but just the one mind. I don't want this impressionable young Sword thinking this is all we do."

Fulten muttered to me, insisting it was just one drink and then straight back to the Viking Invader to question the tavern girl. The Dirty Duck tavern appeared a much more respectable establishment. Its roof had been well thatched, and the stone walls crafted neatly. Whilst instruments could still be heard from outside, they were toned down giving it much less rowdy atmosphere. Fulten claimed the tavern was attended by more privileged and advantaged residents within the town. As Fulten proceeded to promote the ambience the tavern had to offer, he was interrupted by the sounds of a distressed woman coming from the back of the Dirty Duck.

The high pitch screams alarmed Fulten who began to dash in its direction. The woman was yelling in the face of a man, beating her fists repeatedly into his chest. More concerningly, a man was faced down on the ground beside them. The man, being struck by the woman, sneered at her frustrations. He was finely dressed, his fair hair neatly tucked into a single ponytail. Our presence had gone unnoticed when the man nudged away the distraught woman before hovering over the fallen man. With gritted teeth, he raised his leg, stamping the heel of his boot into the skull of the helpless person on the ground.

Fulten roared at the man, only to be drowned out by the screams of the woman. Charging forward, Fulten gripped the arm of the attacker, demanding that I see to the wounded man. The attacker submitted to Fulten instantly, making no attempt to challenge him. I turned his victim over. Both his eyes were swollen, and the harsh bruising had amalgamated his face, leaving the lifeless man unrecognizable. Blood trickled from the back of his head, creating a pool around his body. The woman dove down, clutching at the now dead victim. Her satin dress became stained with blood whilst she held the man, crying hysterically.

Glancing up at the murderer, I noticed a sword dangling from his waist. Fulten had already spotted the man was armed. With his free hand, he partly removed the hilt of his own sword, displaying some of its blade.

"Move and I will cut you down!" muttered Fulten harshly.

The attacker remained still; his smarmy demeanour indicated he showed no remorse for the vile assault. His pale beige tunic was neatly presented, and his leather boots freshly shined. The murderer was from wealth, which explained his calmness at our apprehending. Showing a stiff upper lip, he sighed as if he was tired at our engagement. Fulten became irritated by the arrogance on display. Yanking the attacker away, he ordered I stay with the body until he returned.

Before Fulten had chance to step out onto the pathway, the doors to the Dirty Duck flew open. A man dressed equally as elegantly as the one we had detained approached us. He was stocky but short, with a reclining hair line. Like the attacker, he was armed and appeared unfazed by our presence, which caused me alarm.

"Me and my acquaintance were just leaving; be assured we shall not return," he called out calmly.

Fulten snarled back towards the man, "This man is under arrest, now be on your way."

Eyeing me up and down, the elegant man sniggered. "I do not care to humiliate you and this boy."

His confidence gave me chills. Fulten remained composed, offering no submission. The attacker called to his associate before pulling away from Fulten, breaking his grip. He sprinted to the side of his companion, confidently smirking back to me and Fulten.

Fulten ordered me to draw my sword. My hand jittered pulling its hilt out from my scabbard. The murderer casually drew his sword, prompting his associate to do the same. Fulten yelled over to the men, "You will stand down, or you will fall."

The murderer laughed, running his hand down his ponytail. My stomach ached with nerves and fear. I retreated, standing beside Fulten, glancing at him for reassurance. The stand-off was timely. Fulten must had noticed my anxiety by the blood draining from my face; he nodded, attempting to offer me reassurance.

Resting his blade against his face, Fulten was composed and prepared for combat. My heart palpitated as if it was going to burst from my chest.

"Last chance: is there anything I can say or do to avoid bloodshed?"

Both men glanced at each other, bursting into more laughter, clearly confident of their abilities. Fulten lowered his chin into his chest, lining up his targets. Dashing forward, he delivered his first strike, swinging his sword, aiming at the smug ponytailed man. The impact of their swords clashing forced Fulten's opponent to stumble back. Fulten swung his body around and swiftly lunged forward, kicking the second, shorter, stockier man in the stomach. Both the men were now disoriented by Fulten's fearless assault. My tutor took a step back, his sword upright, ready for the next challenge.

Regaining their composure, both men separated, now stalking either side of Fulten. A voice called out from behind me: "You OK, young man?"

It was Pip, concerned by my lack of contribution. I glanced back at him, unnerved, mindful of the rattling blade in my hand. My legs felt filled with stone; I couldn't move. Fulten stepped forward, colliding with both his opponents. Slicing his sword from one to another, he rapidly struck both blades held by his adversaries. Fulten's heaviness and rounded shape had no influence over his swiftness, leaving both men flinching, powerless to deliver a counterattack.

Exhausted, both the assailants retreated, giving them a short distance between themselves and Fulten. Locals spilled out of the tavern, animated by the events that were unfolding. Some even cheered, insistent on seeing violence. Fulten was unfazed by the growing crowd; however, our combatants appeared egged on by their audience.

The shorter, stockier man began to breathe rapidly, gritting his teeth. I was close enough to hear Fulten mutter, "Forgive me father, for my sword is yours."

Letting out an almighty roar, the stocky man charged forward, his sword above his head. Fulten calmly eyed up his oncoming threat, stepping aside, leaving his enemy to hit nothing but air. One handed, Fulten hooked his sword, connecting with his target. The steel blade sliced through the top of the man's head, removing his scalp. Blood trickled from the wound, leaving him dazed, before dropping to his knees. Collapsing, the crowd cheered at seeing the dead body, bleeding out on the cobbles.

Upon witnessing the horrific death of his companion, the man with the ponytail ran forward at Fulten. Each swing of his blade was induced by vengeance. Fulten deflected every one of his assailant's strikes, before stepping in and driving his sword through the throat of the once arrogant and undeterred man. Fulten withdrew his blade, leaving the man to crumble onto the ground. Blood gushed from his punctured neck; Fulten prevailed victorious.

Paying no attention to the boisterous crowd, Fulten demanded I return to the lock up and notify Sergeant Hock of the evening's events. On notifying Hock, he dispatched Lev to assist Fulten in clearing the scene. I was ordered to remain at the lock up and await my tutor's return. Once out of sight, I wretched, emptying my stomach over the gravel.

An innocent called out to me; "Are you sick, Jep?"

I turned to see Blair, the servant girl, standing behind me.

She began to giggle at my misfortune, "Don't worry; I won't tell anyone, they all throw up from time to time."

I glanced back her, displaying a half-hearted smirk.

"Don't pity yourself too much, I expect my future tutor to be made of better stuff," said Blair, enthusiastically.

Blair had removed the edge from my thoughts. I remained at the rear of the lock up awaiting Fulten's return. On his arrival he had very little to say; insisting that I get some rest, he dismissed me to my quarters, with no mention of what had happened outside the Dirty Duck tavern. Standing by my hut, I glanced up admiring the full moon that lit the night sky. Water filled my eyes, leaving a tear to run down my cheek.

9

THE RED LEAD

My heavy eyelids were the consequence of my restless mind. I could hear the birds from my quarters; the night sky had lightened. Chenchi was sleeping the other side of our chambers, unaware of my twitchiness. Hota was still out, after taking over from last night's patrol. Visualising the victim's distorted face plagued my mind. I pictured the heel of the murderer indenting the helpless man's skull. With sweaty palms I decided to get dressed and had concluded that I was out of my depth. I knew that I would need to seek an audience with the governor, to finalise my decision.

Walking across the rear yard, the lock up appeared peaceful. There was no movement from the other quarters, so I assumed I would be the first on parade that morning. Last night's banquet still littered the table. Only a few days ago I would have scavenged any remains of food, but I found myself feeling revolted at its presence that morning. The door creaked open. Isa entered, apologetic for disturbing the silence. She began to clear away the remains of the feast. Tying up her long golden hair, she timidly glanced up, catching me watching her.

"Can I get you anything?" She offered.

"You should not wait on me; I am a nobody," I replied.

Isa stood upright, baffled at my response. He timorous manner instantly changed.

Placing her hands against her hips, she said. "What utter nonsense, is there a reason for this sulk?"

I shamefully removed eye contact, glancing down to the floor. Isa came closer, standing in front of me. She questioned my sombre mood, listening to my quandary.

Isa listened, allowing me to rant about my limited time as a Blue Sword. I bared everything to a woman to whom past conversations were sparse. I told her every trouble that filtered through my mind, from Gil to the horror I had witnessed on my previous duties; I even mentioned my over fondness of Lady Ivy. Isa patently awaited my silence, before delivering her verdict.

"You're afraid," she said softy.

"I am a lot of things, but I am no coward," I said brashly.

Isa seated herself on a stool beside me. "You fear that you are not capable, that you do not belong."

I shrugged my shoulders, like a petulant child, not wanting to acknowledge there was truth in her words.

Isa leaned her face closer to mine, pressing me to make eye contact. "I have seen many of you enter those doors, all proud and self-assured. Most are from noble blood, with status to their name. But most fail and are truly lost. Blue Swords are there for the people, a last hope. If you gain their trust and belief, you, Jep, will triumph. When it counts be their saviour."

The doors to the parade room opened; Isa instantly got to her feet. On seeing Fulten enter, she nodded at me, smiling, before continuing her chores. Fulten requested that Isa left us to speak alone. Before leaving I called to her expressing gratitude for her encouragement.

Fulten rested against the table, examining my demeanour. "You are unsettled."

"I am disappointed," I replied.

Fulten sighed; "Do you know, the first time I was on patrol, me and my tutor came across a woman being fondled by a group of travellers in the square. I was certain she was there against her will, so insisted we intervened. My tutor declined his duties and wanted an easy life, so his disposal was that the woman must be paid, when finished with. As we walked away, she glared at me as if she was screaming, silently. The next morning her body was found beaten and bruised by the river."

Fulten paused, with tears forming in his eyes. I remained silent, incapable of taking my eyes off him, waiting to hear the moral of his story.

Clearing his throat, he continued. "You, Jep, did not leave your victim to die that night in the passage, your intrusion may have saved her life. That is why I wanted you to pass the trial; that is why I insisted on being your tutor. You see it's our split decision that echoes fate."

Fulten gently stood from the table; taking a deep breath he wiped his eyes with the palm of his hand.

As he went to leave through the door, I shouted to him. "Last night I froze!"

Fulten turned to face me; "Name me a Blue Sword that hasn't. You will act when required."

Fulten left the parade room, leaving me to reflect. Lev slammed open the door, surprised to see me there so early. He approached the table, annoyed to see that last night's feast had been cleared.

Looking over at me, he smirked. "So, I hear you saved Fulten last night from some outsiders. I also heard that the dead man's wife was rather attractive. Take my advice, don't hump a grieving woman: they talk too much."

Chuckling to himself, Lev left the parade room. I assumed the consequences of my lack of involvement in last night's events would have meant my name was mud around the lock up, but it seemed Fulten had upheld my dignity. Sergeant Hock and Chenchi arrived for morning parade.

Chenchi slumped down onto the stool, peering over to me. "So, it seems you do have a hair or two on that ball sack."

Hock started on the briefing, finalising with the outcome of last night's incident.

"So, gentlemen, the significance of the story is leave other men's wives be, or you end up dead. Right, Jep, I am afraid it is time for the aftermath. The governor is awaiting you on the upper chamber, in the detector room."

I made my way, still confused by all the credit I had received for being so inadequate. It was obvious Fulten had indicated my competence, however unjustified. Still it spurred me on, altering my mindset on giving up as a Blue Sword. Panic shadowed my brief euphoria, knowing I was on my way to join the governor.

Approaching the top of the staircase I could hear voices: the gruff tone of the governor, along with Fulten and a voice I was unfamiliar with. Knocking at the door I apprehensively awaited my invitation inside. The atmosphere was rather tranquil, considering the governor was present. Fulten stood on my arrival, his mood more jovial. He welcomed me, insisting I came inside. I instantly glanced over to the governor, who was seated behind a table. He remained formidable, refusing to loosen in my company.

Fulten introduced the unfamiliar man. "Jep, may I introduce to you Flint, once a very capable Sword of Stanford, now a detector in the city of Alma."

Flint, stood to greet me, surprisingly warm and eager to meet me. Like Hota, he was well groomed, his hair brushed forward and clean shaven. His piercing blue eyes complemented his appearance. He wore a neat black tunic, with an arming sword attached to his leather belt.

He spoke plainly and got straight to the point. "It sounds as if your initial night patrol was an eventful one, two dead. That elicits a lot of writing. But still, I am satisfied with Sword Fulten's account."

Excitedly Fulten patted Flint on the back. "There is no cause for concern, Jep, this is merely decorum. Flint was as pure as you once, until he was influenced by me of course."

Flint smiled, glancing at Fulten in admiration. Adamant he was content with our actions from the previous night, he insisted on his return to the city. Walking towards the door, the governor called to Detector Flint.

"May you remind the chief of our existence, and that there are requirements outside of Alma?"

Flint paused, acknowledging the governor's request. "Sir, Fulten, Jep. I wish you good day."

With Flint vacant from the room, the governor began to question me on my thoughts from last night's events. Before I could speak, Fulten interrupted the conversation, applauding my efforts. The governor took Fulten's words as truth.

Once the governor dismissed us from his company, Fulten pulled me aside in the corridor. Unfocused on the last night's duties, he demanded I attend the Viking Invader Tavern, to question the lead on Lady Ivy's missing father. About to show my gratitude for his compliments, he insisted I left right away.

Elevated, I made my way towards the tavern to speak with the red head. There was an eerie mood amongst the townsfolk. Some appeared unnerved by my presence. Rumours of last night's deaths had clearly been articulated around Stanford. The people were edgy, rather than dismissive, having been reminded of consequences. Their reactions gave me a sense of authority, making me feel rather superior.

Boldly I strolled into the empty tavern, noticing the red head I had come to question. She leaned forward, placing her elbows on the table, smirking at my approach. I tried to remain stern and composed, signifying I was there only on official purposes. She didn't lose eye contact, staring at me with her pale, freckled face. Slightly biting her bottom lip, she gave me lustful flutters.

Clearing my throat, I attempted to speak in a much deeper tone than normal. "Good day to you. I need some answers."

The red headed girl giggled, standing upright. "Straight to the point. Well, a girl requires warming up."

She toyed with every word I said, flirting and playing me, forcing me to lose concentration. Her insistence on learning each other's names, made the attempt at questioning her much more personal. The name Jen suited the red head. The mention of her past lover, Elis, toned down her flirtatious behaviour.

Now, much less formal, Jen began to cooperate with my questioning. "The man only had time for one thing, his cock. I was yet another one, fooled by his charms."

"Do you know where he is now?" I replied.

Jen paused, sighing as if she had grown uninterested with my company.

"It is important I speak with him," I insisted.

Jen was attentive to my desperation to locate Elis, remaining silent, assessing whether to aid my investigation.

Self-assured, she said. "You are clearly unaware of the way to a girl's heart. Now if I was to suggest some flattery or indulgences, maybe then my tongue would loosen. I have been keen to see the current production being displayed at the local playhouse."

I was adamant Jen was playing with me; however, my inquisitiveness determined my agreement in accepting an evening in her company. I told myself I was meeting her purely for the benefit of the investigation and not to indulge my lustfulness towards the red head. I left to brief Fulten on my progressions, slightly unnerved by his reaction to my personal arrangement with Jen.

Fulten was still rather upbeat and appeared satisfied with the reason surrounding my planned engagement with Jen. If anything, he was delighted that I had used my initiative and showed commitment to the investigation. With Fulten's approval I felt a little excited to be spending the evening with Jen. Before I could prepare for the evening, Fulten insisted that I meet with Lev by the stables. It was to be my first instruction in riding, and something I was rather apprehensive at doing.

Hota was already at the stables, awaiting Lev. He couldn't help but comment on the permanent smirk I was unable to remove from my face.

"What pleases you, Jep?" said Hota.

"Not the thought of getting on the back of one of those," I replied, glancing over to Lev, attempting to saddle a rather boisterous horse. "I do fear, however, I may have got myself in a little bother."

Hota sniggered. "Now why doesn't that surprise me."

Hota was already aware of the current investigation, regarding Isaak, Lady Ivy's missing father. He was impressed to learn that Fulten had allowed me ownership over its progression. Telling him of my new lead, he was already familiar with Jen.

"I have known Jen for many years. We used to quarrel as children. Be mindful the girl does come with quite the reputation, but then, which tavern girl doesn't."

Lev overheard the conversation and began to mock me. "You will itch for years to come with that one."

Snapping back, I insisted it was nothing more than to progress the very stale investigation. Hota then presented me with a conundrum, making me aware of Chenchi's fondness for the girl.

Lev was quick to break my tension; "That is why the big man is always scratching at his ball sack."

As insensitive as the conversation was, Lev offered no insult; it was merely his way -and a way I was becoming more accustomed to. His humour had taken my mind off the matter in hand. The magnificent creature glared at me from inside its stable. Lev chuckled, seeing the apprehension on my face. The gravel churned behind me; Chenchi joined us at the stables. He looked unimpressed by the task that had been set.

Calling to Lev, Chenchi boastfully announced his expertise at horse riding. "I was a Baron's guard, there is no reason for me to be here. I have ridden some of the best thoroughbred stallions in Thear."

Lev glanced at Hota, smirking; "So I have just heard. Sounds like you have mounted many mares in town."

Chenchi frowned, confused by Lev's wit. Hota encouraged Chenchi's debate, agreeing that he was just as experienced at riding horseback. Lev sighed, succumbing to their complaints. He glanced over to me, offering him the least resistance. Taking the easy option, he called me over. Lev pulled the reins of the heavy black stallion, who was clearly unimpressed by the disturbance. The horse reared onto its back legs, thrusting back its head. I stumbled back, concerned by Lev's lack of control.

Lev sniggered; "Jep, meet Spike. He is a little stroppy but just needs some tender loving care."

Lev began to caress the agitated horse's face, settling him down. It was apparent that Lev was very fond of the horses and it was refreshing to see his more serious and passionate side on display.

"That's it, easy boy, easy," muttered Lev to the horse. Lev glanced at me, slowly waving me to step closer. "Right now, steady does it, nice and relaxed; if you get uptight, so will he. Gently take his reins and talk to him."

Cowering forward, I took hold of Spike's reins. The metal buckle rattled, caused by my shaking hand. Lev murmured for me to remain calm. Whispering to the horse, I slowly reached out my arm to pat his neck. Disturbed, Spike reared back onto his hind legs, forcing me to lose grip of his reins. I panicked, stumbling back, falling on my buttocks. Roars of laughter came from Chenchi, whilst Lev rapidly stepped forward, grabbing hold of the horse's reins. Settling him down, Lev looked down at me, sighing, insisting that I try again. I nervously lifted myself to my feet.

I overheard Hota silence Chenchi' s mockery. Taking hold of the reins, I was able to get my hand across, gently touching Spike's muzzle. Lev encouraged me to get one foot into the stirrup. I swung my leg over the horse's back and was now mounted on Spike's saddle. A little unsettled, he began to thump his back leg into the ground. Lev demanded that I remained calm and spoke to the horse. Stroking his crest, Spike began to breath less frantically. The feeling was surreal, like the horse was slightly accepting of me. We had found common ground, mutual respect.

Lev glanced up at me, proudly smiling. "There, you are now as one."

Setting off around the courtyard, Hota gave me an approving nod. By late afternoon, Lev was satisfied with my progress and dismissed us form the stables. Closing the gate on my newfound friend, I glanced into his eyes. I then realised I had a new companion.

10

THE PLAYHOUSE

Wandering the streets under a night sky, my excitement to meet Jen the tavern girl was filtered out by feeling exposed. My Blue Sword tunic made me a representative, a figurehead. However, without Fulten's guidance, I felt inept and vulnerable. I played out numerous events in my head, which were all reminders of how incapable I was, as a Sword. Fulten was surprisingly relaxed about the idea of me facing the public alone at night, giving me strict orders to return once having the information I required. Part of me couldn't help but feel that was his way of testing me, associating it to my ongoing trial.

The market traders had cleared their stalls for the day, yet still locals lingered around the square. From the far side of the market square, I could hear raised voices. A man's deep, gruff voice drowned out a high pitch agitated woman. Some of the townsfolk glanced at me uneasily, awaiting my intervention. Inside I wanted to flee back to the lock up and call upon my tutor, but I knew that wasn't an option. Taking a deep breath, I made my way to the source of the disturbance.

The magnitude of the man covered the woman from my sight. His agitated demeanour and aggressive tone made him a threat. On closer inspection, I released my grip on the handle of my peace baton. The brute was very well known to me: it was Chenchi. His visible veins pressed from his bald head. To make matters worse, the woman he was in dispute with was Jen, the tavern girl I was on my way to meet. She glanced around Chenchi's wide body, upon seeing me approach. It took Chenchi some time to stop his vile insults, before looking back at what had taken Jen's attention.

Grinding his teeth, he rolled his eyes on seeing me behind him. Sighing, he shook his head in disbelief. Jen, on the other hand, saw her opportunity to tease him further.

She grinned, before darting around him, only to meet me with an overfriendly welcome. "Oh, you are dashing," she taunted.

Ignoring her compliments, I pleaded to speak with Chenchi alone; he raised his hand dismissing my request.

Stepping closer, he spoke: "You are welcome to the whore," he muttered.

Pacing off, he headed across the square, red faced and angered. I was unsure how to react. I needed the evening with Jen to ensure I discovered more about this Elis character, yet I didn't want to worsen the already fractious relationship I had with Chenchi.

Having little choice, I decided to remain with Jen. She made little of her altercation with Chenchi, linking my arm and insisting I take her to the Playhouse. Jen's appearance distracted me from Chenchi's upset. Her red hair flowed loosely down her purple silk corset. Her dress tightly hugged her body, displaying her seductive, curved figure. Walking towards Main Street, Jen was quick to dismiss her relationship with Chenchi, indicating it was nothing more than a fling.

Jen was insistent on using the passage by the Viking Invader Tavern as a short cut to the Playhouse. The dim, narrow pathway reminded me of my first night in Stanford, the evening where I intervened with three men taking advantage of a local girl. I pictured Linc, the man who led the attack, rumoured now to have a vendetta with me. Unaware of my unease, Jen's flirty behaviour distracted my anxieties.

The Playhouse was a grand sight; The wooden doors posed as an entrance to the glamorous, bustling foyer. The room was filled with stalls, selling a variety of beverages. The floor had been decorated with rose petals, to set a romantic ambiance. Everyone was dressed in their finery, mingling amongst each other, socialising. My own attire attracted the attention of some of the locals, all keen to offer their greetings. I felt out of place, inferior to the lavish company in the room, but Jen relished in it. She skipped around, like an excitable child, insistent on showing me the stalls containing wooden toys and memorabilia.

Queuing for our tickets, the usher waved me forward, refusing to serve anyone else. With my natural modest nature, I attempted to discourage the man; however, Jen pulled my hand, leading us to the front of the line.

"No charge, sir, I assure you that your seats will allow you to have an unobstructed view of the stage."

Before I had time to protest, Jen snatched the tickets from the seller's hand. Mingling in the foyer, some locals offered me wine in exchanged for them to voice their grumbles. The hospitality was remarkable and something I was enjoying and slowly becoming accustomed to.

The attention on myself was soon diverted at the announcement of the Baron and his wife Lady Ivy. Hearing their names called made me feel on edge. Ivy's beauty took my breath away; her thin head scarf complimented her fresh, leafy green eyes. Even the presence of her stout husband, Baron Asher, could not dilute her exquisiteness. Asher strutted with his rounded belly hanging over his leather belt, savouring the attention from the locals. With one hand he scratched at his bushy, black beard and the other waved casually around the room.

My heart raced, seeing them notice me from the other side of the foyer. I was slightly relieved to see that Gil, Asher's head guard, was not present, replaced by two unknown men standing either side of the Baron and Baroness. Approaching, Ivy squinted, giving both me and Jen a second look.

Asher greeted me as if he had never met me before in his life. "Always reassuring to have a Sword in the room. I trust you are being entertained well?"

Ivy remained silent, disapprovingly eyeing Jen up and down. Her demeanour towards Jen took me aback, whilst Asher was keen to make further conversation.

Arrogantly demanding more wine, one of the ushers instantly handed him a beaker. He glared at me, guzzling down its content, some of the wine splashing onto his beard.

"I know you: didn't you attend to the bastard boy who stained my floor with blood?" said the Baron.

Ivy swiftly interrupted; "This is the Sword who is leading the investigation into my dear father."

Showing little interest, he glanced around the room, "Splendid, useful to have fresh eyes look over it; I fear some of your companions may have become slightly decayed."

His attention then drew to Jen. Asher chuckled; "And I do recall you, young lady."

Jen responded with a curtsy, grinning back at Baron Asher, flattered by his recollection of her.

"If I remember rightly, you have a had a thing for a few of my guards in the past."

Asher sniggered, only for his behaviour to be excused by Lady Ivy. Embarrassed, Jen glanced back at me, uncomfortable with his remarks. As with most of our encounters, Asher left me feeling enraged.

To my relief, the usher informed Baron Asher that his seat was prepped and ready. I glanced over to Jen, who was looking back at me shamefully.

"Everyone has a history they wish to rewrite," she said timidly.

I offered her no judgment; it had merely intensified my hatred of Asher. In truth it was slightly refreshing to see Jen's sensitive side.

"You do not need to justify yourself to me. The stout pig will do anything to tease," I said sternly.

Still keen to watch the performance, Jen requested we take our seats. The stage was magnificent, made of the finest wood. I was enthused to be directed to the front row, as if I was someone of importance. I felt conscientious of my large shaped head, blocking the view of the audience circled behind me.

Seated in a high rising gallery, Baron Asher bellowed down at the performers, inciting laughter from the spectators. My involuntary snarl was broken on seeing his wife, Lady Ivy, glancing back down at me. On locking eyes, Ivy swiftly looked away, focusing her attention on the stage. My curiosity got the better of me, and I found myself having a peek up towards the gallery, where she sat. Now and again I caught her glancing back down at me and Jen; I had to force myself to face forward, as I did not want to appear peculiar.

At the end of the production, I insisted that we make a hasty exit, keen not to have any further engagement with the Baron. Jen saw this as an indication of me wanting to take the night further, requesting we attend the Viking Invader tavern. Carelessly accepting her proposal, she took my hand, excitedly dashing through the audience. Part of me felt hesitant about continuing with Jen, however I considered the reason for the arrangement. Jen led me to the Viking Invader, and I followed with no objection, aware that flowing drink was the key to loosen her tongue.

The atmosphere in the tavern was rather boisterous for my liking. Self-conscious of the crest displayed on my tunic, I was apprehensive and felt on edge. Drunken women flirtatiously teased me, diverting their attention from their own men, causing animosity. Jen's over-friendly attitude towards me reduced the tension and it wasn't long before the novelty of my presence had worn off. Now sat discreetly in the corner, Jen began to stroke her fingers around the back of my head. Nibbling at her bottom lip, she stared at me, seductively. The ale had made me feel lightheaded and my common sense diminished rapidly, yet I still had awareness of some unwanted attention, observing me from across the room.

A familiar and unfriendly face glared back at me. The bruises on his skin were the result of an injury I had inflicted. Linc, the man who had attacked me on my first night in Stanford, eyed me from the other side of the tavern. My senses numbed, but encouraged by liquor, allowed me to return the hostility. I eyeballed him, frowning, refusing to disguise my annoyance. Jen glanced back at the source of my irritation, quick to deflect my attention back onto her.

"You will have no quarrel in my quarters," she said.

Still eyeing Linc, I replied, "The turd will slit my throat in my sleep, if I stay here."

Jen sniggered; "If you leave here, you will end up with his dagger in your gut; stay with me the night. He would not dare shed blood within these walls."

Jen was right: even Linc was not foolish enough to challenge a Blue Sword in the company of this many witnesses. I had no choice but to accept her offer, an offer that was rather endearing. Jen stood from the table and took a few steps, before glancing back at me, nodding for me to accompany her. Following her behind the serving table into a narrow corridor, my eyes became fixated on her rear, complimented by her satin dress.

Locking the doors to her quarters, Jen stared at me silently. The chemistry between us was electric. Rushing forward, she pushed me against the wall in her room. Nibbling at my neck, I became aroused by her confidence. Dominantly, I took hold of the top her arms, whilst looking into her eyes. Forcing her back, our bodies slammed against her door. Firmly I gripped the back of her loose, flowing hair, prompting her to exhale. Passionately we locked lips, tightly kissing, whilst my other hand wandered up her dress. Nudging me back, Jen removed the straps to her dress, allowing it to drop to the floor. Seeing her curved naked body, I had no choice but to take her. Rushing forward, I hoisted Jen, clutching her smooth bum. Tightly wrapping her legs around my waist, I rapidly pulled down my linen trousers. With each thrust, she moaned, digging her fingernails into my neck.

The following morning, I woke to see Jen seated at her dressing table, brushing her hair. Seeing her curved, pale, naked body eased the ache in my head. On discovering me awaken she glanced at me, pausing, assessing my mood. Responsive to my smile, she sprinted over, launching herself on the bed, straddling her legs over my body.

"I trust there are no regrets then, Jep?" She said.

I smirked up at her; "Only a throbbing head."

Stroking my chest, Jen looked at me thoughtfully. "Rumours about me are unkind, I am not the girl you think I am."

Whilst leering at her naked breasts, I replied. "Men speak ill of what they cannot have."

"I have loved once," she said sombrely. Remaining silent, I gave her the opportunity to elaborate. "The man whom you wish to speak about."

"Elis?" I replied.

"Yes, Elis, the real reason for which you entertain me," she said.

The passion between me and Jen was undeniable, but she was right, it was the reason I had accompanied her last night. Jen made the awkward truth bearable, by being forthcoming about Elis.

Bitterly, Jen said. "He left the town in the arms of a whore; she was from the same village as Elis. I have no doubt she now cares for his bastard, in their homeland."

"What is the name of this village?" I replied.

"Whiten; it is north of the river."

Sitting up, I leant my torso against the wooden bed frame. Jen had become open about vital information I needed for the investigation, so I took the decision to push the questioning further.

"Did you ever meet his master, Isaak?" I asked casually.

Jen sniggered; "The Baroness's father? Why yes: he was a cantankerous old git. He never approved of Elis courting me, I was accused of being a distraction."

My desire to repeat last night's events with Jen, made me refrain from pushing her any more. My eagerness to impress Fulten and Lady Ivy with the fresh lead was overshadowed by the fact that I lusted after Jen. A loud bang on Jens door brought our time to an end.

In a bleak tone, a voice called from outside the room. "Jen: get to work.",

Jen smirked at me, leaning down for a kiss. "I do hope that we do not become strangers."

Leaving the tavern, the grim old man who served me on my first night in the Viking Invader sighed on seeing me. Glancing at my uniform, he offered no respect.

He muttered; "You lot are all the same."

Choosing to ignore his remarks, I sheepishly left the tavern. Keen to go unnoticed, I walked with haste through the square, refusing to make eye contact with any locals.

A chirpy voice spoke out to me. "Oh dear; look at the state of you."

I glanced up to see Blair, the young servant girl, stood holding the hand of her mother Isa.

Isa yanked her daughters' arm in a way to reprimand her for her manners. Blair paid little notice, nodding her head from side to side, giving me a disapproving look.

"Fulten will have your guts for garters," said the mischievous girl.

Isa crouched down, facing her daughter; "You will mind your words, child."

Stuttering, I began to justify my outing, only to be interrupted by Isa. She was insistent that my previous whereabouts were nothing to do with her and wished me good day.

Anxiously I entered the parade room. Lev and Fulten were seated, finishing off last night's scraps. Lev chuckled on seeing me, glancing back and forth between me and Fulten. Fulten gave me a bleak look, then dismissively turned back around to continue chewing on a chicken leg in his hand.

Lev sniggered; "I can't wait to see this."

Fulten sternly ordered Lev to vacate the room.

On his way out, Lev stopped, giving me a firm pat on the back. "I hope she was worth the sores, pup."

Blushingly I stepped forward, closer to Fulten. Leaning down to grab a stool, Fulten demanded I remained standing. He glared up at me, frowning at my presence.

Staring forward, he muttered. "Do you think me unreasonable?"

"No," I sputtered.

Now eyeballing me, he said, "So why do make me look an arse?"

Refusing to allow me to speak, Fulten began to rant about his evening searching the town for my whereabouts.

Fulten said, "I decided not to interrupt your shenanigans on learning from the tavern keeper that you were occupied in relations with our potential witness. Do you not understand the consequences of your actions?"

Pleadingly I replied: "I am truly sorry; I was unaware that affairs with witnesses were forbidden."

Now standing, Fulten yelled; "They're not forbidden boy, just unethical. I am more concerned by your reckless indulgences with the locals in the tavern; did you know that Linc was there? He could have splattered your skull across the wall."

Fulten's fatherly criticism, however harshly delivered, was meant in good faith. He was clearly worried for my wellbeing, rather than the fact I had taken advantage of my position to seduce Jen. My cowering expression gave him the remorse he wanted from me. Sitting back down, he exhaled, taking a sip of ale from his beaker. My silence gave way, allowing for the tension to pass.

More steadily, Fulten said, "Now please tell me your heedless behaviour was not for nothing: did you learn more of this Elis boy?"

"He is believed to have headed North, back to his home village," I replied.

"Alive," said Fulten, sharply.

Gulping, I replied, "Yes, the tavern girl said he left with another woman."

Fulten glanced up at me, frowning. "You mean Jen? Respectfully you can at least refer to her by her name. I will relay your lead to the governor. In the meantime, I suggest you focus your attention on the combat room, a severe session in there ought to detox your mind."

II

MEANS AND RULES

The ale oozed from my pores, leaving my skin clammy and stale. With each strike of my baton on the wooden block, the vibrations rattled through my body. I was keen to work hard and ensure that Fulten would notice my efforts, along with my commitment to advancing my abilities. Aware of the loud footsteps coming from behind me, I remained focused on the target, continuing to assault the block with passion and accuracy.

"Did you take her?" The voice behind me called out.

Turning, Chenchi stood before me; the night before he was restless and agitated. The vein was attempting to erupt from his red, balding head; glancing to the ground and then back at me, he repeated his question. Unsure how to answer, my silence and reluctance to reply aggravated him further.

"Are you deaf, turd? Did you take the whore?"

My uneasiness and lack of response was not intended to frustrate him further, I was keen not to lie, along with showing consideration for his feelings. It was apparent his flame for Jen had not extinguished.

Stuttering, I answered. "It wasn't like that."

Raising his head, he glanced to the ceiling before taking a deep breath and lowering his voice. "Just tell me the truth, did you spend the night with Jen?"

Gulping, I sheepishly replied, confirming his disgust. Before being able to justify or reason with the giant, Chenchi marched forward, his face scrunched and flushed. Cupping his hand, he took hold of my throat, forcefully slamming my body against the cold stone wall; I gasped for air at the tightness with which he gripped my windpipe.

With gritted teeth, he placed his face closer to my own, exhaling his breath onto my skin. Rage had engulfed this man mountain and I was helpless to react; the tighter he squeezed on my throat, the more I knew I was finished. He showed no intention to end his attack, stimulating my own hostile response. Clenching my fist, I drove my hand into his groin, making him release his grip; stumbling back he folded over, grabbing at his testicles and panting.

Aware that the impact of his assault had caused me to release the hold I had on my peace baton, I scrambled onto the ground to retrieve the weapon. I knew full well that his reaction would be consumed with utter rage; my only hope would be to even the odds, for I was outmatched by the brute. Displaying my show of strength, I raised the baton above my head, warning him off any further combat; however, his disgruntled growl showed me he was far from deterred. Standing upright, he snarled at me like a tormented bear.

Salvaged by my friend, Hota burst into the room, flabbergasted at what he witnessed.

On seeing our standoff, he yelled: "You fools, what is the meaning of this?"

Strutting over he yanked the baton from my now limp hand, "Have you two gone mad, risking it all for some tavern girl? The governor doesn't care for either of you; he will be sure to dismiss you if he learns of this."

Chenchi remained fixated on me, breathing heavily. I was uncertain if he had heard Hota's words. Stepping closer, he nodded his head, whilst eyeing me up and down. Hota reiterated his concerns, demanding that Chenchi was to yield.

Chenchi remained silent, his magnitude intimidating, leaving me feeling uncomfortable.

Eventually he broke his silence, gruffly muttering. "You are welcome to her; we may honour the same crest, but you are no companion of mine."

Stomping out of the room, Hota gave me a grave look. I asked him for reassurance that Chenchi would eventually pacify; however, Hota offered me none, only advising that I should keep my distance and allow Chenchi to settle.

Hota insisted that I attend the parade room, as requested by Fulten. Once inside, I noticed that Chenchi was already seated. Wiping the sweat from my brow, I refused to make eye contact with him. Sitting on my stool, the floor vibrated from Chenchi's restless leg-twitching. Fulten was next to arrive, offering me no greeting, leaving me to feel like the villain in the room. Sergeant Hock followed; I took slight comfort in knowing that he disliked everyone equally. Insistent on hurrying proceedings along, Hock demanded our attention for briefing.

After a rushed briefing, Fulten demanded I meet with him in the rear yard, equipped for patrol. The walk into town was a rather quiet one; Fulten made no attempt at his usual small talk, and I figured it best to remain silent, so as not to irritate him further. My sombre mood was slowly being replaced by annoyance and hot-headedness. Sighing like a sulking child had little effect on Fulten; he glanced, raising an eyebrow at my self-pity, shaking his head in dismay.

Defiantly I asked: "Am I allowed to know where we are going?"

Fulten sniggered. "The Grand Hall; it is only right that we inform Lady Ivy of our planned trip."

In a change of tone, I replied: "A trip, where?"

"Too follow up on your lead, in the village of Whiten. It is crucial we speak with this Elis boy."

"We?" I said enthusiastically.

"You retrieved the information; It is only right that you learn of its meaning."

The thought of seeing Lady Ivy made me feel apprehensive; the previous night, Ivy seemed a little dismissive and rather unimpressed with the company I had kept. Ambitiously, I considered that her awkwardness might have been a result of her slight jealousy over seeing me with Jen; realistically it was more likely caused by her disapproval of the way in which I was conducting the investigation into her father's disappearance. Approaching the gates of the Grand Hall, I voiced my concern to Fulten, telling him of Lady Ivy's rather brief tone.

"Lady Ivy is an honest woman, with the utmost of morals. I could only imagine she was disappointed by your grooming of a witness."

Confirming my concern, Fulten haughtily opened the gates. I became distracted by his smugness at the sound of a chilling yelp coming from the far side of the courtyard. Fulten looked at me alarmed, before dashing in the direction of the disturbance, each squeal followed the sound of slapping; the high pitched, horrific cry reminded me of a wounded animal. Fulten came to a halt, leaning out his arm to stop me getting any closer to the source of the noise. A plump, balding man, wearing torn rags, crawled slowly on the gravel, the cuts from his knees staining the stones with blood. Drool dripped from the mouth of the distraught man; he glanced back, cowering before the attacker who stalked him. Gil stood over the man with tightened lips, egged on by two youthful looking, impressionable guards.

Gil raised his arm, holding the handle of a leather, studded paddle; viciously he struck the helpless man's back, tearing through the cloth and slicing his skin. The trembling man murmured; his stuttering words too unclear for me to make out what he was saying.

Fulten yelled, "Gil, have you no compassion? The man is lame."

Halting his attack, Gil's attention turned to Fulten. "This half bred stole from the Baron's grounds; we have no quarrel, and you have no authority here."

Crawling towards Fulten, the quivering man sought his aid, but Fulten looked down at him in sorrow.

Pleading with Gil, Fulten begged, "His name is Moon, he doesn't understand; please, I beg of you, let me return him to his mother. I will ensure your kindness is well compensated."

Gil paused before glancing at his influenced guardsmen. Turning back to Fulten, he sniggered, "Crazed or not, this thing will receive the Baron's justice; I think three more lashings ought to do it."

Fulten's lack of response forced me to plead with him on Moon's behalf; I insisted that we could not stand by and watch this horror unfold, but Fulten furiously demanded my silence.

Gil chuckled, prompting laughter from his guards. Moon latched onto my objections, glancing up at me with sunken eyes. Helplessly I looked away, unable to make eye contact with the terrified man.

Fulten clutched my shoulder, "We must leave."

Taking my final look at Moon, he began to grunt, before hysterically sobbing, anticipating our departure. My eyes began to well as we crossed the courtyard.

Stepping further way, my body jolted at hearing a further cry from Moon. Fulten yelled for me to stop, but I had no choice but to sprint back towards Gil. Once again, his arm was raised, ready for his next strike on the helpless man. Bellowing, I rushed the head guard, driving my shoulder into his waist, making him lose balance. Both of us crashed to the ground, but he was much quicker to his feet; now standing over me, Gil was red faced and angered. Panting, he grinded his teeth, placing his hand onto the hilt of his sword. Drawing his blade, he towered over my body, ready to slay me on the ground next to Moon.

Quick to react, Fulten had also drawn his sword, now pointing the tip to the side of Gil's neck.

"Give me a reason, Gil, and I will leave your head here on the cold stone."

Gil sniggered, whilst sliding his weapon back into its scabbard. Fulten demanded that I get to my feet and walk towards the gate, without any further quarrel. Gil scowled at me, watching me step away under the protection of my tutor. Fulten marched across the courtyard, meeting me at the gate of the Grand Hall. I again begged him to aid Moon's release.

Fulten yelled, "You will learn you place, boy, or you are finished. If you cannot accept things for the way they are, then you shall not continue this journey."

Lifting my head, I glanced up at the window above the entrance to the Grand Hall. Lady Ivy stood staring back at me; her hand covered her mouth, alarmed by the dramatics that had unfolded within the grounds of her own home. Looking back at her distress, I understood my failure to save Moon was the harsh truth of the predicament I was now in. The oath I had made to protect the weak and vulnerable was not as straightforward as I may have interpreted.

Pacing back through the square, Fulten made no attempt to alleviate the heightened tension between us. I was uncertain as to whether he was maddened at my brash and reckless actions, or that he had allowed Moon to become susceptible to Gil's temper. Doubt and self-loathing scattered around my mind; for the first time I concluded that the crest I represented was nothing more than a gimmick, second best to the evil that truly ruled over Stanford.

Breaking the silence, I boldly asked, "Will he kill him?"

Sighing, solemnly Fulten replied, "No, but I have no doubt that he will leave him scarred. Come, let's return to the lock; I need wine."

Fulten's sorrow was the reason for my lack of further questioning; running his hand through his thick, wavy hair, it was clear he was as devastated as me at our lack of intervention. On the edge of the Finch estate, Fulten came to a standstill, to clarify our quandary.

He exhaled, glancing between me and the ground. "We have no authority over the Baron and his guards, they are protected by an agreement written many years before my service began."

It was clear even Fulten was questioning his decision, so considerately I lowered my tone; "Why raise your sword to Gil?"

"That was different: a threat against a Blue Sword is as good as a threat against the crown itself. Plus, foolishly or not, I admire your spirit."

The dimmed sky was a good reflection of my gloomy mood; thoughts of Moon, left at the hand of that vile creature, punished my mind. Suppressing my emotions was the sound of further dramatics, coming from a home within the estate. The inability to ignore distressed voices was becoming far too common. The single high-pitched scream prompted Fulten to roll his eyes, frustrated at this ongoing, demanding day. Sighing, Fulten nodded his head, indicating our investigation into the distressed cry, coming from a nearby stone-built house. Fulten assertively knocked at the wooden door, causing a young child inside to cry; the lack of greeting indicated the household was reluctant to come to the door.

Growing agitated, Fulten bellowed. "Open the door, or I will kick it down."

The door flew open, and we were eventually met by a rather obnoxious, elegantly dressed man. His well to do voice stuttered on eying up our tunics. Straightening his faded white chemise, he nervously rested his arm in the archway of the door, attempting to appear relaxed. His obstruction of the doorway made it obvious he was keen to engage outside his home. Fulten grew weary of his false charm and barged past the man, insistent that he heard a disturbance from inside the home.

Following Fulten into the living quarters, the pompous man remained adamant that all was well inside his well-presented home.

"Gentleman, I believe you're wasting your time; I assure you there are no issues within these walls," he claimed.

Fulten sternly replied, "I know what I heard; where is the child?"

Smugly, the man said, "She is with her mother, feeding."

Fulten examined the room, before stomping towards a closed internal door; he ordered that I was to remain with the man, who now appeared more unsettled and unnerved by Fulten's relentlessness. His attempt to make idle small talk escalated my already irritable mood, leaving me to demand his silence.

Now attempting to plead, her husband began to try to justify the injuries. "You understand, these common women aren't accustomed to our ways, they need persuasion from time to time. Now please if you would allow us peace, I will ensure that the Baron learns of your thoroughness and professionalism."

Fulten ordered that I apprehend the women's husband; leaning out to grip his arm, he resisted, thrashing his hand back, refusing to be detained. Realising that his appeal had fallen on deaf ears, he arched his body upright, disgruntled, before spitting in my face. The harsh day's events had taken its toll, and I reacted, allowing my enraged temper to cloud my judgement; pushing the man off his feet, he fell backwards onto the ground. Straddling his torso, I began to deliver punches to his face, picturing Gil's reflection with every blow. My uncontrolled behaviour was drowning out the yells that came from the man's wife, as blood began to drench my fists.

Yanking my tunic, Fulten pulled me to my feet, removing me from the blood-stained man I had beaten brutally. Spluttering, he begged for mercy, barely able to lift his head to plea for his life. Fulten shouted in my ear, ordering that I yield; his magnified voice brought me back to reality, whilst I glared down at the beaten man and the wounds which I had inflicted. My chest heaved; witnessing his wife leaning down, clutching her child in one arm and her now disfigured husband in the other, her haunting cries made my spine shiver.

Gripping my shoulder, Fulten gently spoke, "We will receive no gratitude here."

Ushering me outside, Fulten momentarily paused, allowing me to settle. Circling my fingertips around my eyes, I tried to make sense of my indignation.

Softly spoken, Fulten turned back to me and said, "Let us end this troubled day."

Snapping, I replied, cynically. "Walk away again, like we did at the Grand Hall? Yes, let's leave another one in the hands of a beast!"

"You will mind your words. Now tell me boy, what would you suggest?" said Fulten brashly.

Shaking my head in disbelief, I replied sullenly; "I don't know; the lock up to be judged?"

Bitterly Fulten clapped his hands together, "Now isn't that an idea? Without the woman's oath we have nothing, only an ill vented man returning to his wife, furious at spending the night in a dungeon. You tell me, Jep, who do you think will be truly punished?"

Facing up at the sky, I exhaled, feeling disjointed. I found no words to answer; Fulten stepped closer, aware of the reasons behind my rash and emotional state.

Calmly he said, "There are means and there are rules; we abide by both, my young Sword. Your sensitivity is noble, and something rarely found in a Blue Sword of recent. Allow me to guide your path; I swear, I will offer you clarity."

It was a hard concept to understand, but one I would need to recognize and appreciate if I was to continue wearing the crest of a Blue Sword. Fulten reassured me my naivety would blossom into knowledge and acceptance. In the meantime, I would need to discover if I had the stomach to fulfil the oath I had made.

12

THE BARON HILL

FESTIVAL

Summer was in full bloom and my reputation amongst my companions was bolstering, Fulten was satisfied with my progress and my interactions with the governor had remained sparse, which could only have been a positive sign. He had agreed to grant myself and Fulten leave, in order to travel north in search of Elis, the only lead I had for Lady Ivy's missing father, Isaak. Since the incident in the courtyard at the Grand Hall, involving Gil brutally punishing Moon, I had seen little of Lady Ivy; on occasions she had attended the lock up, pressing the need for us to leave and locate Elis; however, the governor was insistent that all Blue Swords were to remain in the town until the Baron Hill festival had passed. It was rumoured that the up and coming festival was giving the governor sleepless nights.

My relationship with Chenchi remained fractious; our conversations were somewhat brief and to the point. Hota remined one of my closest friends; his additional mentoring had improved my ability to read and write, along with my capabilities with a sword. As for Jen, she was still very much a lit flame in my life, but selfishly she only fulfilled my lustful cravings, leaving me pining for the forbidden fruit that was Lady Ivy.

It was the eve of the Baron Hill festival; the humidity made my quarters unbearable, especially with the stench that oozed from Chenchi's pores. I decided to head out for a stroll, wandering over to the stables, keen to settle and seek comfort from my horse, Spike.

Gently patting his mane, I heard a clatter from the far side of the stable; putting it down to scavenging rats, I gave it little attention. The second clang encouraged my curiosity. Stepping closer to the cause, I had stumbled across a rumour, one that I had speculated on in my head since arriving at the lock up.

Isa the servant woman blushingly pulled down her dress, whilst Fawkes scrambled to pull up his trousers before turning around, exasperated at my interruptions.

My initial pause sparked agitation from the fearsome Blue Sword; "Turn away, boy; have you no shame?"

Witnessing Fawkes's capabilities on my first evening in Stanford, I was quick to do as asked and rapidly stepped away. Fawkes was swift to catch up with me. "Stop," he ordered; "In the confines of this establishment, men's tongues have a habit of becoming loose; I care not for gossip or idle chat. It would be rather unpleasant if I was made to repeat myself; do we understand one another?"

Timidly, I replied. "Yes, my mouth is shut."

Fawkes, smirked chillingly, "Good, then I will have no desire to rip out your spleen."

Fawkes ushered me away, insistent that I return to my quarters.

Wearied eyed, I was awoken by an erratic Hota, hurrying me along, ensuring that I made morning briefing. Chenchi remained his usual ignorant self, only speaking to me for the purposes of formal and needed conversation. Once we arrived in the parade room, I noticed Lev, Fulten and Fawkes were already seated, prepared for the day ahead. Fawkes harshly eyeballed me, giving me a mental reminder of the threat, he had made from the previous night.

Taking my seat, the eery silence reflected the tension in the parade room that morning. Fulten eyed me up and down, ensuring I was dressed correctly and prepared for the coming day's events.

Hota leaned over, whispering in my ear. "The calm before the storm."

Sergeant Hock opened the door, followed by the governor. Hock made it difficult to gauge his true mood; most the time he stomped around the lock up, sour faced and sullen, rarely making time for anyone. The governor scanned the room, his fierce eyes squinting at each of his Blue Swords, ensuring we were all present and correct.

Harshly, he relayed the morning briefing. "The day which we all detest has arrived; blood will be spilt, bones will be broken, and one way or another the Baron will claim the will of the people. The only thing I ask of you is to protect each other."

The senior Blue Swords mocked the governor's speech, jeering his pathetic attempt at motivating his men. His underwhelming words provided me with little encouragement; they did however leave me even more intrigued by the Baron's festival and reputation that had spooked the more senior Blue Swords. Hota glanced at me with raised eyebrows before Hock took his position in the centre of the room.

Following on from the governor, Sergeant Hock spoke, "We have been informed that Asher's champion event will take place at midday as yet we haven't been made aware of any challenger. I have no doubt that some pompous, overprivileged turd will step forward, keen to make a name for themselves. You will honour its heritage and refrain from interfering. Be mindful of numbers, I don't want you filling my dungeon with boisterous drunks that have had a fondle with the local tarts."

Looking over to Fawkes, Hock nodded, giving way to him. Strutting forward, he addressed us, with his permanent snarl displayed from his chiselled jaw line.

As always, he kept his words brief and straight to the point; "Fulten, Lev, heavy armour and horseback; pups as you are, you will be on static posts."

The bleak briefing left me feeling even more uneasy, after being dismissed from the parade room. Convening at the stables, the more experienced Swords began to suit up their heavy amour.

Muttering to Hota, I asked, "What is the champions event?"

Chenchi, eagerly answered on Hota's behalf, "It's a right to challenge Asher's head guard; to succeed would mean a right to the post themselves."

Hota interrupted, smirking at me. "Fancy it Jep? We all know you would love to remove Gil's head."

"Gil wouldn't even flinch," Sniggered Chenchi, quick to mock my inexperience.

Biting back, I replied, "Rumour has it he would much prefer to confront one of his deserters."

Chenchi raised his upper lip, forcing Hota to intervene. "You boys, play nice; today is not a day for a quarrel, we must forget our differences and aid one another."

Fulten quashed the frictions between me and Chenchi by revealing himself, mounted on his horse, his armour glistening from the reflection of the sunlight. We glared at him in awe; however, his moment of supremacy was cut short by Lev's humour.

"Poor beast, having to tolerate you straining its bones."

Even Fawkes managed a half-hearted smirk at Lev's ridiculing of Fulten. Brushing off the remarks, Fulten halted his horse next to where I stood. Tilting his head back, observing me from his helmet, he sentimentally wished me well, as if he was riding off to battle, unaware of what fate had in store for us.

The three veteran Swords rode out from the courtyard, like a formidable force to be reckoned with; their presence would certainly result in heads being turned. I felt admiration for each one of the tutors and hoped that one day I may be as skilled and reputable as they had become. Chenchi insisted that we head towards the festival site; he had received orders from Fawkes on our required postings.

Hota held back, keen to offer me a word of warning about the upcoming event.

"Be mindful, Jep; I have seen this thing go sour in the past. Folk have a funny way of becoming much bolder once influenced by their fill of mead; stay sharp."

Hota's advice made me all the more nervous about the Baron's Hill festival; seeing the crowds flocking towards the market square made the atmosphere more intimidating. Chenchi strode through the large groups of people, dismissively moving them aside, to aid his way through. As much as the bitterness between us had escalated over the past few months, I was pleased to have this Titan on my own side.

Children excitedly rode their fathers' shoulders, all strolling towards the far side of the square, keen to get the best views from the hillside where the arena had been erected. The swarms of individuals forced us to a standstill; the sight of the locals gathering in their masses was overwhelming. It seemed as if the whole town had descended upon the festival to enjoy the celebrations, financed by the Baron.

Chenchi turned back to me and Hota, "Look at them, a bit of song, dancing and the fools forget all about the taxation he squeezes out of them."

The people seemed high spirited and excitable; the event had gathered all the people together and it was a day where all stood equal. Whichever part of town they lived in, they flocked together all with the aim of enjoying the entertainment that was on offer. I observed a little boy, his face beaming with happiness, as he gazed up at his father, gripping his hand with unconditional love. It made me think of my own father; he would often amuse me by taking me to our village gatherings. He eased my anxiety of the crowds with his formidable presence. Since he had passed, leaving my mother and sister behind, I was the one that carried the burden of shielding my family. I missed the security which my father had offered. Now I stood, guarding the community in which I served, wearing one of the most prestigious uniforms in the land; something I was certain my father would have been proud to witness. Straightening my back I shivered, thinking of the honour I had brought to his memory.

Overlooking the arena, situated back from the massed crowd, Baron Asher leaned back in his chair, casually glancing down at his people, dressed in his finery. Even his lavish maroon tunic could not hide his gut, which bulged over his thighs. Lady Ivy positioned herself upright in her chair; her plaited hair ran neatly down her back, covered by a flowered head garment which complemented her beauty. Ivy's glowing smile enlivened the townsfolk; enthused, they waved excitedly towards the podium, bowing, and curtseying to the gracious Baroness and Asher.

Hota caught my stare. "Those curious eyes of yours will be your downfall."

Still squinting up at the podium, I causally replied, "You sound like Gil."

Hota, cleared his throat, rapidly replying to my comparison, "Not at all, I cannot deny her splendour; it is almost tragic that poor woman of her breeding, having to lay each night with that pig."

Hota grinned, pressing his tongue into his cheek. "I do believe the other lady in your life desires your attention."

Hota had spotted Jen, making her way through the crowd towards me; her tightly fitted corset emphasised her large breasts, gathering chants from some of the local men. Ignoring their remarks, her glare remained fixed on me. Giddily smirking, Jen bit her lower lip on catching my eye.

"The ideas that are racing through my mind," she said, playfully, looking me up and down.

I glanced at Chenchi, whose natural grimace was now focused on Jen. I attempted to play down her flirty behaviour, keen to not tease Chenchi further; however, she refused to allow me to brush off her compliments, leaving me to be saved by the governor's arrival.

"Jep, when you have finished toying with the over- friendly locals, may I suggest you get your arse to the fixed post," said the governor, sternly.

Jen giggled at the governor's irritable mood. Seductively she approached him, pouting her lips, "I do love it when a man is wound up tight; they need releasing."

Awkwardly, the governor downplayed her provocative comments, blushing and glancing at the ground. Stuttering, he repeated his order for us to withdraw from the arena.

We stood in line, spread out, but still within earshot of one another; me, Hota and Chenchi were now positioned by the meadow, situated some distance from the townsfolk. On slightly higher ground, I had a full view of the arena, observing the rather excitable crowd, chanting and cheering along with two foolish dwarfs, playfighting with sticks, keen to humour the spectators. Five of Baron Asher's guards, armed with long swords, lined the edge of the arena, separating their master from the local people. Gil had now taken his stance beside the Baron; unlike Asher he found little amusement from the act humouring the appreciative townsfolk. Prepped for combat, his black tunic was covered with a shiny, steel chest plate of armour.

Glancing beyond the meadow, I could see Carre's farm; it reminded me of the hospitality both he and his wife Dam offered me on my arrival at Stanford. Although keen to repay his kindness, I had neglected to attend West farm and look in on the humble couple. Hota coughed, gaining my attention; he discreetly smirked, nodding his head in the direction of the Baron's platform. Lady Ivy was staring at me; she began to grin on seeing me notice her gaze. Our very brief and infrequent interactions since the night at the Playhouse had left me assuming she was displeased with me; however, catching her watchful eye made me overthink her thoughts and intentions. Returning a fleeting smile, I felt aware of the potential eyes that could be observing our momentary contact.

Seeing Fawkes, mounted on his horse, far side of the arena, offered me reassurance about the potential upcoming hostility, rumoured to be the outcome of the day's festivities. The last strike of the drum silenced the people. Asher pulled himself from his chair, prompting the townsfolk to glare up to the Baron, listening intently, as he introduced Father Arrend to the arena.

The priest wandered into the centre, smiling as he circled with his arms outstretched, displaying himself so all could see him. The spectators applauded; he was respected and loved by the people and this was apparent in the response he had received.

Raising his hand for silence, he called out; "My dear residents, may I welcome you to the Baron Hill festival, brought to you by the gracious Baron Asher himself. In the past I may have defied these traditions, yet now I am able to see the congregation of this magnificent town as one; may God bless you all."

The crowd congratulated his brief but effective speech. I found myself feeling sickened by his overpraising of the Baron, yet I had learnt that this town was much like a theatre performance, and I had finally accepted and understood the part which I played.

Asher now moved to the edge of his platform, peering down at his people at the end of his nose; arrogantly he raised a single finger, ending their applause to Arrend. They paused in silence, gripped by this pretentious fool.

"Enough of these pleasantries; now is the time for a real spectacle," he shouted.

The people cheered. Announcing and applauding his champion, Gil casually stepped forward, unimpressed by the roaring crowd; he observed their admiration, returning a raised upper lip, unmoved by their response.

Gil strutted down to the arena, rotating his shoulder, preparing his body for combat. I glanced over towards Chenchi, whose expression displayed only hatred towards his previous mentor. I thought back to the day of the trials, when I overheard the feud between Chenchi and Gil, all fuelled by Chenchi's relinquishment of the Baron's guard. Chenchi's loathing of me had made it hard to discover the truth behind their quarrel. With Hota refusing to indulge in gossip, the only way I would be able to learn of Chenchi's past would be through manipulating Jen further, relying on her divulging of their past pillow talk.

The Baron's hand gesture brought the cheers from the crowd to a halt. Smirking, he glared around the arena.

"Who will challenge my champion? Is there a man amongst you who has the courage and the ambition to take his place and join my entourage?" he called.

The people glanced among each other quietly muttering, whilst Gil scanned the spectators, waiting to learn the identity of his challenger.

"No one? Surely there must be a valiant knight amongst you, capable of slaying this veteran?" shouted the Baron.

Sniggering, Gil looked back at Asher, shaking his head in disappointment, "I do believe your townsmen are cowards, my lord," he yelled.

Then a voice came from outside the arena, catching the attention of the people, including my own governor.

Emerging from the crowd, dressed gallantly in pristine heavy armour, a man, not much older than myself, stepped forward with a raised arm. Swaggering forward boldly, he flung back his head, clearing his long, wavy hair from his eyes. Entering the arena, he towered over Gil, relaxed and proud, before announcing himself to Baron Asher.

In a pompous tone, he said, "My sword is yours, my Lord."

Asher tilted back his head, grinning at the challenger, "You are courageous, boy; do you carry a name?"

"Oser, son of Wald, my Lord," He said confidently and smugly.

"Very well, I accept your sword, Oser, son of Wald."

With that, all the bystanders began to jeer and chant, stamping their feet; the tension around the arena began to magnify. Oser eyed the crowd, lapping up their cheers; Gil rolled his eyes at his boastful challenger, unconvinced by his egotism.

The drums began to beat, intensifying the build up to the battle. I noticed the governor exhale, unmoved by the unnecessary proceedings. I couldn't help but feel slightly enthused at the prospect of seeing Gil fall at the hand of this young, self-assured warrior.

Hota glanced over to me, nodding his head, with his lips clutched together, "The boy is already dead," he muttered.

Oser began wafting his sword from side to side, whilst eyeing up Gil, their steel chest plates, shimmering in the sunlight, forcing me to squint to see both fighters. Gil took his stance, drawing his sword, calmly resting the blade against his thigh, unimpressed by Oser's attempt at intimidating tactics.

The audience began to settle, allowing me to hear the whistle of Oser's blade hitting the air. Gil remained composed, calmly awaiting the showboating to end. Oser opened his stance and pointed the tip of his sword towards Gil.

"Be assured, I intend to make this swift," called Oser to Gil.

Charging forward, Oser roared, rushing towards Gil, swinging his blade. Oser thrust his sword downwards, forcing Gil to flinch, struggling to defend his attack. The clash of the steel encouraged further hails from the locals, excited by the potential of this young contender.

Gil stumbled from the impact of Oser's strike. I glanced at the Baron, who frowned towards Lady Ivy, clearly worried by Oser's promising start. Oser stepped back, giving Gil the time to regather his concentration. Smirking, the challenger was confident he had unnerved his opponent, Snarling, Gil then took the fight to Oser. Evenly matched, both fighters delivered a medley of strikes, neither one appearing to get the upper hand.

Showing signs of exhaustion, Oser began to pant. Gil was tactful, aware of his combatant's fatigue; he allowed Oser to deliver pointless, frenzied attacks. Effortlessly Gil dodged every one of Oser's desperate blows. Growing restless, Gil lunged forward, butting the hilt of his sword into the face of Oser. The crowd exhaled as the drained challenger dropped his sword to clutch his face. His opponent now unarmed, Gil took his opportunity to floor Oser, kicking him in the stomach, knocking him off balance.

The crowd gasped with anticipation, prompting my stomach to tighten. Oser scrambled around on the floor, disoriented by the blood impairing his vision. My stomach tightened on seeing Gil stalk up behind the helpless man; glancing to the crowd, guardians covered their children's eyes, aware of the reputation of this brutal guardsman. Oser came close to gripping the hilt of his sword, but Gil prevented his comeback by driving his blade into the elbow rivet of Oser's armour.

Yelping, Oser's agonised screams silenced the arena. Gil withdrew his blood-stained sword, raising it in the air, roaring to the stunned crowd. The Baron's applause momentarily distracted the head guardsman, who turned back to see his wounded challenger dragging himself across the grass, away from his victor. Gil chillingly approached Oser, unmoved at his struggling attempt to flee. I glanced at the governor, awaiting his order for intervention, but none came. Oser was left to face his fate. Tormenting the helpless challenger, Gil stalked his fallen adversary to the edge of the arena before thrusting his sword downwards into the rear leg rivet of Oser's armour.

It was gut wrenching to observe; the crowd exhaled in disgust. The haunting cries from the brave young challenger made me feel nauseous. With his foot, Gil pushed Oser onto his back; lifting his head, Gil glared in the direction of the woods. Some of the townsfolk turned their heads to see what Gil had fixed his attention on. I followed his gaze, which ended at Chenchi. Showing little concern, Chenchi returned the snarl which he was receiving from his previous tutor.

Gil lifted his sword above his head, then with malice drove his blade down in the centre of Oser's face. Gritting his teeth and hauntingly eyeing Chenchi, he twisted the steel, allowing the blood to splash onto his own face. Chenchi nodded his head, sniggering, before slowly clapping, sarcastically applauding the head guard. Baron Asher roared down to his henchman, proudly cheering him on his victory; this prompted the spectators to reluctantly applaud.

Servants dragged away the lifeless, bloodied body of Oser, whilst Asher wandered to the edge of his podium to address his townsfolk.

Arrogantly, he called down to the people, "Is there another who will face my champion?"

The eerie silence gave him the response he expected.

Showing no compassion, he said, "I thought not; please enjoy my festivities, drink and be merry."

The tolerant crowd continued with the festival, clearly forgetful of the brutality they had just witnessed. The afternoon was spent with a variety of games, local men competed in acts of strength including rope tugs and grappling events, coin was gambled on cock fights and dice rolls.

All too soon, the jovial atmosphere began to turn, woman and children began to depart from the arena, leaving drunken men, staggering and wandering in search of trouble. Anticipating the change in mood, the Baron retired with Lady Ivy, heavily shielded by his guardsman. Pockets of feuds began to break out between the people, and it became more apparent that the crowd were transforming into a mob.

13

RIOT

Fulten charged his horse towards a group of quarrelling men on the far side of the arena from where I stood; his presence was enough to defuse the initial altercations, prompting the men to separate. As the sun lowered on the horizon, so did the mood; tensions were beginning to run high. Two large bands of men stood off from each other, hurling abuse. Fulten, Lev and Fawkes had situated themselves in the middle, staring down the main perpetrators. The governor ordered me, Hota and Chenchi to join him.

Firmly he said, "Right, these feral bastards are about to turn on us; I want you to line the route between the horses. Only let woman and children through, I don't want this to spill over into the square."

Chenchi led the way. His enormity gave me confidence as we took up our positions. Fawkes, Lev and Fulten integrated our line, creating a neat divide between the arena and the market square. The very few remaining woman and children rushed towards us, keen to escape the brewing tension. I was stood next to Fulten, who was still mounted on his horse in the centre of the line. The governor paced up and down behind us, anxiously awaiting the reaction from the crowd.

The violence began to escalate, with pockets of fights breaking out between the local men; the majority fought with their fists, however a few had escalated the carnage by collecting fallen tree branches to use as weapons; some even removed timber from the arena, keen to arm themselves.

Fulten glanced down at me from his horse, "Stand fast Jep, they will soon turn their attention to us."

My stomach griped, and my bowels loosened with a mixture of worry and anticipation; Fulten's prediction was right: the first few men began to approach our line, all hyped and encouraged by one another. Consumed by a concoction of mead and revolt, some of the peasants began to hurl abuse towards us; this promoted more of the quarrelling men to unify and direct their feud at our line.

With numbers growing, the governor yelled, "Draw your batons; if any of them get close, engage them."

Our show of strength elevated their temporary hatred of us; displaying our batons had proven to be futile, leaving the growing mob undeterred. Shouting abuse and spitting in our direction, I counted at least forty hostile locals; however, it took time before any of them plucked up the courage and dared to break away from their own rabble to encounter us. The first peasant stepped forward; his bald head matched his rounded, plump face. Growling, he was missing most of his teeth; as foam accumulated around the corners of his mouth, moving forward he broke away from his own group, edging towards our line, egged on by the mob.

Now stood between us and the hostile crowd, the rotund peasant taunted us, his cheeks reddening with loathing, offering us combat. Lev grew weary of the man's misplaced courage and rode forward to meet him; offering the peasant no words of advice, he slammed his peace baton down, striking the thug on the top of his head. Blood gushed from the wound inflicted by Lev's assault, causing the mob to became even more antagonistic. The governor bellowed at Lev to withdraw. Hearing his order, Lev obliged, casually riding back towards our line with a smug expression on his face. I glanced at the injured man, who was grounded and dazed by Lev's attack.

"What was that?" called the governor to Lev.

Unnerved and carelessly, Lev replied, "I didn't like the way he looked at me."

Lev's actions sparked a reaction from the angry mob; a handful of men began to charge forward keen to engage us in retaliation, some in possession of wooden planks and sticks, whilst others held back, throwing loose rocks in our direction.

Some of the rubble landed just short of the governor, prompting him to yell his next order, "Go meet the bastards!"

Turning to face Hota, he nodded his head at me, curbing my fears. With a surge of courage, I moved forward, remaining in line with Chenchi and Hota. Fulten, Lev and Fawkes had galloped forward, already engaging the mob.

The mounted Blue Swords drove their batons down at members of the crowd, causing some to flee. Bodies crashed to the ground, whilst some of the people remained able to swing their makeshift weapons towards our horses. Joining the altercations, I stumbled across my first combatant; the scarred, skinny peasant eyed me up with intent to challenge me. Charging towards him, I ducked, avoiding his clench fist. Swinging my body around his, I slammed my baton into the rear of his head, leaving him beaten and floored. The next peasant dashed towards me; swiftly I raised my foot, kicking his stomach, leaving him grounded. My third struggle was with a much stockier and stronger looking townsman; gripping both my arms, his squeeze left me incapacitated, unable to use my baton. Lunging forward I crashed my forehead into his nose, hearing the bone crunch, forcing him to release his hold of me.

I found myself lashing out at anyone who came close to me; I lost count of the number of peasants I struck with my peace baton. Seeing Fawkes in the distance, struggling to keep the mob at bay, it was clear we had become overwhelmed. Hearing the governor's orders faintly over the roaring crowd brought relief; he demanded we withdraw. Turning to retreat, Chenchi was to the side of me. He towered over his foes, swinging his baton around his head, hitting anyone that came near him.

The noise from the unrest was surreal and delayed as it echoed through my ears. Panicking, I searched for Hota. A handful of men bunched up and circled around each other, delivering kicks to the ground. I plunged my way towards them, aware that their victim was likely to be a fallen Sword. My fears were true; Hota had been floored. His arms guarded his head, whilst he thrashed around on the ground, attempting to avoid the brutal stamping, inflicted by the animated men. Learning of my friend's predicament, I charged his attackers with my baton stretched out above my shoulder. Driving my arm down, I repeatedly struck them individually, aiming only for their heads. The ones left standing became fearful by my enraged and frenzied attack; they fled, giving me the time to help Hota to his feet.

Bloodied and bruised, Hota was still coherent and with my support, he was able to withdraw from the remaining mob. Now regrouped, and fortunate that the hostile crowd were holding back, the governor was able to consider his next strategy.

Fawkes dismounted from his horse, gripping Hota's face. "Head back to the lock up; one more hit and you're useless to us."

The governor witnessed Fawkes's order to Hota. "Lev, get him back, see that Isa attends to his wounds and evacuate the square on your way; I fear they will breach us shortly."

Leaving with Hota, Lev rode towards the square; our numbers had now dwindled at a time when exhaustion was setting in. We had little time before the mob would retaliate and engage us once again, so the governor ordered that we regain our line.

The night sky had darkened the arena; the only light came from the burning torches that illuminated the square behind our line, making the atmosphere more unnerving. The undeterred mob responded to our heavy-handedness with jeers of loathing and hatred; glancing at the tip of my baton, the blood had already begun to dry on its shaft. A few wounded locals staggered around the edge of the arena, refusing to participate in any more of the hostile antics. With an intensified roar, the remaining mob rushed forward, charging at our line. Hitting anyone and anything in sight, I felt a surge of rage engulf my body. Bellowing, I attacked anyone that came too close, my aching and throbbing body upheld by my will to survive.

Through the clutter of men, I laid eyes on one whose reflection gave me chills; he glared at me, keen for me to notice his disturbing stare. Seeing his menacing eyes, backed up by his thick, stocky frame, my spine shivered. Tightening the grip on my peace baton, I felt my unoccupied hand wander to the hilt of my sword. Linc wanted my blood, after my interventions left him beaten and downtrodden by Blue Sword, Fawkes. Fulten had previously warned me of his lust for vengeance; following his apprehending in the town armed with a mace, intended for me, this was his perfect opportunity to carry out his desires. With the other Blue Swords occupied, I was left alone to meet the ex-guardsman.

Linc's reputation left me feeling afraid and outmatched. I exhaled, trying to determine a strategy to outwit him but in the current atmosphere it was difficult to think rationally. Linc smirked, sensing my apprehension to challenge him. Raising a plank of splintered wood his smirk transformed into a snarl. Instinctively I drew my sword, fearing for my life; Linc sniggered, clearly unimpressed at my reliance on a blade to favour my own odds. Frightened by the display of my sword, the crowd around me retreated before my escalating actions. Linc, however, remained undeterred, slowly approaching me, closing the gap between us. The band of rioters, including Linc, came to a startling standstill; some began to retreat towards the hill behind the arena. To my relief, Linc himself gawked behind me; his attention had now been diverted to a more concerning enemy.

Turing my head, I counted eight riders galloping towards the arena. The men were being led by Baron Asher; his ceremonial tunic was now covered by a steel chest plate. Gil was amongst the guardsmen, still dressed in the blood stained, heavy armour from his earlier battle. Their presence caused the mob to retreat and reform, but this time their mood had changed; they were no longer filled with resentment. They looked amongst each other, now alarmed and fearful at what faced them. Their reluctance to fight prompted the governor to order us to fall back to our original line.

Joining Baron Asher, Gil sniggered, ridiculing us for the lack of control over the townsfolk, Chenchi spat on the ground, reacting to Gil's mockery. Fulten noticed my sword in my hand and leapt down from his horse; gripping its hilt, he sternly demanded that I yield my weapon. Unimpressed by its presence, he was unaware of my reasons for drawing it against the mob.

"Swords at the ready," shouted Asher.

The governor strutted over to the Baron, glaring up at him. "There is no need for a slaughter, they're drunken peasants, nothing more."

Gil calmly rode forward, ignoring the governor's plea with Asher. Glancing back, he eyed the governor up and down, before defiantly pulling his sword out from his waist.

Some of the crowd began to flee towards the woodlands; however a few remained, still spirited and undeterred, overwhelmed by false courage, which had been boosted by ale and mead.

Baron Asher glanced down at the governor, dismissively shouting for us all to hear him. He said, "You have failed to maintain order in my town, which means I invoke crown law. A few heads today deters a revolt tomorrow."

The governor sighed, glancing to the ground, before looking back at his Swords. Reluctantly he demanded we fall back, allowing passage to Asher's guards.

Smirking, Asher called out to his guards, "Only a reminder is necessary."

With the order, Gil charged forward, followed by the remainder of the guards. The lingering mob gasped at what they saw riding towards them. Attempting to flee in panic, they began frantically stumbling and trampling over each other, all desperate to escape the impending onslaught.

Charging in single file across the line, Gil led the assault, driving his sword down on top of any local who was unable to escape. The haunting squeals echoed in the arena as the guards sliced through the peasants like fruit, leaving the ground filled with corpses and blood. I closed my eyes, unable to observe, as Gil circled the arena picking off any stragglers. The Baron, watched the attack, carelessly picking food from his teeth, showing no remorse for the barbaric actions he had ordered.

Fulten touched his forehead, sullenly making the symbol of the cross as Gil returned, showing no remorse for the carnage he and his men had left behind. Passing Chenchi, Gil glared down, wiping his blood-soaked sword across his own thigh.

The governor stood snarling as the Baron rode by, unaffected by the consequences of his command, "You entertain them, then you butcher them," bellowed the governor.

Asher leant over his horse's mane, snidely saying, "May I suggest next year you maintain order."

I stared over at the arena, distressed by the bloodbath that now covered the ground; some of the fleeing peasants had returned to assist their fallen companions.

Yelling over to our position, one stuttered with emotion; "You bloody animals, how did it come to this?"

The governor demanded our attention; insisting that Fawkes and Chenchi were to attend to the wounded, he ordered me and Fulten to patrol the market square to ensure that people had dispersed and returned home.

Fulten, jumped down from his horse, handing her over to Chenchi in order to convey the dead away from the arena. Walking towards town, my speech was halted by the horror I had witnessed.

Fulten turned to me: "I am proud of you, Jep; you kept your nerve."

I replied, "The bastard needs to die."

Realising what I had just said, I anxiously awaited Fulten's reply; pausing, he muttered, "That he does, that he does."

We both remained silent walking towards the square, in an attempt to create our own equilibrium. I allowed my mind to wander, glancing up at the stars illuminating the summer sky. I thought of comfort, picturing Lady Ivy: her reflection was shrouded by another, and that other was Jen.

14

SETTLE THE ENEMY

Fulten's chest plate clattered against his body as we strolled through the market square; limping, Fulten turned to me. "I fear I am too old; this armour, it is meant for a young man's shoulders."

Fulten had been alive for nearly forty years and spent at least half his time serving the Blue Swords; he was a great tutor - at times his teachings had left me exasperated and bewildered, but he had taught me to be resilient, a trait that was required for becoming an established Blue Sword. He promoted my over-sensitivity, urging me to not allow my role in society to dictate my natural character. I always trusted his judgement and admired him, almost like a father.

Hearing the distressing moans of wounded men coming from the arena, Fulten was quick to sense my unease.

"Come, let us find some tranquillity," he suggested.

Leaving the square, we followed the path leading towards the church. Fulten was a religious man and had made no attempt to disguise his fondness of father Arrend; he measured his faith against all the actions he took when carrying out his duties. Walking up the steep slope towards the church, Fulten disclosed that we were leaving for Whiten in the morning, to locate and question Elis regarding Lady Ivy's missing father, Isaak. My smile reflected the excitement I felt, enthused by the thought of leaving Stanford for a while.

Fulten gazed up at the church tower, admiring the crucifix that glistened in the moonlight; exhaling, he grinned and closed his eyes, enjoying the moment of peace.

Whispering, he said, "When the pieces are jumbled, this is where I come to put them back into place."

"It's pleasant here," I replied.

Fulten sniggered, "That it is, that it is."

Our moment of harmony was interrupted by the sound of footsteps; gently turning around, Fulten sighed at the company that had interjected on our serenity. Gulping, I instantly felt alarmed by the face that looked back at me with hatred and animosity.

Linc stood before me, backed by two other men, who appeared rather anxious by our immediate stand-off. Eyeing me, Linc snarled, showing little concern at Fulten's presence; it was clear he was after one thing: my blood.

Fulten's demeanour suddenly changed; his usual stringent mindset had shifted to a more uncaring tone. "It seems our day's struggle is far from over, young Jep."

Disrespectfully, Linc shouted, "The fight is not with you, old man; feel free to leave us and look in on that queer priest."

One of Linc's associates timidly begged for Fulten's pardon at Linc's remark, excusing his behaviour as drunken and foolish, but Fulten responded to Linc's bad taste rather unusually. Withdrawing his sword, he tossed the weapon onto the ground, in reach of Linc.

Sniggering, he gazed at Linc, "Surely you are not reckless enough to challenge a Blue Sword, unarmed?" said Fulten, confidently.

Linc chucked, glancing between his companions, who did not share his humour and took a step back.

Leaning down, Linc gripped Fulten's sword. Holding it out, he familiarised himself with the weapon; concernedly, I stared at Fulten, unaware of his reasons for now arming a man who wanted me dead.

Fulten's relaxed tone changed as he frowned, turning towards me. "Now settle the enemy."

Slowly nodding, Fulten stepped back, now leaving me and Linc alone in the standoff; stutteringly I called back to Fulten, pleading for reassurance.

Fulten ignored my appeal, bellowing, "Draw your sword, Jep; strike down this man who challenges our crest."

Removing my sword from its scabbard, my hand shook, prompting Linc to sneer at my anxiety; peacocking, he waved Fulten's blade from side to side, displaying his familiarity with a sword. Panicking, I charged forward, recklessly swinging my blade towards Linc.

Composed, he stepped to the side, leaving me to chop thin air. We began circling one another before engaging in a combination of attacks, neither one of us gaining the upper hand. The second medley of strikes between us provided no victor; evenly matched, our steel clashed, both desperate to land a finishing blow.

Tiring, we separated, eyeing up each other's footing. I thought back to the teachings Hota had given me, and his guidance on remaining composed. Linc dashed forward; this time it was his turn to be reckless. I sidestepped him, leaving my leg out to meet his charge. Linc crashed to the ground, scurrying to turn himself onto his back. I saw my opportunity; pouncing forward, I pointed the tip of my blade against his throat. Glancing down, I noticed Linc had lost grip of Fulten's sword. He snarled up at me, showing no fear of death. Thoughtlessly I looked over to Fulten, to see his reaction at my success.

My careless act left Linc taking full advantage of my naivety, chucking dirt in my face. I stumbled back, disorientated. Linc had now regained his stance and was rearmed with Fulten's sword; growling he raced forward to deliver his killer blow.

Fulten bellowed, "Move out the way, man!"

Clearing my eyes, I had no time to configure my defence; losing my footing, I panicked as I stumbled back onto the ground. Linc vaulted, gaining momentum to finish me off. Instinctively, I pointed my sword towards him, creating a barrier between us. Observing the dread in his eyes, he was aware his hasty action could not be reversed, and that he was going to fall, impaling himself on my blade.

The steel crunched, penetrating through bone and tissue. My breathing calmed at learning of his incapacitation. Face to face, he glared at me, gasping out air. His red eyes stared down at me, before blood began to trickle from his bottom lip, splashing onto my head. Shoving his dead weight to the side, I rushed to my feet, letting go of the hilt to my sword. Gawking down at his lifeless body, initially I felt relieved by my victory. Fulten approached, removing my sword from Linc's chest.

Unable to remove my gaze from Linc, the triumphant feeling became shadowed by truth; truth that I had never taken the life of another man.

Sensing my incredulous mood, Fulten handed me back my sword which he had prised from Linc's corpse. "Each life you take is another scar on your soul; your salvation is your reason for doing it. He wanted your blood, Jep, and what for? Linc had always been a pawn for the devil and you have returned him to his master. You have my permission to sleep easy this night."

Returning to the lock up, it was not long before word of my triumph had spread. Lev had been dispatched to clear up the scene. Sitting in the parade room, Chenchi entered, glancing at me, unexpectedly keen to talk.

"I hear you drove your sword through Linc," said Chenchi.

Staring at the floor, I nodded.

Impressed, Chenchi scrunched his mouth; "Linc was a capable warrior; like me he was mentored by Gil."

Sniggering, I was not in the mood to entertain his attempt at conversation; sarcastically I replied, "Yes; Gil, your mentor, so why is it the man wants your head, Chenchi?"

Peeved, Chenchi stomped towards the door. I called out to him, allowing my careless attitude to prompt my next words. "I will learn the truth, that I swear."

Chenchi slammed the door shut, displaying his disgruntlement. I took a sip of ale from one of the beakers left over from the evening feast as the door re opened. I assumed it was Chenchi; I prepared myself for further confrontation and sneered towards the creaking door. Blair looked back at me, bemused by my uncommon ignorance.

Scratching at her matted, scruffy hair, she said. "Shouldn't you be happy? I heard that you just killed a man?"

Sombrely I replied, "It's not all it's made out to be."

Brazenly, Blair hissed at my grumbling, "Oh come on, you really need to shore up if you want to be my tutor."

Grinning at her impudence, it was hard not to find Blair entertaining; her naive wit, along with her brash attitude, made her quite the character. She adored the Blue Swords and had made it noticeably clear that she would not allow her gender to dictate her future.

Fawkes joined us in the parade room, his skin stained with blood, for clearing the bodies from the arena. Sitting at the banquet table, he began to pick at some left-over cheese and bread.

"You need to bathe," said Blair.

Fawkes sighed, "You need to sleep. Does your mother know of your wandering?"

"You should ask later," replied Blair, defiantly.

Coughing, Fawkes glanced at me in astonishment at the young girl's cheek; attempting to hold in my smirk, I clenched my lips together, staring at the ground.

"Your quarters, now," ordered Fawkes.

Insistent on the final word, Blair reminded me of her advice to toughen up, should I wish to one day be her tutor. Chuckling, I wished her goodnight, before being left alone in the room with Fawkes.

Rushing down his food, Fawkes chewed at the bread and guzzled at the remaining mead. Leaving the table, I walked towards the door.

Fawkes called over to me, "To think: it wasn't that long ago I stopped that turd from bashing in your skull, and on this night you drive a sword into his heart." He took a gulp of mead, before finishing his sentence, "Not bad, not bad at all."

The words he used were sparse, but to receive a half-hearted compliment from Fawkes felt rather rewarding. Heading to my chambers, my body throbbed and ached from the day I had endured.

The following morning, I woke surprisingly unregretful of Linc's death; if anything, I felt a tad pleased by his demise at the hand of my sword, even if part of the victory was down to luck. Initially enthused by the thought of leaving town for a while, I glanced over to Chenchi, snoring from the other side of our quarters. I was unaware that my glare was being observed by Hota.

"You know, it's not noble to kill a man in his sleep," said Hota, sarcastically.

Sniggering, I replied, "My hands wouldn't fit around his neck; you look tender."

Hota leaned up in his bed, squirming as he stretched his back. His face bruised from yesterday's assault at the Baron's Hill festival, graciously Hota glanced at me:

"I saw the way you fought my attackers; you saved my life, brother."

Interrupting Hota, I replied, "I wouldn't be here if it wasn't for you, now enough, you would have done the same."

Grunting, Hota gripped his side, "He was impressed with your triumph over Linc."

"Who?" I replied.

Hota nodded his head toward Chenchi; "The man whom you have grown to detest; your dislike for one another is pitiful."

Sniggering I replied, "The man tried to choke the life out of me over a girl; besides I don't trust him, something isn't right; he knows more than he lets on."

"You bedded his woman; as for his loyalty, I can only assume you're referring to Gil?" said Hota.

My reluctance to reply answered his question. I was aware of Hota's allegiance to Chenchi, so I thought best of it not to continue expressing my views, stirring a pointless debate. Getting dressed, Hota quizzed me on my impending journey to Whiten.

"My father is accompanying you on your investigation; I am sure he will be eager to thank the man who saved his son's life."

Surprised, I asked the reason as to why one of the Baron's guardsmen would be joining us on our search for Elis.

"You don't think Asher would allow his most valued possession to travel alone with two strange men, do you? He doesn't trust the Blue Swords, nor does he enjoy the nag of his persistent wife; this will be his only compromise," said Hota.

"Hmm, I'm not sure Fulten will approve," I replied.

"Fulten will have little choosing, it's been agreed with the governor," said Hota.

My stomach fluttered on learning that Lady Ivy would be joining us in travelling north of the river; initially I felt enthused about the opportunity of spending more time with her, away from her vile husband, but then I considered her distant and rather dry approach at our recent meetings. Hota had previously spoken at length about his father, discussing his father's morals and dislike at some of the Baron's attributes; his extensive service to Asher had made him more of an advisor than protector. Baron Asher was said to have trusted Hota's father's judgment, and respected his seniority, allowing him to step down from public duties.

"Was your father amongst the riders who charged the crowd yesterday?" I asked Hota.

Sighing, Hota replied, "My father would not entertain such barbaric orders; he may still serve Asher, but he does so on his own terms."

"He sounds remarkable," I said.

Proudly, Hota replied, "That he is."

My guilt was the reason I hastily attended the Viking Invader Tavern; my relationship with Jen was far from blossoming, but still I was keen to keep our encounters stable and ongoing. She sprinted from behind the serving table in order to greet me that morning, kissing me for the whole tavern to witness; she cared little for the thoughts and reactions of the local people.

"Must you go?" she pleaded.

Ensuring her loyalty, I snidely demanded she invited no other into her bed if she wished to continue our arrangement. Jen giggled, promising herself to me; it was apparent that she saw our relationship as something more than I did.

Jen questioned me on the rumour that Lady Ivy was leaving town to accompany us to locate Elis. Jealously she threatened to gouge out Ivy's eyes should she offer me any flirtation.

"Don't think I haven't noticed the way in which that precious whore gazes at you," said Jen.

"Enough; Lady Ivy is the wife of the Baron. Besides, the only interest I have is locating her father," I replied, slightly flattered.

Jen exhaled, uncomfortably glancing to the floor. Picking up on her awkwardness, I demanded to know the reason behind her sheepishness.

Guiltily, she looked back at me; "I fear you will not be content when you determine the truth."

Gently kissing my cheek, Jen sombrely stepped back; frowning, I demanded to know her understanding of the situation. Teary eyed, she remained silent.

"What do you know?" I shouted, startling some of the locals drinking inside the tavern.

Growing weary of Jen's reluctance to elaborate on what she had said, I raised my voice again, causing her to tremble. The horrified expressions of the onlookers prompted me to withdraw, feeling confused and frustrated by Jen's lack of explanation. Walking back to the lock up, I knew that I ought to relay Jen's slip of the tongue back to Fulten, but I was afraid that this would prolong our trip and jeopardise my chances of spending time with Ivy. Still unaware of what I could gain from further interactions with the Baron's wife, I decided to keep my mouth shut and allow my dangerous desires to run their course.

15

THEAR

Arriving back at my quarters, Hota was outside splashing water over his face from the barrel at the side of our hut. Sensing my irritation, he followed me inside, observing me gathering my belongings for the trip to Whiten.

"What is troubling you, Jep? I though you would feel excitement about leaving town for a while," said Hota, chirpily.

Shaking my head, I replied, "It's Jen."

"Ah yes - tavern girls have a way of making you miss them," chuckled Hota.

"It's not that; she mentioned the investigation- she knows something," I replied, sternly.

"What did she say?" asked Hota.

"That's the thing, she didn't make any sense," I said, frowning.

Hota sighed, "She is a tavern girl, with a reputation for her loose, idle words; think nothing more, now go, enjoy glaring at Lady Ivy's arse."

Fulten was already at the stables accompanied by the governor. Red- faced, he was animatedly raising his concerns over Lady Ivy joining us on the road to Whiten. Fulten insisted the journey was no place for the Baron's wife, reminding the governor of the threats we were likely to face. "Shadow crooks, the paths are swarming with them," said Fulten, heatedly.

The governor's self-righteous response indicated his mind was made up. "Well, Lady Ivy should feel herself lucky to have you escorting her along these potentially turbulent roads; besides, I have been advised that Ricard will be riding with you. I think the Baroness has all the protection she needs."

Sighing, Fulten offered no further argument, grunting as the governor left us to saddle our horses; Fulten huffed and nodded his head, as he steered his horse away from the courtyard. I held back with Spike, giving him no excuse to vent his frustration out on me.

Lady Ivy and Ricard, Hota's father, awaited us at the front of the lock up. Ivy smiled on seeing us ride out from the courtyard; she was mounted on a fine grey horse. Her delicate brown hair spilled from the hood of her black cloak. Ricard eyed me up and down, rubbing at his greyed beard; his wrinkled skin reflected his age and experience. His guardsman's tunic was neatly pressed and tightly fitted. Glancing down at his waist, Ricard's sword was shielded by an exquisitely crafted scabbard, marked with official embroidery. He welcomed Fulten in his gruff voice, initially paying me little attention. Fulten did not waste any time in endeavouring to deter Lady Ivy with warnings of potential hazards the journey had to offer.

Disregarding his cautioning advice, Ivy introduced me to Hota's father, Ricard. Leaning out to meet my hand, Ricard smirked:

"So, you're the boy who came to the aid of my son; for that my sword will forever be yours."

Fulten rolled his eyes; downtrodden on the lack of response at his discouragement, he interrupted the niceties and insisted that we leave. Riding through the square, the townsfolk cheered, offering their blessings to Lady Ivy before she was halted by a local man, prompting Ricard to brashly step in and engage him.

"Step aside, old man," he ordered, sternly.

On seeing it was Pip, Fulten rushed forward, "He offers no harm, he is a local tradesman."

Wittily Pip replied to Ricard; "Old timer, you don't look too fresh yourself; I wish to gift the Baroness bread, that's if the guardsman doesn't remove my headfirst."

Ivy graciously accepted the bread and placed it into her saddle, before wishing the charming old man good day. Leaving the main gate, it felt good to be out of Stanford; I felt an instant relief to be rid of politics and procedures for the time being.

The land of Thear was separated by a great river. I grew up north of the river and until my journey to Stanford had never wandered south. Not only did the water mark a divide in land, it also divided wealth. The north was covered by farming territory and home to mostly commoners, working the vast amount of land to supply the south with trade; the north was poor and lawless, unlike the south-occupied by rich settlements, along with the great city of Alma that housed the queen of Thear. I had learnt that Alma was where the Blue Swords grew. I was keen to explore the lavish, misshapen terrain in the south, and visit the reputable city. Fulten assured me that my time would one day come to seek guidance from the council of Blue Swords located in Alma.

However, intrigued as I was by the south of Thear, I felt enthused to be heading north, back to familiar ground. It was a two-day ride to Whiten; its location was north east, the opposite side, from my own village of Somerby. Now away from Stanford, we picked up the dishevelled path, surrounded by lush green fields, bordered by fresh hedgerow. Fulten led the way with me by his side. Fulten enjoyed speaking of the sources behind the Blue Swords and I was rather intrigued to learn of its past. The land had been controlled and tormented by tyrants who dictated the lives of all who occupied the land.

Fulten relayed that a man named Michlob grew tired of seeing the throne only interested in its own assets, and decided to lead a group of men, vigilantes, whose vow was to carry out justice on the ones who preyed on the weak. Michlob and his followers became famous through the city of Alma, prompting the people to revolt against the crown. Civil war was avoided by appointing Michlob and his men the title of guardians over the city, giving birth to the Blue Swords.

Proudly Fulten continued: "To this day, our own leader Chief Muir heads the queen's council."

The clouds began to redden through the blue sky; night was creeping up on us; in the distance a figure staggered towards us. Fulten glanced at me, suspicious of the on comer. The frail man wandered towards us with his head down; posing little threat, his rags were dirt stained and torn. His persistent cough prompted us to allow him space as we passed. Ivy glanced down at the stranger, clenching her lips, sympathetic to the feeble wanderer. The stench of urine did not deter Ivy from stepping down from her horse; greeting the frail man and removing the bread gifted to her by Pip, she handed him the loaf. His eyes lightened with joy at her charitable gesture; her act of kindness matched her angelic beauty- that's why I was growing to adore her.

With the light fading, Fulten brought my attention to a dishevelled plaque on the ground, at the edge of the path. The sign read Hook Cross; it was the name of a village I had passed through on my way to Stanford. I remembered the tavern, occupied by degenerates, and bandits seeking trouble. Before I could relay my experience, Fulten insisted we boycotted the village, clearly already aware of its reputation. Ricard offered no argument, agreeing that our presence would attract unwanted attention.

Naively, Ivy said, "The village will most certainly have an inn for us to rest."

Ricard replied, "My Lady, once word is out of your presence, the village will be plagued with shadow crooks. I think it best we set up camp away from the road."

Sniggering Ivy said, "But my dearest Ricard, we have the company of two Blue Swords, surely that will be a deterrent for thieves?"

Intervening, and offering no explanation, Fulten snubbed Lady Ivy's argument and agreed with Ricard; pointing to an opening in the hedges, he advised that we rest the far side of the road's borders.

A dyke sheltered by trees and hedgerow provided us with adequate cover. Fulten demanded that I start a fire, insisting that I kept it minimal and the flames low. Sitting around the fire, Fulten offered around his leather bottle filled with wine. I began the conversation, asking Ricard about the reputation of the shadow crooks.

"They claim to be free men, but they're nothing more than savages, taking whatever, they desire. Their tactics are brutal, making them feared amongst defenceless villages."

Intrigued, I replied, "They are not known in the north; why do they stay south?"

"Because, my boy, that is where the coin is; besides, regal henchman guard the river crossing. Mark my words, they are growing in numbers and will soon be regarded as a threat to the whole of Thear," replied Ricard.

"Nonsense," interrupted Fulten, "They are nothing more than forgotten Vikings; simple folk, they will never intimidate the crown, let alone the Blue Swords."

Sniggering, Ricard screwed up his mouth, offering no deliberation, before resting his head against his saddle and drifting off to sleep.

After several sips of wine, Fulten was the next to close his eyes; it was not long before his rounded gut pressed his snoring. Lady Ivy paid me little attention; she clutched at her knees, shivering as she trembled, peering up at the rustling leaves.

Glancing over to her, I asked, "Would it settle you my, Lady if I stayed awake while you slept?"

Abruptly, she replied, "I was raised on a farm; believe it or not, I am not as feeble as one may think."

Surprised by her reaction, I said, "Have I wronged you, my Lady?"

Sneering, daunted by my forwardness, she stuttered in her response, "Now why would I even concern myself with your behaviour?"

"Ah, now we are getting somewhere," I replied, sarcastically.

Flabbergasted by my uncommon tone, Ivy arched her back, exhaling, calculating her reply. "Well, as a member of your establishment, I think your rather unorthodox dealings with a certain tavern girl are somewhat questionable."

"You speak of Jen?" I said.

Faltering, Ivy replied, "Yes, Jen. I mean, I see the appeal- the woman is rather seductive in her manner, but to bed her for gain, it feels deceptive." Still uneasy, Ivy continued to mumble out her words, "Not that any of it is my concern, of course; you are a grown man, and you can court whoever you see fit."

Suspecting an undertone of jealously, I relished seeing her off guard and slightly irrational. Learning that she had an opinion at all over my relationship with Jen, was enough to make me assume that she had grown rather fond of me and that there was a small possibility that my feelings for her could be reciprocated. Unamused by my questioning,

Ivy stubbornly nestled into her saddle, wriggling her body under a thick sheep skin blanket. Unaware of my stare, I looked over to her, admiring her splendour, thinking of how someone so precious could be wed to someone so wicked.

Passing by the Hooks Cross, the pathway was lined with tall trees, shielding us from the scorching sun. Lady Ivy was ahead, contently riding alongside Fulten; however, me and Ricard had fallen back slightly, but remained in sight. Ricard spoke proudly of his son, my closest friend Hota, reminiscing with stories of when he was a boy, dreaming of one day following his father's footsteps of becoming a protector, and serving in the Baron's guards.

I deceptively took advantage of his mention of the Baron and decided to manipulate the conversation on to Asher and Gil.

"From what I have learnt about your son, I just couldn't see Hota abiding by Gil's inhumane approach; the way in which he charged upon the townsfolk at the festival, it was sinful," I said, eager to hear his own views.

Shaking his head sullenly, Ricard replied. "Gil was raised on hate; his older brother showed him little affection, beating and abusing the boy. I am afraid it turned his heart black. Asher, who was also a boy at the time, was his only confidant. I served under the baron's father, as his headguard, for many years. Gil was my apprentice; I tried so hard to relieve the boy's anguish, but my efforts were in vain. Once Asher took over from his father, he stood me down and appointed Gil as his head guard; it was inevitable really, once Gil got his claws into Asher, his path was destined to become destructive."

"Why do you stay?" I said, gently.

"I stay because I swore an oath. I pray, one day, that Lady Ivy will be free from Asher's torment; until then I sleep easier knowing I am close by."

Ending our conversation, Fulten yelled for us to hurry forward. Ricard raced forward in order to close the gap between himself and Lady Ivy. I was quick to follow; Fulten pulled at his horse's reins, attempting to steady his stallion from what had spooked it. Two men stood under him, both bloodied and petrified; they were heavily armed, dressed in claret coloured unformed tunics, like the one worn by

Asher's guards. The outline symbol of a hawk on their helmets indicated they were regal guards, employed by the crown.

Their heavy panting and over excitement made it difficult for us to understand what or who had inflicted their injuries. Ricard grew impatient, and demanded they settled.

Catching his breath, one of the regal guards sputtered out the reasons behind their frantic behaviour. "We were ambushed at the river; I counted over twenty of the bastards, it's rare they ever attempt to cross."

Fulten interrupted, "Who, man? Speak clearly."

"Shadow crooks, they slaughtered my band; we must flee, they are mounted."

Ricard encroached on the conversation, "Have they ridden from the north?"

"Yes!" shouted the guard, "They will be upon us, any time now!"

Ricard turned, glancing at Fulten, "It seems their plague spreads; we are outnumbered, we cannot protect the Baroness."

Fulten scratched at his beard, considering his next plan; hurried along by the guard, he was forced to think sharply. "There could be survivors; we will take cover in the trees, allowing them to ride by. Jep, you take the path back to Hooks Cross- branch off at the opening before the village, I want you to cross the river downstream."

Ricard sternly disagreed with Fulten's orders; "This is madness, I will return with Lady Ivy to Stanford."

Dismissively, Fulten replied, "You will not outride them, this is the only way." Glaring back at me he relayed his demands, abruptly. "Jep, ride cross country to the eastern bridge, then head north once you get to the river; seek sanctuary in your home village, and wait for me there."

Nervously stuttering, I replied. "But I can help…"

"Go now, boy, if they discover the Baroness she is as good as dead. You must go now; ride, Jep!"

I glanced over to Ricard, seeking reassurance; sighing, he gave me a reluctant nod of his head before looking at his Baroness, displaying an uncomfortable grin. Ivy peeked over to me; her face was pale as she nervously bit down on her bottom lip. Fulten leant over, smacking the rear of Ivy's horse, prompting it to hurry along. Anxiously, I gave Fulten a final nod of my head before racing off to catch up with the Baroness. Teary eyed, Ivy looked at me in desperation; she was afraid, as was I. My little experience was now our only hope.

16

THE SHADOW
CROOKS

The hooves from our horses churned up the mud as we sped along the path; the opening between the trees was in sight. Ivy began to slow down; staring ahead in dread at who obstructed our path, looking between the Baroness and our dilemma, it felt as if time had slowed down. Bringing our horses to a halt, two figures had intentionally blocked the opening. They grinned, relishing our fearful reactions. Both dressed in animal skins, their faces blackened with dirt elevated their terrifying appearance; the taller man of the two rested a long-handled axe across his shoulder, whilst the other held out a worn, short sword.

Confident in their stance, they sniggered, thrilled that we had fallen into their trap. The shorter one of the two stepped forward, perverted in the way he glared at Lady Ivy; eyeing her up and down, he made his warped thoughts known.

Gruffly he said, "Give over the whore, ride on, and you can live."

Chuckling, his companion stepped alongside him. "We don't wish to fight a Blue Sword today, so as a compromise, you may watch us fill her up; I might even let you have a go after."

Ivy turned her head to see my reaction to their offer; snarling, I brought their foul chuckling to an end. My initial dread had been surmounted with pure loathing and a wanting to end these vile creatures' lives. The consequences of my potential failure spurred on my bravery. I jumped down from Spike, yanking out my sword from its scabbard. Focused, and now with a true reason to fight, I knew what had to be done.

Approaching the barbaric men, I allowed my repugnance of them to spur on a quick attack. Repeating a trick an old foe had taught me, I drove my foot into the loose soil, kicking it into the shorter man's eyes. His distress distracted the much taller and leaner man armed with an axe; before he had chance to realise, I had lunged forward, driving my sword forward towards him to pierce his face. Still attached to my sword, he crumbled to the ground as the blood poured from either side of the steel; swiftly I yanked my weapon free, ready to meet the now recovered shorter thug. The sight of his deceased associate spurred on his rage filled attack. Now accustomed to this type of confrontation, I promptly slid myself around to his side, leaving him hacking nothing but air. Swinging my body around to counterattack my adversary, he met me, blocking my assault. My relentless combat training aided me in outmatching the man who had threatened to bring harm to the woman whom I had grown to adore.

Incapacitating him, I swung my sword, slicing his thigh. Screeching, he released the grip of his sword, clutching at the open wound on his leg. Losing balance, he stumbled backwards on the ground, as the blood seeped from between his fingers.

Crying out, he looked up me, glancing at my now blood smeared blade; "Killing me will bring you no satisfaction," he pleaded.

Scowling, I glared down at the man before gripping both my hands tightly around the hilt of my blade. Raising my sword, intent on driving the steel through his heart, I said, "This will give me much satisfaction."

Lady Ivy called out to me, "No, Jep, be merciful; enough blood has been spilt."

Hearing her tranquil tone was enough for me to yield my sword; the fallen man began to show his gratefulness for my exoneration. Blubbering, he began to recognise my generosity.

Placing the tip of my sword against his throat, I demanded: "Your name?"

"Seth, sir, "he mumbled.

"Well Seth, if you ever threaten to harm her again, I will cut out your innards and feed them to the buzzards, now go and pray you don't bleed out."

Seth rapidly hobbled away, sheepishly glancing at Lady Ivy as he passed her; observing him flee, I wiped my blood-soaked blade across the grass. Ivy stared down at me, her eyes filling with tears and her mouth scrunched, attempting not to sob.

"My pleas have been known to fall upon deaf ears," she stuttered.

"I am not the Baron," I said sternly.

Riding through the fields, glancing back, I was keen to know we weren't being followed. I could not help but consider my tutor's fate: Continuing to glare at the horizon, I wanted so much to see him appear. Ivy must have sensed my unease, attempting to soothe my mind, reminding me of Fulten's gallant reputation. Part of me considered heading back towards Stanford, for reinforcements, but Fulten's orders kept me resilient to do what he had asked of me.

The sun had faded away in the distance, and dusk was upon us. Lady Ivy shivered as the air became chilly and crisp. I noticed a ditch, enclosed by a hedgerow off the main track.

"We should settle their till morning light, my Lady," I suggested.

"I don't think it wise to stop," Ivy opposed.

"It won't be long before it is too dark to see the path; we can't risk injuring the horses. If we don't light a fire, we will be hidden."

Tethering the horses away from the ditch, I removed their saddles, to soften the ground where we were to lay. The moonlight shone down, and stars scattered the clear, summer night sky, leaving enough illumination to see each other. Ivy offered me some cheese she had in her saddle; my inability to accept her offering raised her concerns.

"Do you think of Fulten?" she said, gently.

Sighing, I replied, "He is a noble man; even though I tolerate his harsh criticism, I owe him everything."

Smiling, Ivy said. "Yes, he is stringent, he would have been proud of you today for saving my life."

Forgetting my place, I gazed at her intently, watching her shiver. I felt nervous at the idea of offering her comfort.

Glancing to the ground, she prompted her wish for intimacy, whispering, "Will you hold me?"

Clearing my throat and hesitating through my surge of nerves, I moved closer towards her; sitting beside Ivy, my stomach fluttered as I placed my arm gently around her shoulders.

Nestling her head into the side of my chest, we sat quietly, peacefully. Peering down, I noticed she had closed her eyes. Keen to cherish this stolen moment, I did not take my sight off her, savouring having her in my arms.

The night had been serene; as the dawn sun appeared on the horizon, Ivy woke in my arms. Swiftly removing herself, her unease prompted me to come to. She became insistent on our haste to leave and get to the crossing. Riding along the edge of the river, little was said between us.

The bridge was a welcoming sight; its huge stone boulders neatly joined Thear's north and south divide. Smoke drifted from a wooden hut close to the entrance of the bridge. Lady Ivy insisted that she spoke with the regal guards. On hearing our approach, two men, dressed in regal tunics, exited the hut. Their overt staring at Lady Ivy left me feeling uncomfortable and irritable; I brushed off the dirt covering my Blue Swords tunic and directed Spike forward.

"Steady your eyes, you are speaking with the Baroness of Stanford."

Lowering their head, they cowered; fixing their gaze to the ground, stutteringly one of them replied. "Forgive me, my Lady, we should have known, anyone who keeps the company of a Sword was bound to be of importance."

Ivy rode up closer to the guards, sternly saying: "All women are of importance, you fool."

Both the men remained reluctant to make eye contact with her; moving off, Ivy began to cross the bridge. I halted my horse by the guard's side.

"Have you had word of an attack from the eastern crossing?"

They looked at each other, baffled at my question; the one closest to me replied. "No sir, not a soul has passed through in days."

"Shadow crooks have taken the bridge; I suggest you remain vigilant. Send word to Alma of the ambush," I said, authoritatively.

Before riding on, one of the regal guards called out to me, sullenly. "Are there many dead, sir?"

I turned back, pausing whilst thinking of Fulten;, I replied: "Let us pray not."

He gloomily looked at his companion before I turned around, leading Spike across the bridge. The vast river ran wild, splintering through the rocks, beneath the stone arches. It was nice to be back on familiar ground; the flat lay of the land was made up of farming fields and wet marshes; to most it was a much more bleak and harsh environment than the lavish forests and greenery that the south had to offer, but to me it was home.

Still at least a day's ride from my village, my thoughts went to ensuring we found a suitable place to set up camp for the night. Peasants strained to observe us from their fields, finding the appearance of strangers on horseback a rarity.

"It feels colder here," grumbled Ivy.

"The flat land exposes you to the elements," I grinned, "the air is clear and fresh."

"Should we not steer clear of the main path?" Lady Ivy replied.

Relaxed, I replied, "Look ahead, my Lady; you can see as far as your eyes will allow you to."

"I sense poise in your tone; it's comforting," she said.

Smirking back at her, I said, "I feel safe here; there is a brook further up the path. We should settle there tonight."

Arriving at the stream, the sight of the muddied water flowing over rotten branches reminded me of my childhood. I thought of when I was a child sneaking out of the village and coming here with my friends, skimming the stones across the water.

Observing my reminiscence, Ivy said, "Do you miss your family?"

Sincerely, I replied. "They will be astonished by the attire I now wear."

Smiling, Ivy replied, "They will be very proud."

Keen not to ruin our moment with talk of Asher, I encouraged the conversation towards Ivy's past.

"Rumour has it that you were once quite the farm hand?"

Beaming, Ivy glanced at the running water, allowing her mind to reflect. "My father had always wanted a boy; after mother died, he and my uncle raised me, keen to ignite my fighting spirit. Well, they did their best."

"You appear sturdy enough," I said.

Huffing, she replied. "You have to be resilient, to stay married to a Baron." Involuntarily my eyes rolled, just at the thought of Asher. "Do you wish to unearth love, Jep? said Ivy intently.

Sighing, I gazed over to her, intensive in the way that I stared. "I fear I may have already done so."

Clearing her throat, Lady Ivy stood up, blushingly looking away; her naive pretence deflected her reply, portraying her misunderstanding of my answer.

"Jen?" she said, complacently.

Becoming more forgetful of my place and caught up in the informal conversation, I remained gazing over at Ivy. "I fear my heart may belong to another."

Aware of my hidden remark, Lady Ivy insisted that we retire for the night; she wrapped her cloak tightly around her body, making it apparent she was in no need of any further comfort.

Washing my face in the stream felt refreshing; I was keen to reunite with my mother looking clean and respectable. Ivy had already saddled her horse, eager to set off that morning. The red sunrise provided a picturesque backdrop for our onward journey; I felt a mixture of nerves and excitement about the reception I would receive from the village folk. No longer a nauseating peasant, I was returning, now displaying one of the most prestigious emblems known to the land of Thear.

Ivy noticed my fidgeting; "You look very gallant, Jep."

Passing off her flattery, I sniggered, casually cupping my hand over my knee, sitting upright.

In the distance, I could see a small group of men blocking our path, prompting me to grip the hilt of my sword. Noticing they were on foot relaxed me slightly. Their heated bickering came to a halt on seeing us approach. Two of the men were dressed in burgundy tunics, both armed with swords that were fastened to their belts; I recognised their dull uniforms to be the mark guardsmen that watched over my village. We had interrupted their verbal reprimanding of two local peasants. The first man towered over the two guards; his thick set elaborated his loud voice as he pleaded his innocence. His accomplice glared up, nodding his head in agreement with his over excitable companion.

Noticing our intrusion, the much heavier peasant flicked his hair to the side, squinting from the sunlight as he attempted to eye me up.

His agitated frown transformed into a sneer; "What the bloody hell are you wearing?" he jeered.

Sternly one of the guards interrupted his insolence. "You will mind your tongue lad; you're speaking with a Blue Sword."

Smiling, I raised my hand, "It's quite alright, judging by his oversized head I can only assume the man is lame."

The shorter ginger peasant cackled at my remark causing his companion to glare down at him, frowning.

"What are these men detained for?" I called to the guards.

"They are thieves sir; they owe coin to the local tavern."

The larger, more vocal man insisted they had been wrongly accused, "We paid the old bastard; more like you corrupt degenerates want the coin."

"How much do they owe?" I said, abruptly.

Looking between each other, one of the guards shrugged his shoulders at his counterpart, before blurting out, "Seven coins."

Puffing, I shook my head, "Seven coins? The little one doesn't look as if he could handle that amount of mead."

Removing a leather purse from my saddle, I began counting out the coins, leaving all four men silently glaring at me in anticipation.

Tossing the seven coins individually onto the ground, I grunted to the corrupt guards; "Take it, their debt is paid, now be gone."

Scurrying, the two guards collected the coins, quick to place them in their sacks. Before leaving, one glanced back towards me: "Forgive my insolence, but have we met before?"

"Yes, I have spent many nights in your dungeon, now piss off before I change my mind."

Leaping down from my horse, the short, ginger bearded man smirked, leaving his companion with a baffled expression on his face.

"Will you not embrace me? I have missed you, Gibbon, your big oaf," I called to the larger peasant.

Marching forward, Gibbon grabbed my waist, hoisting me off the ground. I grunted at his tight squeeze. The smaller man rushed forward, struggling to wrapping his short arms around me and Gibbon.

Releasing his hold, Gibbon began to chuckle, "Be honest, do you think Abbot has shrunk?"

Breaking into fits of laughter, Abbot humoured Gibbon, clutching at his groin. "Not everything is small."

Lady Ivy glanced at Abbot's crotch, before bashfully looking away.

My childhood friends glanced between me and Ivy, intrigued by her glamorous appearance, and confused by our association, before deflecting their attention on the uniform I wore.

Bewildered, Gibbon eyed me up and down, shaking his head. "A bloody Blue Sword, now who would have thought it."

"I fear the Swords have fallen on hard times," giggled Abbot. "So, what's with the girl?" He added, nodding his head towards Lady Ivy.

"That girl is the Baroness of Stanford; you will do well to remember that."

Sheepishly, Abbot began to foolishly bow, apologising for his misinterpretation. Gibbon paid little attention to Ivy's status, he had never been one for titles or authoritative figure heads. He was much more interested to learn the reasons behind my return.

Handing Abbot my horse, he rode alongside Lady Ivy allowing me to bring Gibbon up to speed with our current quandary.

"It all sounds like too much grief to me." Lowering his voice, Gibbon continued, "This Asher sounds like a turd, but then, you are trying to fondle the man's wife."

Grunting, I looked back to ensure Ivy had not heard his reply.

"So, what if this Fulten doesn't arrive, then what?" said Gibbon.

Sighing, I replied, "I don't know, I need to ensure the Baroness' safe return to Stanford."

Changing the subject, I asked for word on my mother and sister.

"Your mother is still as stubborn as ever; as for Emil, she is happy, well apart from some pestering from one of the guards - he has taken a liking to her."

"Who is this guard?" I replied, abruptly.

"He is young, newly appointed. Skinner got him in from the city. I am sure, he will ease off when he learns Emil's brother is a Sword," said Gibbon.

The final leg of our journey consisted of Gibbon and Abbot's insistence on ridiculing me, divulging stories from our childhood to Lady Ivy, leaving me embarrassed and mortified. Ivy relished listening to the tales fed by my old friends; giggling, she pushed for more gossip about my past. The merriment between us closed my mind to the reality which we faced as we approached the entrance to Somerby; it felt good to be home.

17

A MOTHER'S BLESSING

To many, Somerby was just another northern farming village; its bleakness made the depravity apparent. I had known little more growing up and felt rather enthused at the thought of being home. Crossing over the murky stream, I could hear voices from the settlement. Abbot was reluctant to get down from Spike; he relished the attention he was receiving from the local villagers whilst mounted on my fine stallion. Waving down at the young children playing and winking at the local women, he enjoyed the momentary feeling of importance. My home was centred in a row of tattered wooden huts; arriving I tethered the horses to a post fixed into the ground at the side of my mother's hut. I was hit by a wave of nerves at the thought of seeing my family again; straightening my tunic and taking a deep breath, I knocked on the door.

Lady Ivy glanced at me, amused by my fidgeting as I brushed my fingers through my hair. The door creaked open and my sister Emil looked back at me, gasping at seeing me stood before her; paying little attention to the clothes I wore, she embraced me with a hug before pulling back and taking a second peek at the guests I had brought to the door.

"Mother will be pleased," she said. Peering around the corner at Spike, Emil gave me a puzzled look; "Are one of them horses yours, Jep?"

Coughing, Gibbon nodded his head, pointing out my attire. "Never mind the bloody horses, see what your brother is wearing."

Emil eyed me up and down, smirking. "Have you joined the queen's guards?"

"No, you daft bugger, he is a Blue Sword," said Gibbon, firmly.

Lady Ivy stepped forward; "And a fine one at that- my name is Ivy; it is a pleasure to meet you."

Emil raised her eyebrows, struggling to comprehend the sight she was presented with. Abbot discreetly tried to gather my sister's attention, pointing his finger at Lady Ivy; however, his muttering was far from subtle.

Sniggering at Abbot's ineptitude, I turned back to Emil. "Lady Ivy is the Baroness of Stanford."

Emil placed one hand on her hip and began rubbing her eyelids, still bewildered. Quizzing her, I was keen to know if she had seen any other Blue Swords pass through the village. Disappointed by her answer, I insisted that Gibbon and Abbot were to stay behind, whilst I attended the Grand Hall to speak with the ruler of Somerby.

As I stepped away, Emil called out to me. "Mother will want to see you; she prays for you at the chapel."

Smiling back at her I made my way in company with Lady Ivy towards the village square; my return had attracted the attention of some of the locals, their timid reactions on observing my crest were something I had expected. The diminutive, log-built chapel was the heart of the village and had always attracted large gatherings. As the congregation emptied from its doors, I noticed Father Roberts, a rather pious and stubborn individual, stood at the gate offering blessings to the villagers as they left.

On seeing me and Ivy approach, he glared, focusing his attention on my tunic. Paying little consideration to the Baroness, he stared between my face and my uniform, displaying bafflement in his silence.

Squinting, he frowned. "Jep, is that you?"

"It is, Father; my mother, is she here?"

Ignoring my question, he began to chuckle, "The Lord does work in mysterious ways, the troublesome boy I remember has returned before me as a man of principle."

Uncomfortable at his compliment, I ignored Ivy's sniggering and repeated my question, this time more abruptly. "My mother?"

"Yes, of course, of course your mother is praying, I suspect she will be at her usual place at the front of the chapel."

Walking inside the chapel, Ivy struggled to remove the grin from her face. The hall had emptied, leaving my mother alone kneeling behind the second pew. Observing her frail body and greying hair I crept forward, keen not to disturb her prayer. The creaking from the wooden floor caused her to open her eyes and glance back to the aisle. Exhaling, her face lightened with a beaming smile as she walked out from beyond the benches. Meeting me with a tight cuddle, she held me tightly, refusing to let me go.

Cupping her hands over my cheeks she looked up at me, smiling; I noticed her eyes filling with tears before she embraced me for a second time.

"I have missed you, mother," I said, sincerely.

Peering down at my tunic she gently nodded her head, smirking. "I do wish your father could see you standing here; he would be so proud." Noticing Lady Ivy standing close by, she leaned around me to face her. "What beauty you possess. It seems fortune has favoured my son."

Sharply interrupting my mother, I instantly played down the misunderstanding. "Mother, this is the Baroness of Stanford; I have been ordered to escort her here."

Frowning, my mother replied. "To Somerby? Why would any Baroness choose to entertain our village?"

Revealing the reason behind our arrival, my mother played down our predicament and thanked God for returning me home safely.

"I must attend the Grand Hall and seek an audience with Skinner," I insisted.

"Yes, of course you must, although I'm not sure what help he will be, the man is a floundering fool if you ask me," replied mother.

Ivy giggled at her honest and abrupt remarks about the leader of Somerby; it was clear that my mother's charm had won over the Baroness.

On leaving, my mother called to Lady Ivy. "It would be an honour if you could attend supper, my Lady."

Ivy turned back and approached my mother, "Please, your son saved my life, call me Ivy and yes, supper would be delightful."

The Grand Hall was situated at the rearmost point, overlooking the village; it housed Nobleman Skinner, Somerby's rather lenient and merciful ruler. His gentle approach to taxation was well received by the local people, however its consequence was the deprivation of the village. His naivety towards his corrupt guards meant their thuggish behaviour had gone overlooked.

The decaying walls ironically made the Grand Hall appear more bleak than grand; surrounded by overgrown shrubs, the grounds were in desperate need of restoration. I peered into the stables, eager to see if Fulten's horse was tethered, indicating whether he had arrived. Disappointed, I glanced back to Lady Ivy before trudging over the dense grass that covered the pathway and led to the front door.

A well-spoken voice called out to me and Ivy. "The nobleman does not entertain unannounced guests."

Stepping forward, he stood before us arrogantly gazing down over his pointed nose. The guard's burgundy tunic was much more vibrant and fitted tightly, emphasising his lean physique. Running his thumbs over his fair moustache, his posture radiated vanity.

Accustomed to his type, Lady Ivy led the introductions, speaking on our behalf. "I am the Baroness of Stanford; I demand to speak with your Lord," she ordered, matching the guard's pretentiousness.

Sniggering, the guard ran his hands through his fair hair." That does change things, what is the reason we have the privilege of such a radiant Baroness in our village?"

His smugness was unbearable, prompting me to brashly speak out; "Our arrival is not your concern, now beckon your master."

Smirking, the guard dismissively eyed me up and down, "I had heard word that a Blue Sword was wandering the village. I was also informed that you attempted to bribe my men to release some local thieves; not good form if you ask me."

Aware of my intolerance of the guard, Ivy sternly repeated her demand to see Nobleman Skinner; mindful of her irritation the guard obliged, however he remained unhurried and rather pompous in his manner. Slowly unlocking the door, he turned to me and Ivy, glancing at us contemptuously.

"You will wait here; I will enlighten Nobleman Skinner to your arrival," he said, ostentatiously.

Lady Ivy scrunched her face. "The stench of the damp in this place is a good reflection of the guards that shield it."

From the far side of the hallway the self-assured guard summoned us to the dining hall; leading the way, he entered the modest banquet chamber.

Nobleman Skinner stood from the banquet table on seeing Lady Ivy, paying little attention to my attendance. He respectfully greeted Ivy with a slight nod of his head. Skinner was just as I remembered, frail with grey, thinning hair. His tatty robe looked as if it had not been cleaned in a while. The nobleman's faltering manner was rare amongst rulers, yet there was something humble about Skinner; his kindness had unfortunately branded him as weak.

"My Lady, it is an honour to have the Baroness of Stanford in my company, I trust your husband Baron Asher remains well and prosperous," said Skinner, snootily.

His flattering of Asher was repulsive, and I felt my eyes roll involuntarily, which fortunately went unnoticed.

Lady Ivy replied respectfully before accepting his invitation to join him at his table. Once seated, Skinner casually sat back, squinting as he eyeballed me.

"You face is familiar, Sword," said Skinner.

Awkwardly, I looked down at the table, before glancing up to see the smirk on Lady Ivy's face. She was becoming amused by my historic, boisterous reputation. "I was born and raised right here in Somerby; I worry that previously our paths may have crossed," I replied.

Interrupting me, he clapped his hands together, before energetically replying. "Yes, if I remember rightly you were a rather troublesome young man, promiscuous with an eye for the local girls. Your antics resulted in many quarrels."

Lady Ivy coughed, indicating she was keen to get back to the matter in hand. Instantly toning down his excitable recollection, he began to backtrack in a more gratifying approach.

"It is a privilege to have you back home, young Sword, and the markings you display are some of the most prestigious seen within this land."

The Baroness brought the nobleman up to speed with our current situation; ending the conversation, Skinner had agreed to summon me back should Fulten arrive, He appeared sincere and sympathetic to our predicament, offering to send word to Stanford should my tutor fail to appear.

"I will see to it that the Baron rewards you appropriately, Nobleman Skinner," said Ivy, graciously.

"That is exceedingly kind of you my lady, I will see to it that your chambers are prepared at once," replied Skinner.

Stringently, Lady Ivy replied. "There is no need, I will be staying in the village, my lodgings have been arranged. Sword Jep's family have offered me suitable accommodation."

Bewildered, Skinner paused before carefully replying. "My Lady, the slums are no place for someone of your status."

Sighing, Ivy replied. "I spent my childhood surrounded by poverty; I assure you I am not naive. Besides, I have spent the last few years being pampered and smothered; it will be refreshing to become reacquainted with my past."

Astonished, Skinner insisted that one of his guards escorted Lady Ivy around the village.

"I am in the company of a Blue Sword; I have all the protection one would ever need."

On leaving the dining hall, I turned to Nobleman Skinner; "Beg your pardon, but your guard, the fair haired one- his mannerism is rather off-putting."

Skinner stuttered, "You speak of Steffen; yes, I am aware his ways are somewhat unorthodox, but he was hired for a purpose."

On leaving the Grand Hall the guard I spoke of, Steffen, haughtily leaned against the side of the stables, throwing loose grass from his fingers onto the ground. His lingering was clearly intended for our benefit; calling out to me and Ivy, he conceitedly said, "My Lady, do forgive my intrusion, I can't help but find it rather peculiar that the Baroness of one of the most glorious settlements within Thear rejected the hospitality of our Grand Hall, in exchange for the slums."

Ivy sniggered, "Do not flatter yourself, guardsman, the Grand Hall you serve is far from Grand."

Frowning, Steffen glared at Ivy, unimpressed by her sarcastic wit; I found her reaction rather impressive, enjoying the way in which she cut the self-assured guard down. As we walked away, Steffen was intent on stirring up trouble and having the final word.

"Do wish your sister well, won't you, Sword?" he said, snidely.

Lady Ivy knew I was going to react; leaning out, she gripped my arm and shook her head. Her prevention of my short-tempered reaction gave me a moment to pause and settle; casually strolling up to the egotistical guard, I glanced to the ground before eyeballing him with malice.

Mirroring his arrogance, I gruffly said; "You whine a lot for a village guard; it will serve you well to learn your place."

Annoyed by my disdain he clenched his mouth, muttering: "Indeed."

Returning to my home amongst the slums, Lady Ivy embraced the poverty of where I had spent most of my life; entering our hut my mother was preparing a stew on the fire pit. Abbot and my sister Emil were seated on the bench humouring Gibbon as he relayed one of his long winded, farfetched tales. On seeing Lady Ivy present, Abbot leapt up from the bench, offering his seat to Ivy. Watching the Baroness interact with my family, I could not help but feel contented; the conversation flowed naturally, and I could see my mother was beginning to take a shine to her. It was clear Ivy held no prejudice for the conditions with which she was surrounded, her ability to adjust to any situation was one of the reasons the people of Stanford could relate to her and in turn adore her.

During our supper, my mother saved me from yet another embarrassing childhood story relayed by my friends Abbott and Gibbon; insisting I help her clean the cooking pot outside, I was able to escape their teasing. Feeling her beaming gaze, I smirked back asking her what was on her mind.

"My son has unearthed love," she said, tenderly.

Sniggering, I stuttered, "I do not follow."

"Lady Ivy, she feels it also," said mother, stringently.

Looking around, I whispered, "Mother, she is a Baroness and wed to one of the most influential men in the land."

"She observes you through a loving eye, the way in which I looked at your father," she replied.

Sighing, I said, "You drink far too much mead, mother."

Having the final word, mother replied, "Maybe I do, but remember these words, a heart will only follow truth, it will merely tolerate circumstance."

Returning inside, it was now Emil's turn to enlighten Lady Ivy of my past; however, the cackles of laughter roaring from the table at my expense were refreshing to see. Gibbon demanded that we were to attend the Bull Horn tavern to continue our merriment; however, my objections were quickly overruled by Lady Ivy's enthusiasm to explore her brief touch of freedom a little more.

18

STOLEN MOMENT

My family home was rather modest, with one chamber separated from the rest of the hut; mother had become insistent on allowing Lady Ivy to take her bed for the night.

"Will you not accompany us to the tavern?" Ivy asked mother.

"My dear, my weary bones are fit for cooking and praying; please go and enjoy the gaiety, I will ensure your bed is prepped for your return."

My final plea with Lady Ivy fell on deaf ears, she was caught up in the moment and encouraged by mead.

Ruffling my hair, Gibbon teased. "Steady yourself, man, and unwind; that uniform has made you uptight."

"You don't have to protect a Baroness," I mumbled, sarcastically.

Tearing the laced sleeves off her dress, Ivy said. "This night, I am no Baroness."

My sister glared at Ivy in awe of her confidence and poise; leaving for the tavern I ran my fingers over the hilt of my sword remembering my tutor's teachings to keep my blade close. Gibbon stomped through the village, boisterous and excitable, leaving Lady Ivy and my sister Emil linking arms, giggling like children. I felt uneasy and vulnerable; my tunic was already attracting attention from the locals. As chants came from some of the village men admiring Ivy's beauty, I found it even harder to relax.

Arriving at the run-down tavern, it was not dissimilar to the condition of the Viking Invader in Stamford. The dark and dingy tavern was bustling with life and the rowdy atmosphere was escalated by a folk band, passionately banging at their drums. Gibbon strutted to the serving table using his thick set to barge his way through. Most of the locals' wandering eyes began to settle on seeing that Ivy and Emil were in my company. Abbot knelt on one his stumpy legs, offering Ivy his hand. Accepting his offer, she joyfully joined him as they began to dance arm in arm; her beaming smile lit up the tavern. It was the happiest I had ever seen the Baroness; she looked free and untroubled.

Abbot's hardened reputation kept the local men at bay from attempting to engage with Ivy, leaving me feeling slightly loosened. Gibbon leaned against the serving table glaring at Ivy.

"She wants you, Jep; I tell you now, she wants you to take her."

Gasping, I choked on my beaker of ale, "She has a husband," I replied, firmly.

"When has that ever stopped you in the past? Besides, you told me the man is a pig, I imagine a couple of thrusts and it is all over. Give the woman a damn good seeing too."

Chuckling, I looked up at my childhood friend; "I have missed you, Gibbon."

It was not long before Lady Ivy returned to the serving table looking rather worse for wear: her elegant hair was now pressed against her forehead and her dress dishevelled. Slightly slurring her words, she begged for me to dance; Gibbon encouraged her persistence, leaving me to follow her to the centre of the tavern. My heavy footing made my dancing rather undesirable, however Ivy's grin was infectious. Forgetting our quandary, time stood still; this blissful stolen moment between us was euphoric, leaving my mind to venture away from Fulten.

Coming to a standstill, Ivy frowned whilst glancing around the room.

"Do you feel unwell my Lady?" I asked.

"No, your sister: where is Emil?" she said concernedly.

Peering over to Gibbon, he was engaging in some drunken ramblings with some of the locals. Marching over to Abbot, I asked him if he had seen Emil; his slurred, uncertain reply prompted me to step outside the tavern, followed by Ivy and Abbot.

The sounds of commotion came from the rear of the chapel; the whimpering sounds of women's voices reminded me of my interventions between Linc and the peasant woman on my first night in Stanford. Racing over to the graveyard, my sister Emil stood being held at the mercy of Steffen, the pompous guardsman who had already encouraged a grievance with myself. Seeing his hand cupping the throat of my sister filled me with rage. Now aware of my presence, he released his hold of my sister, refraining from tormenting her further.

Emil ran to the arms of Ivy who embraced her with a comforting hug. Steffen straightened his tunic before pressing his palm down on his hair.

Gulping, his attempt at deflecting his behaviour onto my sister endorsed his snide attitude further. "Your sister is nothing more than a tease, I am afraid I grew weary of her leadings."

Stalking towards him, I clenched my fist tightly. Ivy called out to me, but her pleas of peace went unheard. Glancing back at my sister, I saw the fear in her eyes as she trembled because of the conduct offered by this obnoxious predator.

Seeing the wrath displayed from my snarl, Steffen cowered, flinching on my approach; "Be mindful of your actions; we are sworn to protect, not inflict."

Thrusting my head forward, I struck the bridge of his nose; the crunch from the cracking bone left Steffen dropping to his knees, clutching at his face. The seeping blood trickled down his tunic as he glanced up at me in desperation.

Leaning down, still scowling at him I sternly muttered, "If your wandering hands ever meet my sister again, I will choke you with your own balls. Do we understand one another?"

Cowering, he stuttered in agreement before scurrying away. Emil ran towards me, wrapping her arms around me as she sobbed into my chest. Peering across Emil's shoulder, Ivy glared back at me nodding her head, surprisingly appearing satisfied by my actions.

"About time someone dropped that weasel bastard," bellowed Abbot.

Arriving back home, mother embraced my teary-eyed sister before taking her to bed; I headed outside to clear my face in the water barrel by the side of our hut. Sighing, I approached my horse Spike, gently stroking his mane. Hearing the front door creak open, I assumed it was my mother checking up on me, however turning around I saw Lady Ivy stood glaring back at me. Raising her hand, she gently cupped her palm against my cheek; the contact caused my heart to beat faster. Leaning forward I met her, kissing her soft and delicate lips. The tranquil intimate moment sent flutters through my stomach before she eventually broke away, smiling back at me.

"I thought you would be disappointed of my actions this night," I said.

"You fight when you must, and I can't fight my desire for you, Jep."

Leaving me outside, Ivy left me pondering over our encounter; the intimacy of our stolen moment left me feeling ecstatic and forgetful of our reality. Returning inside my mother and sister were sleeping peacefully. Approaching the archway that separated the chambers which Ivy was occupying, I glanced over to her intently as she perched on the end of the bed.

Sighing, she muttered, "Jep, do you ever wish you could flee from it all and start over?"

"I do; destiny took me to Stanford, to you," I replied.

Placing her fingers against her mouth, Ivy tensely gazed at the floor, before speaking. "My life is dominated by jealousy and control, the clothes I wear, the company I keep. Yet here I feel so free, I can be me."

"Would you ever leave?" I replied.

Sniggering, Ivy glanced up at me, rolling her now teary eyes. "What a delightful thought; if I were to leave how would I ever learn the true fate of my father? Goodnight Jep."

Laying down on the hard floor, I contemplated Lady Ivy's words; her vague confirmation of the rumours surrounding the Baron's foul behaviour towards her were hard to stomach. I took the comments she made about staying to learn her father's fate to mean that she too had her suspicions about Baron Asher's capabilities.

At first light I got up from the floor, glancing over to my mother and sister, who were still peacefully sleeping. It was a motivating reminder of my need to complete my trials and become an established Blue Sword, to ensure they were provided for. After checking on Lady Ivy, I snuck outside our family home keen to attend the Grand Hall and check to see if Fulten had arrived. Unconvinced and anxious, I wandered through the village square observing the morning traders setting up their stalls.

In the distance, racing down the hill towards me, Abbot ran. His short stumpy legs struggled to keep up with his will to meet with me. Panting and struggling to catch his breath, Abbot wiped the sweat from his forehead.

Frowning, I glanced down at his thick, ginger beard now covered in mud stains. "I am guessing you never made it home my friend?" I said.

Huffing he replied, "No, my night was spent in the square but that is not why I come to you. Your Sword; he has arrived."

Brashly, I said, "Fulten? Are you sure the man you saw was a Blue Sword?"

"A rounded man with a beard, not too dissimilar to my own, he had the same markings as the ones on your chest. He woke me up with his reckless riding, charging through the village like a man possessed."

Sprinting, I dashed up to the Grand Hall, relieved at the sight of Fulten's horse tethered in the stables. Entering the open door, I excitedly raced down the hallway into the dining hall. Stunned by my erratic interruption, Nobleman Skinner and Fulten were seated, eating, and becoming acquainted.

"Jep my boy, it appears you have made quite a name for yourself here; where is the Baroness?" said Fulten.

"She rests at my home, with my mother and sister," I replied.

"Rather peculiar that she chooses a night amongst the common folk rather than the comforts of the Grand Hall, nevertheless she is safe and unharmed," he bellowed across the table.

Skinner glanced at me disapprovingly; "There is the matter of the assault on my guard."

Rising from the table, Fulten smirked, "Well if he challenged a Blue Sword, he should think himself lucky to have his head; besides I can vouch for Jep, he would have only done what was necessary."

Clarifying my reasons, I called over to Skinner. "Your guard harasses my sister."

Mortified, Nobleman Skinner glanced down at the table.

Fulten hit the table with his fist, concluding the matter. "There we have it, your guard leaves my boy's sister be and he keeps his head; now come, Jep, we must collect the Baroness and leave."

Swanning out of the Grand Hall, Fulten's arrival had raised my spirits further; following him strutting to the stables, I smiled, enthused to see him safe.

"I was worried you wouldn't make it," I said to Fulten.

Unknotting his horse's reins, he glanced back at me with one raised eyebrow.

"Do you think a band of amateurish crooks are a match for me and one of the most skilled guards in Stanford? I disapprove of your doubt," Fulten replied, sarcastically.

"Where is Ricard?" I replied.

"Against his own objections, I ordered him back to Stanford and if we do not return in the coming days, to bring reinforcements."

"So, what now?" I said eagerly.

Exhaling, Fulten replied, "Whiten is less than a day's ride; if we leave now, we will arrive before nightfall."

Returning to my family home, I had mixed emotions. I was glad to see Fulten alive and well yet the thought of leaving Somerby made me feel rather sullen. On learning of Fulten's plan, Lady Ivy eagerly prepped her horse for the ride ahead. Fulten politely engaged in formalities with my family, but he was twitchy and wanted to leave. Now seated on our horses, my mother stood between me and Fulten.

Glancing up at me, her eyes filled with tears. "Now you do what must be done; do not allow your past to determine your outcome, my son is as worthy as any other man."

"Never a truer word spoken, madam," agreed Fulten.

Peering over to my tutor, she spoke sternly. "Be patient with him, his heart his clean and meaningful."

"And that is why he will make a fine Blue Sword," replied Fulten.

Lady Ivy was saying her final goodbyes to my sister Emil, someone of whom she had grown fond during our brief time in Somerby, before graciously expressing gratitude to my mother for her warm hospitality. Fulten's insistence to depart left me riding away, mirroring my mother and sister's teary eyes. At the outskirt of the village, a voice called over, bringing us to a halt.

"Leaving without saying goodbye? You bloody Swords are all the same," called Gibbon, sarcastically.

Gibbon stood grinning, towering alongside my good friend Abbot. Introducing them to Fulten, he greeted them with courtesy.

"You must come to Stanford, visit me soon," I said, eagerly.

Abbot sighed, "You know, Gibbon, he isn't one to travel, he likes his home comforts."

Fulten interrupted before I had chance to reply, "It is a shame, the Swords are always seeking new men to try-out." Turning back to me, he continued, "Now, Jep, it is vital that we leave."

"Well it can't be that challenging, if they insisted on allowing you in," said Gibbon, sardonically.

Leaving Somerby, I held back, allowing Fulten to bring Lady Ivy up to speed. He was keen to learn of our own dealings and listened intently, whilst Ivy praised my bravery in tackling the Shadow crooks that had challenged us on the road outside Hooks Cross. Glancing back to me, he gave me an approving nod, showing his proudness at my ability and willingness in keeping the Baroness safe.

19

EDGAR

Following the narrow and rocky path, we were surrounded by flat land covered by crop fields. Fulten came to a dramatic stop; he peered between me and Ivy appearing rather uncomfortable. Concerned, Lady Ivy eyed him up and down.

"Are you unwell?" she asked.

Grunting, he jumped down from his horse. "I fear that Skinner's eggs have not agreed with my delicate stomach, do excuse me."

Shuffling towards the hedgerow, Fulten disappeared out of sight. Chuckling, I glanced over to Lady Ivy who met me with a cold expression. Aware that Fulten was currently occupied, I nervously broached the previous evening's intimate moment between us.

Ivy's reluctance to look back at me gave me an indication of her thoughts. Sighing, she raised her chin in the air, appearing rather irritable at my reminiscence.

Breaking the awkward silence, Lady Ivy spoke in pompous tone. "It has been a while since I have overindulged in such merriment, I can only assume that my consumption of mead left me vulnerable to the irresponsible behaviours I pursued."

Exhaling, I frowned, shaking my head, "Well I can only apologise for aiding your irresponsible behaviour," I replied, sarcastically.

"Oh, do be realistic, Jep, what did you think would come of it? That we would ride off together and live happily ever after? I am the Baroness of Stamford, and you are…" Pausing, she stopped herself finishing her sentence.

"I am what? A peasant?" I replied, abruptly.

"You are a Blue Sword. I cannot deny my fondness for you, but what happened in Somerby was a mistake and will not be repeated. Please can you not see the position you put me in?" Ivy gently muttered.

Sternly, I replied. "What position? You are just fearful of your pig-headed husband."

Leaning closer, it was the first time I had ever seen Lady Ivy scowl, "You will mind your words, do not forget your place."

Our confrontational encounter was interrupted by a rather relieved looking Fulten. Unaware of our exchanged of heated words, Fulten leapt back onto his horse with a smug expression on his face, insistent on continuing our journey. I decided to hold back and allow Ivy to travel alongside my tutor. Livid with the Baroness's dismissive tone, I sulked, and like any man in search of restoring his dignity, I considered my options. Allowing my buried, selfish, and arrogant mindset to take over, I began to think of Jen and her seductive smile along with lustful gestures; that was all complemented by her sensual physique. My mind was made, no more pining and yearning for a Baroness who was out of reach; upon my return to Stanford I had decided I would commit myself to Jen.

Fulten glanced back at me, ordering me to pick up the pace so he could bring me up to speed with his conversation with Lady Ivy. Fulten declared his concern surrounding the Shadow Crooks.

"It was naive of me to be so dismissive of Ricard's warning about the Shadow Crooks; their assault on the Regal guards indicates that they are getting braver," said Fulten.

"What will you do?" asked Lady Ivy.

"Once we return to Stanford, I will send word to Alma; it is imperative that Chief Muir is made aware of their escalation."

The greying sky indicated rain was on its way, and our road had now transformed into sludge. Fulten pointed to the horizon, stating that Whiten was close by; stopping, he glanced across the depleted crop fields to ensure that we were not being followed.

Arriving in Whiten, the modest settlement was a true reflection of the deprivation in the north. The backdrop of dark clouds was fitting to the dwindling huts spread throughout depleted ruined walls. Ivy placed her fingers under her nose, keen to alleviate herself from the potent stench caused by rotting animal carcasses. Our presence had prompted the fearful locals to retreat into their homes. Fulten pointed over to one of the larger wooden huts, keen to direct our attention to the crucifix symbol carved onto the door.

Stepping down from our horses, the door to the makeshift chapel opened. A short, plump man with thinning hair bellowed over to us.

"Don't you be leaving them beasts there, this is holy ground," he said bitterly.

Fulten approached the red-faced podgy man, "Are you the priest here?"

Huffing irritably, he replied; "That I am, now move them horses, this is not a blasted stable."

Showing her own irritation, Ivy marched towards the priest. "As a representative for the church, I find you flippant and vulgar. Now, I am the Baroness of Stanford and unless you wish for me to inform the church of your abrupt and unwelcoming tone, I suggest you mind your manners and listen to what my companion has to say."

Scrunching his mouth, the priest glanced back to Fulten, bewildered by his reprimanding. In a more pleasant tone, he requested the reason for our arrival in Whiten. Fulten led the conversation, informing the plump priest of our requirement to speak with a local boy.

"We believe a boy named Elis is staying here in Whiten."

Touching his head, the priest signed the cross before glancing up the sky. "The boy you seek is here; well at least his body is here, I laid him to rest yesterday."

Deflated, Ivy rested her head on the saddle of her horse; on seeing her upset I called to the priest, demanding to know the circumstances surrounding Elis's death.

Directing his answer to Fulten, he nervously replied, "I do not feel it is my place to speak of the boy; his father lives in the home behind the chapel. I am sure he will be enthused by your attendance."

Leading the horses around to the home of Elis's father, our silence reflected our shock. Hearing Lady Ivy gasp, I noticed her eyes watering.

I gently offered her comfort by saying, "We will find your father."

She peered up at me with a half-hearted smile displayed on her face, whilst Fulten glared back at me, frowning at my offerings of false hope.

A wrinkled, grey haired man opened the door to Fulten's knock; glancing down at my tutor's crest, he smiled, displaying lack of teeth.

"Finally; I was hoping you lot would arrive. My son's murder cannot go unpunished."

"Murder?" Fulten queried.

"Yes, my boy was found decapitated by the brook. I demand the head of his attacker, an eye for an eye."

Uncomfortable, Fulten glanced back at me before reluctantly agreeing with the old man. Playing on the grieving father's thirst for revenge, Fulten insisted on asking him some further question surrounding Elis.

Entering Elis's family home, it seemed as if our hardship was something we had in common – that, along with sharing the bed of the same woman. Lady Ivy apprehensively sat on the suspiciously stained bench and was quick to refuse a cup of mead offered by the peasant man. Fulten intuitively began to question Elis's father on his son, however he shrewdly concentrated on his murder before mentioning his association with Lady Ivy's father, Isaak.

"Oh yes, he spoke constantly of this Isaak fellow; he even went to visit him from time to time."

Ivy sat upright, "My father, he is here in Whiten?"

Frowning, Elis's father replied, "No, no, I didn't say here in Whiten. It was north of here- some farm." Pausing, he scrunched up his face, desperately trying to recall the name.

"Edgar?" Ivy interrupted.

"That is the one. Edgar farm: at first, he went there a lot to see this Isaak but then just stopped going. He changed - he was anxious about something. I thought he was just pining for that tart he had met back in Stanford."

Fulten's inquisitive questioning left Elis's father teary eyed and even more insistent on receiving justice for his son's murder. Leaving Elis's family house, Fulten glanced back at me, perplexed. Eventually he shared his puzzlement, explaining that Elis's brutal decapitation was the likely action of thieves or bandits.

"Such an unclean death; the boy was obviously butchered by savages." My silence caused him to question my reluctance to comment. "Do you not agree?" asked Fulten.

Nervous at challenging my tutor's assumptions, I replied, "Something feels wrong; Elis's departure from Stanford has gone unnoticed for a while, yet we come searching for answers and he winds up dead."

Brashly Lady Ivy interrupted, "Let me guess - my husband sent men here to kill the boy; I fear that your theories grow weary."

Ivy then leapt onto to her horse dismissively; I thought it best to consider my place and not react to her snide remark. Fulten scrunched his mouth, uncomfortably and suspicious of the current tension between me and the Baroness.

Leaving Whiten, Lady Ivy made it clear she wanted to ride alone by purposely creating a gap between me and Fulten and I felt it was wise to allow her to reflect and have some time alone. Fulten muttered over to me, trying to make sense of her bitter mood, concluding it was down to her anxiety over what we were likely to discover at her family farm. The darkening clouds mirrored the repetitively dull scenery. Slowing down, Lady Ivy eventually gave us the chance to catch her up, giving us the indication, she wanted to talk. "Edgar farm was named after my late grandfather and our home for many years. My father moved us to Stanford after his relationship with my uncle grew toxic. His willingness to return could only mean he was desperate."

Fulten compassionately placed his hand on the Baroness's arm. "We will learn your father's fate together; you are not alone, my Lady."

Squinting, I noticed smoke smouldering in the distance, camouflaged by the dark cloud and lightly falling rain. Lady Ivy followed my gaze, causing the colour to fade on her face. Noticing her panic, Fulten demanded we hurry.

"We are too late," stuttered Lady Ivy.

The wooden structure was completely ablaze and too far gone to have any survivors inside. Coughing from the smoke, I glanced at Fulten, noticing the flames reflecting in his eyes. He ordered me to search the rear of the farm whilst he attempted to console the hysterical Baroness.

Spike was spooked by the roaring flames, so I leapt down and sprinted around the side of the farm. Peering into the long grass behind the fire, I noticed a separation in the hedgerow. Rushing over, I discovered the corpse of an elderly man; blood stained his white linens and tarnished his grey hair. His severed ears and cut out eyes indicated the barbaric mindset of his attacker. Concluding that the body I looked upon was Isaak, Lady Ivy's father, my stomach griped at the thought of relaying my finding to the Baroness.

Fulten yelled for Ivy to stop, as she rushed towards me, keen to learn of my discovery. Standing, I approached her, grabbing her arms in an attempt to restrain her from seeing the harrowing sight of her dismembered father. Pushing my arms away, Ivy screamed for me to step aside, having no choice, I woefully watched as she glared down at the corpse.

Looking backing at me rather bewildered, she frowned, "This is not my father."

Kneeling before the dead body, Lady Ivy closed her eyes and began to pray. Relieved by her calming reaction, Fulten stood beside me.

"Your thoughts were correct; our investigation has been compromised. We must return to Stanford and inform the governor; we will need assistance from Alma," Fulten said uneasily.

Standing beside Ivy, she looked up to me and Fulten, revealing the identity of the deceased to be her uncle. Fulten offered his condolences, however Ivy's contemptuous tone indicated she was not overly saddened at her uncle's brutal death. The Baroness demanded that we began to search the grounds of the farm for her father. Interrupting her orders, Fulten asked for silence at hearing rustling from the long grass. We nervously glanced over to the direction of the noise, eventually calming, and putting the sound down to animals.

Fulten became restless, pointing out the freshness of the blood that had leaked from the dead man's wounds. Turning to me, he insisted that I hurry the search of the farm along, conscious that the attackers could be close by. Before I had chance to begin my search the rustling from the hedges started once again; charging from the grass a short, rounded man, dressed in animal fur with a blood-stained face came racing towards us. Roaring, he made his intentions apparent.

My slow reactions were spared by the experience and ability of my tutor, who swiftly removed his sword from its scabbard, smoothly swiping his blade upright, splitting our attacker's belly open. Now grounded, the plump man shrieked at the sight of his exposed guts, panting as he clutched desperately at his stomach to stem the bleeding. The blood seeped through the man's fingertips, leaving him glancing up at me and Fulten in dread.

Recognising the man, I frowned. "You; did I not warn you that next time, you would be fed to the buzzards."

Gurning, he was unable to reply. Fulten demanded to know of my previous experience with our attacker. "This is one of the men that challenged me and Lady Ivy outside Hooks Cross; after falling by my sword, he was shown mercy."

Glancing back to Ivy, she stood with her hand over her mouth in astonishment between the bloodied corpse of her uncle and his potential murderer. Fulten's mood changed; he grew irritable and angry.

"Why are the Shadow crooks interfering in our affairs? First the bridge, then the peasant boy and now the farmer; who has hired you?" Fulten yelled.

Spurting blood from his mouth, he struggled to release any words. Crouching down beside him, Fulten offered him a quick death in exchange for answers.

"Damn it man, who sent you here?" Fulten bellowed.

An arrow whistled, released from the direction of the hedges. Accurately it pierced directly into the jugular of the Shadow crook. I tackled Lady Ivy, pushing her to the ground, shielding her body with my own.

Rattled, Fulten sternly muttered, "Take cover by the stables at the far side; move swiftly."

Sheltering the Baroness, I moved hastily behind Lady Ivy. I heard another arrow fly past, narrowly missing my head; glancing back to Fulten he ran towards us, his face filled with panic.

Now covered by the stables, Fulten dived down next, panting and struggling for breath. Peering around, he nodded towards our horses.

"Get the Baroness to the horses and ride quickly; I will create a diversion. The crook is inaccurate with a moving target," Fulten insisted.

Replying, I refused. "No, you are too slow, and your mass has more chance of shielding Lady Ivy."

Frowning at my suggestion, he knew it was a better option; sprinting forward, Fulten and Ivy made a run for it, whilst I jumped out yelling at the top of my voice towards the long grass that sheltered the bowman.

Darting from side to side with a clenched jaw, I was fearfully anticipating the next arrow penetrating my body. Recklessly firing one arrow after another, my sidestepping was enough to make the bowman unsuccessful in his attempts to put me down. Seeing Lady Ivy and Fulten now mounted on their horses, I raced towards Spike still expecting to receive that lethal hit. Muttering prayers under my breath, my legs felt heavy as if they were filled were stone. Panting and breathless I made it to Spike still able to use my arms to pull myself over his saddle, before firmly kicking his sides to hurry our retreat.

Dashing forward, I noticed Ivy and Fulten in the distance glancing back to ensure I was close behind them. Peering back across the flat land, I could see that no one had followed us from the farm. It was a relief to have caught up with Fulten, who gave me an approving nod, clearly impressed by my selflessness and brave actions.

20

INTERTWINED TREES

The rapid ride to Whiten left me feeling rather tender; limited words had been exchanged between us in our keenness to escape harm's way. Fulten was insistent on relaying our findings to Elis's father. Disappointed with our failure to learn more of the circumstances surrounded his son's murder, Fulten assured him that the matter was far from dealt with.

Anxiously we travelled south towards the river crossing; all three of us fidgeted as we glanced across the flat lands to ensure we had not been followed by more Shadow crooks. I never thought I would be so eager to return south where more regal guards patrolled, deterring the roaming bandits. Lady Ivy's blank stare expressed her disappointment with our journey. Fulten's attempt at reassurance by his intention to summon further resources from the city was received with a rather surprising and pessimistic tone.

"Let us be straight with one another: we are none the wiser as to my father's fate and it is rather apparent whom you believe is responsible," said Ivy, bitterly.

Unable to hold my tongue at her disregard for our endeavours I bit back at her; "Let's speak the truth, my Lady; your husband's jealousy gives him motive."

"Enough, Jep, you will remember your place," Fulten replied, sternly.

Bringing her horse to a standstill, the Baroness scowled back at me, "You will do well to remember my husband is your Baron; besides, do you really believe he would set up an ambush that would see me raped and slain? You show your inexperience and naivety."

I had no reply; both Ivy and Fulten were right, I had spoken out of place. My outspoken words reflected my resentment of her dismissal of our kiss back in Somerby. Fulten grimaced, shaking his head in disappointment at my tone, before catching up with Lady Ivy in hope to salvage our reputation.

Crossing the bridge into the south, it was a relief to see the Regal guards had now doubled in their numbers, to deter any further attacks from the Shadow crooks. The guards gave us uneasy stares at our request to camp the night in their company but having two Blue Swords and a Baroness in need of their protection, they had no choice but to oblige. Lady Ivy was offered the guards' quarters and her refusal to have me or Fulten join her reflected her annoyance at my earlier statement.

Fulten sat opposite me, observing my gloomy mood from across the fire.

"You have grown too close to the Baroness; should Asher learn of this, you will be lucky to keep your head, let alone be confirmed as a Sword," muttered Fulten.

My reluctance to reply and change the subject left Fulten sighing at my lack of care for his council.

"Allow me to stay, I will learn who follows our steps and hinders the investigation," I said.

Bluntly, Fulten replied, "No, we return together; it is vital we seek the guidance of the governor. Our only task now is getting the Baroness back to Stanford alive, and for your sake hope she does not spill of your familiarity."

At first light, we travelled the path south towards Hooks Cross; seeing the opening where I defeated the Shadow Crooks who threatened to bring harm to Lady Ivy, she glanced back at me, smilingly acknowledging my bravery; her sincerity broke the awkwardness that lingered between us. Fulten remained cautious and insisted that we boycotted the village, before settling for our final night on the road. I volunteered to remain on watch for the night, keen to make right my previous abruptness towards Lady Ivy. Standing guard, I leant against an old oak tree, listening to the commotion of a nearby owl. Swiftly turning at the sound of crunching leaves, Ivy gently appeared before me.

"Fulten sleeps, so I speak quietly. I am baffled by the relationship we have formed and in truth a little frightened by it also, we will not gain from speaking of what happened in Somerby," said Ivy.

"I have no intention of relaying idle gossip," I replied, flippantly.

"Good, I fear the outcome would be deadly." Placing her hand on my cheek, Lady Ivy became teary eyed. "Be assured my masked exterior will not be a reflection of my true feelings, Jep."

As Ivy turned away, I called back to her. "I will learn the true fate of your father; you have my word."

Grinning back at me, the Baroness crept back towards the camp. Sighing, I glanced up the glistening stars, hovering my hand over the embroidery on my tunic, I remembered how far I had come, and how contented I was. Satisfaction was an unfamiliar feeling and I felt keen not to let it go anytime soon.

I never thought I would be so relieved to see the gates of Stanford; the town sparkled under the clear blue sky. The townsfolk glared at Lady Ivy, flabbergasted by her dishevelled appearance caused by our time on the road. Leaving her at the gates, the Baroness remained composed and grateful for our escort. Fulten offered her reassurance, declaring his willingness to pursue her father's vanishing further. Riding away from the Grand Hall, I could not help but glance back at Ivy; noticing her mirroring my smile, I knew it would be difficult to forget the stolen moments which we shared.

Hota was attending his horse at the stables; on seeing my arrival he grinned, taking my arm as I leapt down from Spike. Fulten was insistent on seeking an audience with the governor, leaving me and Hota to unsaddle his horse.

"My father told me of the ambush you encountered and was complimentary of your bravery," said Hota.

"I am glad to hear of your father's safe return," I replied.

Hota frowned, "We insisted on riding out to aid you, but the governor denied our requests; damn, even Chenchi was keen to assist."

"I bet he was," I replied, sarcastically.

"You remain untrusting; same old Jep. It is good to see you," said Hota.

Footsteps crunched along the gravel in the courtyard; Fawkes walked side by side with Blair- it was pleasant to see her mischievous face. The servant girl eyed up my tunic, grinning at the blood stains she noticed on my uniform.

"Please, Jep, tell me how you killed them?"

Glaring down at the child, Fawkes scowled, demanding she return to her mother. He glanced back at me with his chiselled jaw line, making little of my return.

"Ricard tells me you are good at taking orders; I hope you have brought this trait back with you."

Chenchi appeared from the lock up; his raised eyebrows reflected his surprise at seeing me back from our excursion.

"You made it back; maybe I have underestimated your ability," he said, derisively.

Hota, glanced to the ground, uneasy by the tensions between me and the ex-guardsman.

"Our investigation has been hindered; it seems we have a snake in the grass," I replied, abruptly.

Unable to tolerate the arrogance of the man any longer, I left the stables and headed for the parade room, keen to salvage any left-over food. The only food on offer were some rotten apples and left-over stale cheese, but before I had chance to savour the rather undesirable offerings, a stern voice called for me from the combat chambers. Fulten ordered me to present myself immediately to the governor.

Fulten remained silent as he led me up the staircase towards where the governor awaited my arrival; his refusal to speak was an indication that the governor wanted questions answered, and Fulten did not want to appear to be colluding. Glaring from the smeared glass window, he turned to face me; his stern natural grimace and dark complexion made him all the more formidable and fiercer. Slowly lowering himself down into his chair, he cupped his hands, crossing his fingers.

"Be seated," he muttered, sighing before continuing. "It has come to my attention that your courage may have saved the life of our Baroness; I expect nothing less from one of my Swords. Nevertheless, I have also learnt that Asher is rather displeased with your gallivanting with his wife."

My heart sank into my stomach as I nervously peered over to Fulten, who was seated beside me.

"I do not follow, sir," I stuttered.

Sternly the governor eyeballed me across the table; "I care little for your following, boy, I just need to be assured that there was no lewd behaviour towards Lady Ivy from one of my Blue Swords."

"I can vouch for Jep's chivalrous manner sir," stated Fulten.

"You can vouch for nothing," replied the governor sternly, now staring at Fulten.

Gulping, I replied to the governor, "Sir, you have my word; I have nothing but utter respect and devotion to the Swords: I would do nothing that would bring our crest into disrepute."

Leaning back into his chair, the governor sighed.

"Fulten has brought me up to speed with your findings; the circumstances have made the investigation vastly more complex than it already was, leaving me no choice but to request a detector attend from Alma. You should have returned to Stanford once you had learned of the attack on the bridge, however I am satisfied with Fulten's justifications; as for the Baron, leave his petulant jealousy to me."

On being dismissed from his chambers the governor called out to me before I had chance to leave the room. "Distance yourself from Lady Ivy; this matter must be allowed to settle. If your findings are correct, we may need the aid of the Baron's men to deter any unwanted Shadow crooks."

Acknowledging his instruction, I left, keen to return to my quarters to bathe. Drenching my face in the murky water, I heard footsteps approach me from behind; I turned around to see Chenchi glaring back at me. Unsure of the intent of his engagement, I spat the remaining water from my mouth, frowning and making him aware of my already irritable mood.

Casually, he instigated the conversation. "You are troubled by me, are you not?"

Running my hand through my wet hair, I eyed him up and down with discontent. "I am troubled by your loyalties."

Taking a deep breath, Chenchi shook his head. "I am not your enemy."

Stepping closer to the sturdy ex guard, I sniggered. "We will find out soon enough."

Fulten had authorised my absence from duties, giving me the chance to rekindle with Jen; I was guilt ridden and not because of the kiss I had shared with Ivy, more so because the Baroness's rejection was promoting my egotistical side and prompting me to settle for the tavern girl. Pacing through the market square, I was yearning for lustful intimacy and Jen was perfect for pleasing my desires.

The town had settled since the Baron Hill festival and I had become accustomed to the attention as I walked the streets. The sun was lowering in the distance and the traders had begun to clear their stalls; amongst them was Pip, the energetic old man who was always a pleasure and was known for serving his hot pork slabs. Calling me over, he ushered away his customers, who were haggling with him for a reduced price on his remaining meat.

"Now you look like a man who would appreciate some food; I have no bread, but take a joint of this tender pork," said Pip, as he handed me over a cut of meat. "I hear you are courting the redhead from the tavern, a fine woman if you ask me. Trust me; cook her up some of that chop, and you will have her submitting at your feet, mark my words."

Laughing, I replied; "Do women not adore flowers?"

Frowning, Pip shook his head, "No, my boy, only the soft ones; a real woman like Jen needs meat, big meat," he chuckled.

The charming old man was harmless; on removing my leather purse, Pip refused any payment. "Don't you dare, you returned our Baroness home safe and well."

"How did you learn of this?" I asked.

"Rumours spread rapidly in this town, my boy. Although I imagine the poor girl is at home being interrogated as we speak."

Playing innocent, I replied; "What makes you say that?"

Pip sniggered, "Everybody knows the sacrifice our Baroness makes to ensure this town keeps diplomacy, having to tolerate the vile behaviour of that arse Asher. I have no doubt his jealousy will leave Lady Ivy tormented till winter."

Pip began to anxiously look around to ensure now one was listening in on our conversation. "I say too much, what do I know? I am a foolish old man with a dilapidated mind. Anyway, I must clear the stall; mind how you go."

Leaving the square, I couldn't help but reflect on what Pip had said about Ivy's troubles with the Baron, along with comment she has made during our journey together; did my ill thoughts towards the Baron echo amongst the town? My mind swiftly turned back to Jen. Arriving at the Viking Invader tavern, entering the unusually vacant inn, Jen stood behind the serving table. Her red hair flowed down, covering the laces of her corset, whilst her cleavage spilled from her front; she looked sensual. Coughing to get her attention she glanced up and noticed me stood before her; excitedly she leapt from behind the serving table, racing towards me before jumping and wrapping her legs around my waist.

Undeterred by the small number of customers in the tavern, she kissed me seductively. Her breast pushed against my chest, making me keen to return the passion.

Pulling away, she giggled, "Don't you dare get that meat on this dress." Prising it from my hand, she tossed it towards the old cranky tavern owner. "Have this in exchange for my evening off."

Without awaiting his reply, she firmly grabbed my hand and led me outside.

Wandering away from the centre of the town, Jen was insistent on taking me to her spot in which she enjoyed spending time. Entering the meadow, I glanced over the hill to see Carre's home.

Noticing my attentiveness to the farm, Jen asked. "Do you know Carre and his wife Dam?"

"I do, they took me in on my first night here; I have yet to return and look in on them, but I intend to repay their kindness."

"They are charming," replied Jen. "Carre is a man with great familiarity of this town; I fear one day his knowledge could become his burden," she said, sombrely.

Turning to her, I replied, "Why should a man who harnesses such peace be cursed with a burden?"

Jen glanced down at the ground, sheepishly. The undertone in her words reminded me of her coyness upon mentioning her previous lover Elis before I left for Whiten. Two things stopped me venting my irritation at her refusal to elaborate once again: one was my keenness to not interrupt the mood of our evening and the other was my awareness of having to disclose the death of Elis.

Overlooking the gently flowing river, we sat on the bank, shaded by two entwining trees. The lowering sun on the horizon lit up the water, providing a perfect setting for our courtship. Jen leaned back between my legs, resting her head into my chest, whilst I cupped both my hands on her waist; listening to the sound of the water parting through the loose rocks was peaceful.

Glancing up at the tightly formed branches above our heads, Jen smiled. "The trees clutch each other as if they are in love; have you ever been in love, Jep?"

Exhaling, I paused, mulling over her question. I expected Ivy's name to instantly enter my mind, but Jen's fine company had begun to congest my thoughts. Clutching at her waist, I eventually replied. "Not as yet, but I am hoping it is on the horizon."

Jen leaned around and slapped my arm; giggling, she accused me of being cringy in my choice of words. Intently gazing into my eyes, she moved her head forward and kissed me. The romantic mood was interrupted when she quizzed me on the outcome of my journey to Whiten.

Holding her tightly, I embraced her in preparation for my news on Elis's death. "Jen, we did make it to Whiten, and…"

Interpreting me, she said, "Elis is dead."

"I am sorry," I replied.

"Don't be, his death was inevitable; his constant meddling was only ever going to have one outcome."

Unbeknown to Jen, I frowned down at her. I was keen to interrogate her further on the fleeting messages she relayed to me but keeping the ambiance at that time was my priority; I had allowed my lustful intentions to get the better of me. After a short silence, Jen pushed me back, sitting on me with her legs straddling either side of my waist. Gazing down at me, she bit her bottom lip, leaving her hand to wander over my crotch. After slightly pulling my trousers down just below my bottom, Jen rubbed her hand over my groin before adjusting her dress and pressing down on top of me. Pulling her breast loose from her corset, I caressed her body, whilst she thrust herself intensely on me. We moaned heavily with each sensitive movement, before climaxing together on the riverbank.

Walking back to the market square, we chuckled amongst each other at our bold shenanigans. Once outside the tavern, Jen begged me to spend the night with her; however, aware of the strict rules of the Blue Swords, I regretfully declined her offer.

"I am to be confirmed tomorrow at noon; I want you there for the ceremony," I said. Jen glanced at the ground, attempting to disguise the tears forming in her eyes. Placing my finger underneath her chin, I raised her head and gazed down at her. "I want you there, by my side."

Grinning, Jen looked back at me with serenity. "I wouldn't miss it for the world."

Kissing her gently on the forehead, I began to walk away from the tavern; Jen called out to me. "You say that love may be on your horizon; I say it is standing before me."

Darting into the Viking Invader tavern, Jen left me mulling over her charming words. I wandered back to the lock up, feeling nothing but delight after my evening with Jen; it was soothing to allow Lady Ivy and the investigation to filter away from my mind. I felt contentment and certainty that I was now going to allow my relationship with Jen to flourish.

21

JEN

Returning to my quarters under the night sky, Hota was seated on the terrace of our hut.

Upon seeing my beaming grin, he sneered. "You have the look of man who has conquered; what pleases you so?"

"I have asked Jen to attend our confirmation," I replied, smugly.

Shaking his head, Hota stood to his feet. "Do you think that wise? It will only torment Chenchi."

"I have little care for Chenchi or his sensitivity," I replied.

"You will do as you wish, said Hota, calmly. Opening the door to our quarters, he turned around to address me again. "Jen is a simple girl, with a lust for attention. You are one of my best friends, so I will give you this advice. Enjoy her but be prepared to be dissatisfied; Jen has gathered quite the reputation for one who relishes futile gossip."

Smirking, I looked back at him. "I will be mindful of my manners and refrain from bed talk."

Wishing me goodnight, Hota entered our hut. I shortly followed and got into my bed.

It was the morning of our confirmation and I had awoken after one of the most restful night's sleep I had ever had since arriving in Stanford. Chenchi stood at the edge of his bed, straightening his tunic. Noticing me awake, he glared over at me, red faced and sweaty. His snarl indicated he was in an irritable and foul mood; eyeballing me it was clear the man fished for yet another quarrel.

"I grow tired of your accusations," he grumbled.

Rubbing the back of my head, I prompted a yawn to display my defiance. "I will assume you have spoken to Hota this morning. Your annoyance is with the girl I bed, nothing more."

Noticing his hands shaking, he seemed fidgety and troubled. Keen not to encourage any confrontation before our ceremony, I got up from my bed, turning my back to Chenchi and proceeded to prepare my uniform before getting dressed.

Rushing from our quarters, I saw Hota stood at the far side of the courtyard with his tunic finely prepped and his hair neatly combed. His calm custom relaxed my nerves over our impending confirmation.

"You have come far, Jep; I will be proud to serve alongside you and even more proud to call you a companion," he said, sincerely.

Glancing back at him, I smirked. "I owe my fate to you."

Our attention went to Chenchi, who marched across the courtyard from our quarters; ignoring even Hota's presence, he scowled as he walked by us leaving the lock up.

Shaking my head, I turned back to Hota. "I fear our acquaintance is on the brink of eruption."

Playing down my comments, Hota replied; "The man is tired from his night patrols; come, we must get to the church."

Walking through the square alongside Hota, I heard a chirpy voice call out my name. Turning, I saw an excitable Blair racing towards me; running away from her mother, her mischievous grin was infectious. Isa, Blair's mother, walked in company with Fawkes, who recently had been less discreet about his encounters with the servant woman.

Fixing her attention solely on me, she playfully jabbed my stomach to the horror of her mother. "Here was me thinking you wasn't going to make it," she said, mockingly.

Laughing, I replied. "Charming, I hope I have not disappointed you."

Smirking, she looked up at me squinting from the sun. "Well if truth be told, I didn't think you had the stomach for it, but it seems you will be my tutor one day, after all."

Complimenting Blair on her white dress, it was pleasant to see her out of rags. Isa sheepishly reprimanded her daughter for her impudence; however, I was quick to assure her I felt no offence by her little girl's confidence.

Fawkes casually approached and began ruffling the little girl's hair; "She will make a fine Sword one day," he said, glancing down at her proudly. Looking back at me, Fawkes gruffly said, "I have forgotten the unsure boy I met in the passage that night; make us proud."

Nodding in acknowledgement of his rare compliment, they continued, contently walking together like a humble family. Hota glared back at me, bewildered by Fawkes' brief and sporadic praise.

The town church bustled with the congregation lining the graveyard; locals had flocked to show support for our confirmation. Historically validations in rank were done behind closed doors; however, Father Arrend had modernised the tradition and was keen to allow the townsfolk to be part of the ceremony. The senior Swords were bitter to the now open affair, but I saw the value behind allowing them to spectate the proceedings; after all it was the people we were to serve and protect.

Fulten and Sergeant Hock stood by the entrance greeting the spectators as they entered the church. Fulten smiled, embracing the people with graciousness; however, Hock was unable to hide his usual irritable mood, grimacing at the attendees as they passed by.

Fulten grinned on seeing me approach the doors before checking my uniform was correct by glancing me up and down, like a father would his child.

Hock sniggered, shaking his head on seeing me and Hota, "Look at the state of you two smug turds; I will see you inside."

Fulten chuckled, "Don't mind him, two men cut from opposites cloths, now united by the crest you represent. I am pleased that this day has come; finally, the Blue Swords have embraced this diverse land."

Hota welcomed Fulten's compliments before entering the church. Fulten gazed at me, smiling, resting his hand upon my shoulder.

"You have come so far, my boy; I feel honoured to have witnessed your growth," said Fulten, proudly.

Glancing back at my tutor, I grinned. "This day would not have come without your teachings, let alone your patience."

Raising his eyebrows about to reply, Lev appeared from the church. "What is up with your lover, Chenchi? The man sits in there motionless, as if he is possessed."

Fulten interrupted, "Come, it matters not, this day is yours, Jep. Let us take our seats."

Entering the church, the pews were filled with townsfolk. Being the last Swords to arrive, our entrance prompted their silence. I nervously glanced around the room, keen to see if I recognised any of the spectators. Pip, the generous and humble old man, sat centre within the congregation. Discreetly nodding his head on seeing my gaze, his attendance was a welcome sight. Unable to see Jen amongst the crowd, I was not overly surprised by her lack of timekeeping. Staring back at me from the alter was the governor, seated beside Father Arrend; the opposite expression on their faces were a good reflection of their eagerness to be fronting the local people. The governor's natural scowl made his presence rather amusing.

Taking my seat besides my dearest friend, Hota, I glanced down the front pew, noticing Lady Ivy seated next to her husband, Baron Asher. Catching her discreetly peering back in my direction, it reminded me what angelic beauty she possessed; her long brunette hair flowed down against her green dress. Asher, on the other hand, appeared as uninterested as the governor; he frowned, glaring forward at the altar.

A voice whispered from behind me, "You could have removed that stubble, young Jep."

Turning it was Ricard, Hota's father, smiling back at me. Hota also looked back, admiring my interactions with his father; "I expect big things of you, Jep; this town needs revolutionising with young, prosperous Swords," said Ricard.

Interrupted by Father Arrend, he called for the attention of the congregation; taking one last glance behind me, I felt slightly dissatisfied by the lack of Jen's presence. The pew I was seated on gently rattled, causing me to peer down the bench; the irritating movement was caused by Chenchi, who appeared rather out of character and unsettled. His empty stare at the ground and his pale, clammy skin expressed he felt troubled. I could only conclude that he was anxious about being confirmed as a Blue Sword in the presence of his previous master, Baron Asher.

Father Arrend stood at the front of the altar, smiling as he welcomed the people of Stanford to the ceremony. Opening his service with a prayer, it was not long before he began to show his gratitude for the dedication and fortification the Blue Swords offered the town.

"These courageous men devote their life to ensure the weakest and the most vulnerable have a voice within our society. They carry out their duties in the name of our Father; I urge you all to applaud and honour them, Amen."

Stepping back Father Arrend nodded to the governor, indicating he was to take the altar; rising from his chair our formidable leader stood before the congregation. Glancing around the seated audience, his fixed stern expression made it impossible to second guess his real emotions and thoughts.

His minimalistic speech was far from moving; it was hard to establish whether our governor was uninterested or uncomfortable with public speaking. Ordering myself, Chenchi and Hota to stand beside him, I felt nervous at the thought of facing the people of Stanford. Aware of Asher's jealousy over the time I that I had spent alongside his wife, Lady Ivy, I made a point of not looking in their direction; instead, I felt it fitting to focus on Fulten, the tutor whose teachings had guided my path for the past few months, not only as a mentor but as a dear friend.

As the governor relayed our testament of devotion to the Blue Swords crest, Fulten subtly nodded his head, satisfied by my confirmation. Holding the ceremonial sword to my chest, goosepimples raised from my arm; I felt a sensation of pride, however I could not help but wish to have had my father present to witness my grand accomplishment. Once the governor had finalised our declaration, the townsfolk stood from their seats, giving us their applause. Unable to resist, I glanced over at the Baroness, who did not disguise her delight in our confirmations. Asher reluctantly clapped his hands together, displaying little enthusiasm for our new-found reputable standings.

The people began to empty from the church; Lev strutted towards us, smirking as he continued to sarcastically clap his hands together.

"This is a time for celebration, I suggest we retire to the lock up for wine," said Lev.

I looked over to Chenchi, who still appeared rather unsettled and remained subdued. Fulten slapped my back and demanded my commitment to Lev's invitation of merriment.

"Of course, but please excuse me - there is something I must do," I replied.

"Make it quick, for today you have earned your drink," said Fulten.

Hota noticed me leaving the church and promptly walked towards me, keen to learn of my intentions. "Surely you are not going to miss the wine?" he asked.

"I need to speak with Jen, I want an explanation as to why she remained absent from this affair," I replied, firmly.

Hota shook his head, "She is a tavern girl, you expect too much. But please yourself, just do not leave me to drink alone."

Stomping across the market square to confront Jen, I felt angered by her refusal to attend my ceremony. Thinking the worst, I was convinced that she had toyed with me and that there could be actual truth in the rumours that hindered her reputation. Forgetting my initial intentions towards the tavern girl, I misplaced my double standards and was expecting to find her occupied in the arms of another man.

The tavern was quiet with only a handful of men gambling on dice occupying one table; the cantankerous old man who owned the tavern stood behind the serving table rolling his eyes upon my arrival.

"Since meeting you that girl has become idle; she should be stood here, yet she refuses to leave her bed," he grumbled.

Convinced Jen was going to be entertaining another man, I could not hold back and marched behind the serving table and into the low-lit corridor that led to Jen's quarters. Crashing my fist against the door, I yelled out her name. The silence made me even more furious as I leant my ear against door, expecting to hear sounds of scrambling and panic at my interruption.

Glancing back down the hallway at the old tavern owner, he looked away, keen not to antagonise my indignant state. Turing the handle to the door, I gulped on discovering that it was unlocked. Peering inside, my heart felt as if was filled with lead; blood soaked the ground, spilling from Jen's bed. Stepping closer, my stomach knotted at the squelching caused by my boots pressing down onto the blood sodden floor. My hand trembled as I felt palpitations vibrate my chest; I initially considered walking away, aware that the image I was about to witness would torment my mind for years to come. Jen was laid on her back; the deep gash across her throat had separated her skin and opened the muscle in her neck. Seeing her widened eyes and pale lifeless body within the bloodied sheets numbed my body.

My lack of sensation encourages my legs to give way, forcing me to stumble back against the wall, before sliding down onto the floor. Struggling to catch my breath I felt paralysed and unable to divert my eyes from Jen's horrific fate. Digging my nails into my forehead, I eventually managed to regained control of my body and staggered out of her room. The stench of stale mead mixed with my inability to breathe caused me to be sick in the corridor.

The walls of the tavern span, as the laughs from the men seated at the only occupied table echoed through my ears. Becoming consumed by rage, I yelled for the men to leave the tavern. I could hear the voice of the owner, requesting I calmed down. Ignoring my unwarranted demand, the seated men glanced back at me, frowning, disregarding my order before continuing to engage in merriment and indulge one another.

"Get out," I bellowed for a second time.

Receiving the same reaction, I stumbled out from behind the serving table. Alarmed, the townsmen stared at my feet prompting me to glance down at the source behind their now horrified expressions; it was then I saw Jen's blood staining my boots.

Looking back up with sunken eyes, I chillingly muttered, "I said get out."

The men froze in disbelief; however, my irrational state had corrupted my thought process, as I proceeded to strut towards their table. Removing my peace baton, I slammed my weapon down onto their table, shattering the empty ale beaker. Startled, the men began to flee towards the doors of the tavern. Sullenly glaring over to the owner who stood cowering behind the serving table in astonishment, I ordered him to attend the lock up and request my companions attend.

The eery silence of the empty tavern intensified the reality of what I had witnessed. As I began to feel my eyes fill with tears, the stiff cramps that rippled through my stomach grounded me for a second time. Leaning back against the serving table, I clutched my knees into my chest and began to quiver uncontrollably.

The doors to the tavern slammed open; Hota, followed by Fulten and Lev raced inside to meet me. Hota glanced down, puzzled by my state, before quizzing me on my findings.

Pointing to the corridor, I stuttered. "She is through there."

Lev sprinted down the hallway, returning moments later with a disconcerting look displayed on his face.

Glancing over to Fulten and Hota, he muttered; "Jen is dead, murdered."

Fulten leaned down, gripping my arm and pulling me to my feet; speechless, he gave me a sympathetic look before leading me out of the tavern and escorting me back to the lock up.

On returning to the lock up we sat down at the table in the parade room. Fulten assured me that we would locate Jen's killer and bring him to justice. His reminder of her brutal end made me mull over possible suspects and there was only one that instantly sprang to mind.

Staring back at Fulten, I said, "We will not need to look far, the beast disguises himself underneath our great crest."

Rolling his eyes, Fulten replied. "Chenchi?"

"He had motive," I said, carelessly.

"Your hatred for the man is unjust and so your theory misjudged. If you want to find the person who has slain Jen, you must think like a Blue Sword."

Fulten left me, keen to bring the governor up to speed with my discovery. Sipping back some of the leftover wine I sat in silence, attempting to understand why I felt so saddened by Jen's death; it was only a couple of days since I had kissed Lady Ivy and had arrogantly placed Jen as second best, yet still our intimacy yesterday by the river had left me yearning for her more. The door to the parade room opened and Chenchi entered, causing my guts to wrench; I scowled at the man, making my thoughts apparent.

"I hear she is dead," he said.

Sniggering, I shook my head, glaring at the floor as rage began to consume my body. "You heard she is dead." Leaping towards him with a clenched fist, I landed a punch, hitting the side of his temple. Stumbling back, he felt the impact of my ferocity-filled attack.

Shaking off my assault he blinked, bringing himself back around before standing upright, displaying his sizeable torso.

Snarling back at me he pointed his finger, saying, "You're grief-ridden, so I will allow you that one, there will be no second."

Fulten returned to the parade room; he looked between us, noticing our current stand off before firmly advising me that the governor was expecting my immediate attendance. Both me and Chenchi eyeballed one another as I stepped outside the room.

Opening the door to the governor's chambers he was surprised by my lack of courtesy. Aware of my foul mood, he offered me no sympathy, only ordering me to sit down.

"The tavern girl is dead," he said dismissively.

"The tavern girl has a name: Jen," I replied petulantly.

Sniggering, he stood, turning his back to me, glancing out from the window. "You are a Blue Sword; we lick our wounds and we move on." Turning back to face me, he continued, "You are naive to think this will ever have a happy ending; you have been selected to represent the most prestige crest in the land and I expect it done with dignity."

Calming, I agreed with the governor, offering assurance that I would not disappoint his decision to confirm me as a Sword.

"Do you think me a fool?" he said, abruptly.

Stuttering, I replied, "No, not at all."

Nodding his head, he squinted his piercing his eyes, glaring directly at me. "The Baroness's father, the ambush you encountered and the murder of a farm boy, along with the tavern girl- your investigation is unleashing hell. That is why I am withdrawing you."

Disappointedly, I exhaled, shaking my head.

"Your inexperience will only lead to more death, hence why I have requested the investigation be taking over by the city; they have dispatched a detector to arrive in a day or two. I want you back dealing with drunks and thieves, are we understood?"

Sighing, I nodded my head in acknowledgement to his order. After being dismissed, the governor called out to me before I had chance to leave his chambers.

"If I hear of one more conflict between you and Chenchi, I will have you back in rags," he said, sternly.

Back at my quarters I noticed Chenchi's bed had been cleared; still convinced of his guilt over Jen's murder, I knew I would have to bide my time if I was to keep my post as a Blue Sword. The culpability surrounding Chenchi's involvement in Jen's killing was something I would have to pursue prudently and alone.

22

BACK TO THE BEGINNING

The governor had made the wise decision to move Chenchi into temporary quarters to allow the tension to settle surrounding our tiresome feud. Two days had passed since Jen was found brutally murdered in her room at the Viking Invader tavern; mulling over my comrade's surety of his innocence, even my mind broadened to consider other potential suspects. Contemplating the link between Elis's murder and the ambush at the river crossing, it was possible that the Baron himself could have ordered the killing after becoming aware of mine and Jen's growing closeness. My scattered thoughts caused my head to throb, but still my assumptions continued to return to Chenchi; the question was, did he murder Jen to order, or merely out of jealousy?

It was my first day on independent patrol and due to the recent tragedy, I felt empty; not even nerves flushed through my body that morning as I began to get myself dressed.

Hota stirred before sitting upright in his bed, "It troubles me to see you so sombre, my friend. I heard that the detector arrived last night from Alma," he muttered.

Fastening up my tunic, I replied, "I am sure they will the discover the truth behind Jen's murder."

Sighing, Hota said, "The detector has been called upon for the Baroness's father; they will think little of the killing of a local tavern

199

girl." Frowning, I glared back at Hota, angered by his remarks. "Forgive me, Jep, it was the wrong choice of words; Jen was a great spirit and a loss to the town."

Leaving my quarters my mind could not have been more opposite than the clear sky above. Fawkes eyed me up from across the courtyard, calling for me to remain vigilante on my first day of independent patrol. Sharply nodding my head, I indicated my readiness. Sergeant Hock was already in the parade room and remained silent on seeing me enter; frowning, he glared at me, clearly keen to assess my mood and demeanour. Masking my current feelings, I grinned with confidence and insisted I was ready for briefing. It was not long until Lev joined us in the parade room and his carefree attitude was always good to lighten any uncomfortable atmosphere.

"I will be bound to the lock up today; do not cause me any needless drama," said Lev to me, mockingly.

Hearing several footsteps coming from the stairs outside the parade room, I was eager to learn who else was joining us; the governor entered and like Hock began eyeing me up to gauge my current mood. Behind the governor appeared a man whom I had met before; his handsome looks complimented his well-groomed, dark wavy hair. Detector Flint glanced back at me, straightening his black tunic, before greeting me.

"It appears you have uncovered truths that cannot be hidden, Jep; you have the makings of a detector," said Flint, boasting his own title.

Lev sniggered and rolled his eyes towards Flint. The detector ignored Lev's impoliteness and assured me that he would be carrying out a comprehensive investigation into Isaak's disappearance and the events that unfolded on our journey to Whiten.

"Hurray, we are all saved," said Lev mockingly.

Making little of his humour, I replied swiftly, keen to appease the governor. "My time will be spent learning my trade and ensuring the town is shielded from thuggery; however, I look forward to learning of your findings in the future."

Keen to hurry proceedings, the governor ordered Hock to begin the morning briefing. Hock sat upright at the front of the room, clearing his throat before speaking.

Glancing at me uneasily, he said, "As you are aware a victim of murder was discovered yesterday. The girl was well thought of amongst the locals, so understandably they want answers, and answers they shall receive; I will be taking on the enquiry personally. Also today is the infamous Hunts day, so be vigilant to shenanigans and drama created from the Grand Hall."

The governor glared over to me, reminding me of his advice to distance myself from the Baroness, caused by the damaging rumours of my seclusion with Lady Ivy whilst travelling to Whiten.

Once dismissed I made my way to the courtyard, where Flint caught up with me. Apprehensively he looked around to ensure no one else was listening to the words he was about to replay to me.

Whispering, he said: "You and I both know that the Whiten boy and the tavern girl's death are all linked to the Baroness's father's disappearance. I have no doubt that Hock will write the murder of the girl off swiftly and put it down to an overzealous punter."

"She was no whore," I replied, abruptly.

"I am not saying she was, but your relationship with her has not gone unnoticed and that puts you in a dangerous situation; it is imperative you remain cautious," he warned. Seeing my confusion, Flint continued, "Fulten has told you of the Shadow crooks; they breed like rats and are plaguing these lands. Each day they grow in number and in boldness."

"What does that have to do with Jen?" I replied.

"I suspect they knew of your intention to seek out Elis in Whiten, hence the ambush and then his death. I believe someone in this town guides them, leads them," he said alarmingly.

Leaving the rear yard, I mulled over Flint's warning. It was clear his time in the city had kept his mind open and revived; he was poised and walked with purpose. Glancing back at him from across the courtyard, even though he had an air of arrogance, he was a rather inspiring man to watch. Sighing, I took a deep breath and left the lock up for my first day on independent patrol. The worries I expected to feel were flattened by my racing mind; now more than ever I suspected Baron Asher's guilt surrounding Ivy's father's circumstances and in that equation sat Gil and Chenchi, both capable of being behind the plans that had seen the death of Jen and Elis, along with organising the ambush from the Shadow crooks.

The square was surprisingly more vibrant than usual that morning; gatherings of local peasants had arrived in their masses, all facing the entrance of the market from the town gates. Children sat upon their fathers' shoulders, keen to get a glimpse of the source of what caught their attention. I leapt up on an empty stall table at the back of the square, to see what exited the crowd of men, women, and children. Ricard, Hota's father, led the small parade of riders, dressed in a fine claret ceremonial tunic. He threw loaves of bread down towards the passionate crowd, who cheered and clapped the mounted men.

Gil followed behind Ricard, grimacing as he glared down, unimpressed at the desperate townsfolk. On seeing me observing him from across the square, his snarl amplified, before turning back to Baron Asher who was riding behind him. Asher made his hatred of me apparent through his chilling scowl and refusal to drop his eye contact. Returning with an equally dismissive expression, I stared back at him, without fear or thought of consequences. His rounded gut swelled through his russet coloured fineries; seeing the repulsive Baron and his thug Gil reminded just how much hatred I felt towards them. The thought of their conspiring plans, with Chenchi's participation, made my stomach gripe with resentment. But what was their motive? What could the most powerful man in Stanford want?

The mirrored glares between us became awkward, with both me and Asher refusing to look away; my heart began to race, however I was able to hide my nerves and mask them by the loathing I felt towards him. Any verbal altercations were supressed by the excitable crowd that blocked the gap between us.

"You will give the man a complex," called out an old, crackly voice.

Glancing down, my sneer turned into a smirk on seeing the old humble trader, Pip.

"Asher and his pet have far too much influence in this town, I detest the sight of them," I replied.

Sniggering, Pip said, "Don't we all; they throw out stale bread and this lot think they're gods. Mind you, young Sword, if you are intent on challenging that snake Gil, may I suggest you call upon Fulten first."

"Any man can ram a sword in one's gullet," I said.

Chucking, he replied, "That he can; bide your time."

Peering between Pip and the Baron, I impatiently said, "I don't have time."

Pip paused, squinting at me whilst considering his next words. "If a person is lost, they should go back to the beginning; I understand you have failed to look in on a certain farmer since acquiring that uniform."

Pip vanished into the crowd, leaving me mulling over what the old man had said. His remarks reminded me of a riddle, like the ones Jen had touched on in the past; it was as if he was attempting to give me a clue. Relaying his words in my head, I could not work out what Carre, the farmer, would possibly know that would support my theories. Then I thought back to Jen and what she told me the night before her death, that Carre's knowledge would be his downfall.

The locals began to disperse, so I jumped down from the table only to hear further clattering of horses' hoofs hitting the cobbles; I turned to see who now passed through the square. The burgundy tunic was similar of the uniform worn by the guards that patrolled my home village. I was quick to recognise the rider; his thin wavy hair and underdeveloped moustache matched his upright, pompous pose as he rode haughtily through the square.

Calling out the name Steffen, he glanced back, uneasy at my presence, before slowly approaching me, refusing to dismount his horse.

"What brings you here, Steffen?" I asked.

Nervously, he replied, "The Baron's hunt; Nobleman Skinner was unwell, so I have taken his place."

Sniggering I replied, "Well, better you be chasing fur than my sister. I trust she is well and goes unbothered."

Stuttering, he said, "Yes, of course; I have not encountered her since our unfortunate meeting in Somerby."

Noticing a sword resting against his thigh, I said, "You are not permitted to be armed in this town, remove your blade."

Astounded, he mumbled, "But I am a guard, here on invitation from the Baron himself."

Sternly I replied, "You are no guard here, now remove your sword or I will remove it for you; besides, I am sure that Asher will have plenty of toys for you all to play with."

Steffen bashfully removed his scabbard, reluctantly handing it down to me; smirking, I sarcastically wished him a safe journey before he continued through the square. Strapping his sword to my belt, I also left the market square and headed for Western farm. Glancing across the hill, I noticed the intwined trees that Jen was so fond of. Reminiscing on our evening by the river, I felt saddened and even more determined to trace the person responsible for her death.

Hearing Carre's young boys inside the farmhouse was pleasant; even though my return to their home had been prompted, I was thrilled to be seeing the kind-natured farm owner and his wife Dam. Entering through the creaking gate, I had only made it halfway up the path before the splintered front door was flung open. Smiling, I was anticipating a warm greeting; however, my grin was quickly removed from my face as Carre appeared topless and agitated by my arrival.

Red faced and clearly angered, he frowned, stomping towards me. "You're not welcome here, boy; leave, leave now," he yelled, whilst frantically looking around to see if anyone else was present.

Flabbergasted, I stood speechless as he leapt forward, gripping my upper arm and attempting to usher me off his land; eventually I resisted his manhandling and pulled my arm out of his hold.

"Have you gone mad?" I bellowed.

"I do not want your type here," he shouted.

"My type? You mean a Blue Sword?" I argued.

"I don't give a sheep's arse what you decide to dress yourself in, I don't want you here," he said.

Carre's wife Dam came sprinting out of the house, followed by their two sons. Yelling at Carre, she demanded that he settled and began referring to him as a senile old fool.

"I am no fool, woman, this man has caused far too much death in this town and I want him off my land, now," he roared.

Raising my hands in the air I shook my head, before glaring back at the farmer in disgust. Walking away from his home, he yelled at the top of voice, warning that if I were to come back, he would notify the Baron. Leaving, I felt bewildered at his remark. Carre despised the Baron, even more so than he did the Blue Swords.

Standing at Jen's spot underneath the trees, I squinted as the lowering sun reflected into my eyes from the water's reflection. Feeling even more downtrodden, I wasn't able to make sense of anything. Carre's accusation of the deaths I had caused echoed through my mind and left me feeling foul tempered. I concluded that Carre did have information that I required and one way or another I was going to get it from him. After throwing Steffen's sword into the river, I felt tears form inside my eyes. At the sound of footsteps coming from the meadow, I swiftly wiped my eyes dry.

Lady Ivy appeared; she was dressed in a greying summer gown and her head was covered by the hood of her robe. Her smile indicated she had come in peace and was not going to provide me with further confrontation with which I had become accustomed to that day.

Observing my tension, she said, "My dearest Jep, you look troubled."

Sighing, I replied, "I was unaware of how many enemies this crest would attract."

Softly, she began offering her condolences. "I am sorry to hear of Jen's death; I knew you were fond of her." Dismissively I asked the Baroness what she wanted. Clearing her throat, Ivy said, "I come here with a warning: my husband has become rather irrational since I returned from Whiten. I fear he has conflicting thoughts of our time spent together, when we were secluded from the others."

Sniggering, I stared back at the flowing water. "His jealousy does not come as a surprise; I care little of his thoughts," I said, dismissively. Stepping closer, Ivy pleaded with me to speak with the Baron and asked that I offer him reassurance that there were no inappropriate shenanigans. Scowling back her, I answered in an irritable manner. "Your husband the Baron is a murderous pig, so no, I will not pander to his needs or yours. I have grown tired of saving you, my lady." Hurt by my abrupt response, a tear fell from her eye. Gently nodding her head, she gloomily glanced to the ground.

After a moment's silence, the Baroness took a deep breath and said, "I can only respect your stance on the matter." Stepping away, she called back to me, "Please do not ever allow that tunic to make you lose sight of how truly noble and gracious your really are."

Refusing to look up at the Baroness and acknowledge her gentle words, I remained silent, glaring down at the river, frowning like a stroppy child. I had allowed my dreadful mood to blank my mind to the predicament and danger the Baroness was really in.

23

THE SQUARE

The thunder from Hota's strike echoed throughout the combat room as he struck his baton against the wooden block; seeing me enter, he halted his exercise and began grinning at my presence.

Using his forearm to wipe the sweat from his brow, he said, "Come tell me, how was your first time on independent patrol?"

Sighing, I gloomily replied, "It was much like the other times I found myself wandering alone in this tunic."

Commencing his training, he paused in the middle of a strike, casually saying, "Yes, of course, I forgot: Carre is here to see you; he awaits you in the greeting chambers."

"Are you aware of his mood?" I asked, tactfully.

Shrugging his shoulders, appearing baffled, Hota replied, "He is a farmer - they all seem rather sullen. Do you need my assistance?"

Declining Hota's offer, I anxiously went to speak with Carre knowing full well that one way or another I would be getting the answers I required. Red faced and agitated, he noticed me joining him and shamefully dropped his head.

"Jep, I must speak with you alone."

Sternly I replied, "There is no one else here; speak."

Glancing behind me Carre paused, ensuring I was alone; stepping closer he nervously muttered, "Forgive me for my earlier actions, but I fear that my being here will be enough to see my head removed, it seems that even the walls have grown ears."

Irritably I said, "You are making little sense and I am tired; speak."

Peering around the room, it was clear he felt on the back foot and his uneasiness was not true to his usual boisterous nature. "This town is riddled in corruption and plagued with treachery; I have been informed that you can be trusted."

"That I can, but I am growing weary of riddles," I replied.

Exhaling, Carre continued. "Tomorrow, attend evening prayer and wait for the congregation to empty; there Father Arrend will provide you with the answers you require."

Before having the chance to quiz Carre further, he promptly reached for the door and left the lock up. Standing baffled by his invite, I began to mull over the information he had relayed, considering whether to divulge it to Fulten.

Entering the parade room, Hota stood buttoning up his tunic, "I trust all is well?" he asked.

Shaking my head, I replied, "In truth, I couldn't be more confused."

"Facts present themselves to the patient; right, I must retire - I feel I may have overexerted myself," said Hota, whilst stretching out his arm.

Fawkes walked through the door of the parade and began to pick at leftovers on the banquet table.

Chewing on an apple, he casually said, "I hope all is well and there is nothing to relay."

"No, nothing," I said flippantly.

"Good, Isa tells me we are short of meat; head to the square and replenish our stock. If you hurry the traders shouldn't have cleared their stalls yet," said Fawkes as he left the room.

Unwilling to decline the request made from the most fearsome Blue Sword at the lock up, I left and made my way to the market. The night sky was illuminated from the full moon and the air felt fresh and crisp.

The traders in the square had packed up their stalls, however I noticed candlelight shining from the butcher's on Main street. The sound of drums being struck came from the Viking Invader and it was apparent the tavern was back to normal after being the scene of Jen's brutal murder. A plump, balding man stood sweeping the path from outside the butcher's; the stench of guts and flesh oozed from his white blood-stained robe.

Stringently, he said, "If you're after meat, I only have rabbit and pheasant left."

"Rabbit will suffice," I replied glumly.

Stepping inside, I struggled to avoid treading on the entrails and gristle that covered the butcher's floor.

Startled by the sound of high pitch screams, I glanced outside, noticing the shadows of people reflecting off the walls as they passed the street torches. Glancing at me, alarmed, the butcher eyeballed me, awaiting my response to the commotion. The voices from the flock of gatherers began to overpower the sounds of instruments playing from the tavern; moving outside I used the doorstep of the butcher's to give myself a vantage point over the crowd who had now congregated within the market place.

Peering over the square, a deep voice in an enraged tone called out to the mass group of spectators. Instantly and concerningly I knew that my presence would add further turmoil to the unthinkable and horrifying situation unfolding before me. Being pulled around like prey trapped in the mouth of a vicious animal, Lady Ivy stood helpless at the mercy of her seething husband, Baron Asher.

The Baroness trembled as she grossly exhibited to her people, clothed only in a white linin night dress. Ignoring my griping stomach and trembling body, I frantically ran towards the square, bustling my way to the front of the onlookers, aware there I was about to confront the Baron himself. Steeping out from the crowd, Ivy noticed me and instantly lowered her head, knowing that my presence would escalate her predicament further.

Struggling to catch my breath at the sight of the helpless Baroness, I watched as Asher yanked her slender body violently towards him, causing her further indignity. Quivering, Ivy attempted to pull up the loose strap that had fallen from her shoulder, humiliatingly exposing the top of one of her breasts.

"Let them see your flesh," yelled the Baron.

At least five guards led by Gil stood shielding the Baron. Gil's snarl was enough to keep the terrified local people at bay and controlled. Seeing me standing in front of the gathering of spectators, Asher scowled, staring back at me with sunken eyes.

"Here is your nobleman my love; the brave young Sword shows devotion, standing before me to save his mistress," shouted Asher.

Glancing back at the people, they looked back me in despair as I stood singlehandedly challenging their wicked Baron. Gil chillingly smirked across the square, amused by my boldness and assuming that my death was now inevitable.

"Release her, turd," called a youthful voice from the crowd.

Turning back, I noticed Blair being held firmly by her mother, Isa. The spirited young servant girl wriggled, attempting to break free from her petrified mother's grasp.

Laughing, Asher called over to me, "Even the brat has more pluck than you, boy."

Escalating his aggression, he moved his grip of Ivy's arm and began pulling at her hair. Wincing, Ivy struggled to keep her balance. Now glaring down at his flinching wife, Asher spat in her face, prompting a gasp from the onlookers. Seeing Blair staring back at me in hope, I feared that I was about to destroy her unfounded admiration of me.

Observing Lady Ivy's desperation encouraged me to surmount my fear and return a contemptuous scowl at Baron Asher, "You have allowed ale to dictate your mind; for that reason I will allow you to release the Baroness and be on your way."

Cackling, Asher peered over to his guards; all of them, along with Gil, remained stern faced, unable to see the humorous intent in my demands.

"You are vermin, boy, riddled and nauseating. You want the whore? Come and take her," called Asher.

Pulling the Baroness's hair, he yanked her to the ground, causing her bare knees to sink into the stone cobbles.

Infuriated by his brutality, I gripped the hilt of my sword, pulling it loose from its scabbard. Instantly, I glanced at Gil to see his reaction to my challenge. Refusing to await a command from his master, he grinned back at me chillingly. Slowly he reached around, grabbing the handle of a mace that was strapped to his back. Boastfully, Gil held out the ferocious weapon, displaying the spiked ball that dangled from its steel chain. Losing his grin, he leaned his head forward, glaring at me with malice and intent.

Holding up my sword, I felt it begin to rattle at the shaking of my hand. Asher sniggered, calling out for me to think wisely on my next move, then he vulgarly spat down at his shamed wife. Ivy glared back at me; her desperate yet submissive expression still haunts me today.

I had caused this; I was guilty of falling in love with a Baron's wife and it was now my duty to prevent this act of wickedness. Charging forward to intercept the Baroness, Gil slammed his mace onto the ground, causing the cobbles to crack and the onlookers to gasp once again. Stopping, I knew I had invoked his right to challenge me, as I had threatened to engage his Baron. Pulling his weapon from the ground, Gil now stood between me and the Baroness; he carefully eyeballed me, awaiting my next move. I glanced up at the other guards, in hope Ricard was stood amongst them and prepared to deescalate the standoff, but he was not present, and I was alone to face the most feared warrior in Stanford.

The Baron yelled, confirming my fear. "Shame on you, boy, you challenge your ruler without order. Gil, I demand you disarm this Sword."

"I always knew I would be feeding you to the dogs," muttered Gil.

Swinging his mace loosely over his head, Gil glared at me, thrilled at the terror he witnessed in my eyes. We both knew that his abilities outmatched my inexperience and fleeting time as a Blue Sword but refusing to cower to defeat I tightly gripped the hilt of my sword and mirrored his snarl. Even though I was steps away from God with my tail between my legs, my father had always told me that when death wanted you, it was necessary to give it a good fight first.

Gil unleashed his first attempt to chop me down, thrashing his mace towards me with intent to make my death quick. Determined, I held my sword firmly, allowing the chain to coil around my blade. Rapidly and decisively I yanked back my sword, forcing Gil to lose grip of the handle of his mace.

A brief cheer came from the crowd who were enthused at my capability to disarm the hateful guard, but Gil was too conditioned; he sprinted towards me, whilst removing his sword from its scabbard. Chopping his blade horizontally, he struck me with three hasty attacks; the aggression in his assault made it apparent he was incensed and keen to strike me down quickly, however this also made him unstructured and predictable.

Stepping back, he calmed, and this was when I knew I faced difficulty. Gil eyed my body as he assessed where to attack next, leaving me feeling spooked. Eventually making his move, he swung his body around, looping his sword round before thrashing it at my head. Defending his strike, he swiftly turned his body around and this time hooked his sword towards my chest. Twisting around my own blade, I just managed to meet his blow, but I was too slow to react to his third. Upper cutting his sword, the steel caught my forearm, slicing my skin open.

Feeling the blood seep through my sleeve, my reaction to his fourth attack was delayed; the impact from his steel against my own blade caused my sword to fall from my weakened grip and left me stumbling on to the ground.

Now fallen, Gil began to stalk me; peering down at my helplessness with his serpent eyes, he considered how to fatally conclude our duel. The initial silence from the spectators represented their fears at seeing my defeat.

An old crackled voice called from amongst the crowd; "Stop this madness."

Glancing back at the gathering, I noticed a familiar mature man stagger out to reveal himself. It was Pip, the trader who had recently guided me to Carre, keen to aid the investigation into Ivy's missing father.

The Baron frowned as he stretched his neck to see who had disturbed my ending.

"Step aside old man, you have no place in this act of contentment," bellowed Asher.

Gil ignored the interruptions. Still focused on me, he trod his boot down onto my wounded arm.

Pip yelled, drowning out my moans. "You kill him, Gil, then I will call you out for the traitor you are."

Releasing his foot from my arm, I rolled onto my side, clutching at the injury Gil had inflicted. The head guard had now diverted his attention to Pip and began stepping closer towards the frail old man.

Gruffly, Gil ordered Pip to remain silent; however, bravely the old man shook his head, irritated by his demand.

Arching his back, Pip turned to face his fellow people. "This beast plots treason against Baron Asher and this town."

Pointing his sword, Gil closed the gap between himself and Pip. "I am warning you old man, your tongue will cost you your head," grunted Gil.

Pip disregarded his threat and continued to tout the head guard's intentions, turning to deliver his message to Asher. "He plots to overthrow you, Baron, to appoint himself ruler of our glorious town. He will see us riddled with Shadow crooks and subjects to his order." Peering back to face Gil, he contemptuously muttered, "You grow tired of being the runt, don't you, Gil?"

Enraged, Gil gritted his teeth, taking hold of Pip's scruff. Pushing his sword against Pip's neck, Gil sliced the steel of his blade across the throat of the old man. The crowd inhaled; some even covered their eyes on seeing their townsman clutching at his severed throat.

The blood leaked through Pip's fingertips before he slumped to the ground; his body thrashed and blood gushed from his wound, drenching the cobbles. Some of the people began to scream at the horror they had witnessed unfold before their eyes. Unremorseful, Gil stood over Pip's now lifeless corpse and wickedly spat down on his body.

Glancing to the Baron, I felt certain he was going to reprimand his subject for a such a vile and unjust murder. Having lost his narcissistic manner, Asher looked bewildered as he stared down at Pip's dead body. Glancing back at Ivy, he went silent on observing her trembling and cowering before him.

His brief reflection was short lived, and he was quick to return to his repulsive self. Removing a blood-stained hunting dagger from his belt, he yanked the Baroness into his chest and restrained her body.

Resting the blade against her throat, Asher remained contaminated by hatred and rage.

Taking the opportunity created by the cries echoing from the distraught crowd, I scrambled across the ground to retrieve my sword. Gil was swift, noticing my attempt to rearm and lunged forward, swiping his boot across my face. Feeling my cheek bone dislodge from the impact from his kick, helplessly I laid on back on top of the cold stone cobbles, peering up at the dark sky. It was at that point I accepted defeat.

Time slowed as I froze, listening to the distorted whimpers emerging from the townsfolk; Baron Asher began to yell, silencing their groans.

"Do not think of me as simple, I am aware of your admiration of this adulterous whore. I am your Baron, your ruler."

Turning my head, I blinked away a tear that was the cause of my blurred view of Ivy. The tilt in her head and empty stare indicated that, like me, she had accepted her fate.

The Baron laughed, repeating his intentions in a chilling tone. "You call this whore your princess? Watch me spill her blood."

I was wounded; beaten to the ground, tormented and neutralised. I lay defenceless to defeat invoked by the serpent demon that stood over me; my destiny had been forced into his hands. I could not save her, poor Ivy, she was helpless, and I was her only hope. I had failed her. I managed to lean my head upright to take a final look at her, to see her soft skin, marked with swelling and bruises. She was naked from the waist down, belittled, and frightened. Her eyes were filled with despair. My mind raced, telling me to get up but I was paralysed, trapped within my body.

The blood of a local man leaked from his corpse, as his lifeless body lay next to mine. I started to think of another, someone I had recently lost, someone I thought I loved, and yet another person I was unable to save. I was ready to meet her, to join her in the afterlife.

But then a figure appeared - was it my saviour? He walked with presence as he entered the market square. He shouted to my enemy, ordering them to take the fight to him. My faith had been tested, but this time faith had answered my call. His uniform carried the same crest as my own. It was fair to say my inexperience and brash actions had left me fallen and vulnerable, but he would not fall. He was an expert in his trade, fearless and skilful. Just like me he was a Blue Sword, and he had come to save us.

Removing the numbness from my body, I saw my companion standing between me and Ivy. Noticing my beaten state, he scowled at my adversary with his chiselled jaw line. Fawkes scanned the square, spotting Isa trembling as she clutched onto her daughter, Blair. Nodding his head, he smirked, receiving a mirrored expression from the admiring little girl, Blair.

Turning his attention to Asher, Fawkes yanked his sword free from its scabbard.

"You will release the Baroness," he called.

The Baron glanced at Gil for reassurance, who now stepped before the veteran Sword, his sword lowered, but still displayed.

"You have no authority over my Lord; I demand you withdraw. I will even allow you take this pathetic boy with you," said Gil.

Looking down at me, Fawkes sniggered. "You strike down a Blue Sword; I need no authority."

Gil gave Fawkes a chilling smile, "So it must be," he muttered gruffly.

Gil calmly browsed at the ground before unleashing a swift blow of his sword, intent on ending Fawkes quickly; his dramatic attack was clearly a tactic Fawkes was accustomed too and able to defend with little trouble. Now the pair circled one another, as the square was silenced by their anxious anticipation at witnessing the town's two most skilled warriors face off before them. Peering back at the Baron, he had now released his hold of Lady Ivy, who now looked on with discomfort.

Fawkes took the fight to Gil, swiping his sword either side of the guard's head; his speed left Gil unable to deliver any form of counterattack. With Fawkes leading the battle, he swung his blade repeatedly forcing an uncomfortable Gil to step back. Fawkes danced towards his enemy, composed and precise, making the duel very much one sided.

Getting back on my feet, I retrieved my sword; my consideration to aid my fellow Sword would have been an unwise decision: Fawkes was a noble man and would not have taken well to me assisting and gaining an unfair victory. Glancing back at Ivy, Asher had now stepped back as he looked on in horror at his struggling henchman.

Gil had played it smart, defending each of the Blue Sword's heavy blows; however, it became apparent that Fawkes was tiring. Gil remained crouched down and was now easily blocking each strike that Fawkes had to offer. Taking the upper hand, it was now Gil's turn to lead the contest, delivering a sharp and well formatted attack, slicing his blade repeatedly. Each strike left his steel narrowly missing Fawkes's head. Peering over to Isa, she stared at the ground whilst holding her daughter Blair firmly. Clearly, she feared the worst outcome for her love, Fawkes.

I could feel my heart pulsating through my chest, watching Fawkes pant as he struggled to defend Gil's vehement assault. It was time for me to intervene and aid my saviour. Before I was able to get close, Gil grunted as he violently pulled his sword over his head and chopped the blade downwards towards the crown of Fawkes' skull. With a rapid block, Fawkes gritted his teeth, holding the hilt of his sword with both hands, defending Gil's vigorous attack.

They were now both engaged in a battle of strength; groaning, Fawkes held up his sword, preventing Gil's steel from piercing his head. Overpowering Gil, Fawkes growled as he pushed back, causing the head guard to stumble and leave his body open. Lunging forward, Fawkes kicked his boot into Gil's stomach, forcing the henchman to fall and crash onto the ground.

The crowd cheered, encouraged by seeing Gil's potential defeat; the guard, now grounded, clutched at his winded gut and lay unarmed and at the mercy of the formidable Sword. Righteously, Fawkes pressed the tip of his blade on Gil's throat.

"You yield?" muttered Fawkes.

Snarling, the serpent nodded his head in confirming his surrender.

Fawkes glared across to Baron Asher, calling for him to release the Baroness. Now humiliated and routed, he obliged the senior Sword's request. Ivy remained motionless, distraught, and horrified by the circumstances.

Gil, however, had not accepted his defeat. Disgracefully he pulled a knife from his waist band and promptly lunged upright, aiming the blade's tip towards Fawkes. My experienced comrade was attuned to the guard's shallow response and swiftly raised his own weapon, swiping the blade and penetrating Gil's neck. Fawkes followed through on his blow, allowing the edge of his sword to decapitate Gil, leaving his head detached from its body and rolling across the cobbles of the square. The head guard's bloodied torso dropped to the ground, prompting a careless hail from the local people who were now rid of this wicked tormenter.

The Baron gawked over to his dead henchman's dismembered body. The colour drained from his face, aware of the consequences and now without his most feared asset. My desire to strike him down in the middle of the square was diverted by the sound of horses galloping across the market. Coming to a halt, the governor led the rest of the Blue Swords. Examining the dead corpses of Pip and Gil, he took a second glance of the blood that stained Fawkes's blade.

Fulten glanced, nodding his head on seeing me intact. The governor scowled at the Baron upon observing the condition of the Baroness; she shivered and trembled, displaying her beaten body.

"Somebody cover the Baroness at once," he called back to the line of Blue Swords behind him.

Leaping down from his horse, he strutted towards a concerned looking Asher. The Baron's guards glanced to the ground, refusing to make eye contact with the governor as he stepped through their line with a snarl.

Lev sprinted towards Ivy, swiftly wrapping some animal fur over her shoulders. The Baroness clutched the cloak tightly around her body, sighing.

Baron Asher glared at the governor as he approached and quickly tried implementing his authority. "The people grow hostile; you will provide me with more men to assist my guards," he said pompously.

"My men will not aid you. The crown will be notified of what happened here," replied the governor sternly.

"The crown will disregard such insignificant matters," said Asher.

Sniggering, the governor replied, "I don't doubt it, but your people will not be so forgiving. Your wife is the one they admire and yet you attempt to tarnish her before them; I suspect you fate is sealed."

Turning around, the governor ordered Lev to escort the Baroness to the lock up. As our compelling leader swaggered away, Asher called out to him. "If they revolt, I will call upon you to carry out your oath."

Ignoring the remarks from the Baron, the governor glanced at me and Fawkes, nodding his head, giving us the signal to withdraw.

Shouting for all to hear, he said, "Remove the old man's body from the square."

"What about Gil?" said Chenchi.

"The guard is not my concern," replied the governor.

Before leaving the square, I took a final glance at Gil's severed head; his wide eyes appeared just as haunting in death as they did when he was alive. Exhaling, I felt relief at knowing the serpent had fallen, but with his death came unanswered questions.

24

AFTERMATH

Walking into the parade room, Lev sat sipping back his ale. Already aware of the answer I required, he pointed through to the combat room. Lady Ivy was seated on one of the wooden benches; Fulten was stood over the Baroness, offering her comfort. On seeing me she leapt up from the bench. Embracing me, Ivy tightly wrapping her arms around my body. Frowning, surprised by the Baroness's warmth, I glanced across her shoulder at Fulten who mirrored my expression, shaking his head.

Fulten coughed, keen to break the Baroness's overfamiliar greeting. Peering down at her swollen eyes and purple cheek, I sighed. "Will you ever forgive me? You warned me of his hatred and yet I didn't act."

Stepping back, Ivy glanced at Fulten, now mindful of her impromptu informality. "Have no regrets, Jep, this is nothing more than a crime of passion."

"A crime of passion," I replied abruptly. "I thought the man was going to kill you."

Fulten interrupted. "Once again you will do well to remember your place, young Sword."

Ivy begun defending the Baron, "Did you not hear the poor old man in the square, he outed Gil for treason; my husband is as innocent at the rest of us."

Ignoring Fulten's advice, I replied passionately. "Innocent? Look at the state of your face."

Fulten once again attempted to reprimand my outspokenness, however Lady Ivy was quick to play down my tone, blaming it on the night's events.

"Now I must return to the Grand Hall, I do not wish to cause the Baron any more distress," insisted Lady Ivy.

This time even Fulten interjected, recommending that the Baroness should remain at the lock up. "We have suitable lodgings, my lady; I do feel we should allow Baron Asher to settle."

But with Ivy's insistence on returning home, I was left flabbergasted and speechless. Fulten called in Lev and instructed him to escort the Baroness back to the Grand Hall, leaving even Lev bewildered at his request.

Ivy glared over at me, saddened by my irritation at her decision to return to Asher. Giving me a final look, I noticed a tear roll down her cheek as she left the room with Lev.

Once alone, Fulten dramatically turned to face me. "Is it true? Did Pip disclose that Gil plotted treachery against the Baron?"

Sighing, I replied, "He did, whilst saving my life."

Fulten remained silent, mulling over the rumour I had confirmed was true; I looked at him as he glanced up at the ceiling. I considered whether to relay my invitation by Carre to attend evening prayer tomorrow night. Against Carre's wishes I decided to tell my trusted mentor the truth and told Fulten of Pip's garbled message to liaise with Carre, who had eventually invited me to evening prayer.

"The Cavaliers of Stanford. I should have known, not a thing in this town happens without their knowledge of it," said Fulten.

"Cavaliers?" I replied.

Sniggering, Fulten said, "The Cavaliers are a band of influential locals that formed many years before your time, they meet in secret and not much happens in this town without their understanding. They are a clandestine society; their invite is both surprising and slightly alarming."

"Will you come?" I asked.

Fulten pondered on my question. "If Carre is in fact one of these Cavaliers there will be a good reason he requested you attend alone."

Fulten quizzed me, keen to learn if anyone else knew of my invitation. Finally, Fulten agreed on attending with me, concluding that even the Swords were compromised and insisted on my integrity to keep the invite secret from our fellow companions.

Retiring to my quarters, I left the parade room to see Fawkes stood holding Isa outside her chambers; he held her tightly as she nuzzled her head into his chest. Their love was tranquil to witness.

A voice called out behind me. "Do you not think it is rude to gawk?"

Turning, the governor stood glaring at me with his piercing stare. "Once again, I see you are at the root of the dramatics; I do hope I will not regret having you confirmed. That aside, you stood toe to toe with one of the most feared swordsmen in Thear and yet you live to tell the tale."

I glanced over to Fawkes, "He saved my life, I have no reason to relish in victory."

Stepping closer to me, the governor muttered, before walking into the parade room. "You stood your ground, risked your life for another; that is enough."

Gazing up at the stars that glimmered through the night sky, my head throbbed from the events that had unfolded in the square that evening. I was apprehensive about the impending meeting with the Cavaliers of Stanford and even more anxious about what I was going to learn. It felt deceitful to keep my new acquired leads from my fellow Swords, but with Fulten's knowledge and approval, I felt assured I was doing the right thing.

Footsteps came across the grass causing me to sit upright. Seeing my friend Hota approach was a welcoming sight.

"Your bed is but a few steps away, yet you choose to lay outside on the grass," said Hota, grinning.

"I am finding it hard to settle," I replied.

Sniggering, Hota peered up at the sky. "You duelled with the devil and live to fight another day; be thankful of who watches over you, Jep."

"It is Fawkes who watches over me; I worry he grows tired of conserving my life," I muttered.

Clutching my shoulder, Hota looked down at me, "Your bravery will not always outweigh your ability. You grow stronger by the day and I have no doubt that when the time comes, you will be a valued asset."

Leaving me to ponder, Hota retired for the night. Chenchi wandered through the courtyard; unbeknown to him, I stared over as he strutted towards his quarters. My knotted stomach was caused by my loathing of the man; I knew he was the snake who slithered in the grass.

The morning's red sky was a firm reminder of the blood that had been spilt the previous day. Hota joined me outside our quarters; lifting his head, inhaling, he smiled before insisting we attended the morning briefing. Fawkes and Lev were already in the parade room, awaiting Sergeant Hock's arrival. Lev eyed me up, displaying a cunning grin across his face.

"Let us hope Fawkes does not need to bathe your arse today, Jep," mocked Lev.

His witty humour broke the tension in the room and even received an unfamiliar smirk from Fawkes himself. Lev's mockery was to be expected and something I had grown rather fond of, even if I did find myself at the crux of his wit most of the time. He had a way of enlightening any sour situation and his absurdity was good for morale.

Hock entered, bitter faced as ever and was accompanied by Detector Flint. Flint glanced over to me, looking rather smug, before sitting down and casually resting his feet on the top of the banquet table. Sergeant Hock gave him an infuriated look.

"Please, Sergeant, don't mind me," replied Flint as he rested his hands on the back of his head.

Rolling his eyes, Hock hurried through the morning briefing. "Lev, you will take today's patrols; the governor is keen for you gauge the tone of the locals after yesterday's blood bath in the square. Hota, you will take over at dusk. Jep, Fulten has requested you remain with him at the lock up, after the stir you caused yesterday, I think it is wise you remain unseen for the time being."

As the room emptied, I purposely loitered around the banquet table, picking at some old grapes left over from yesterday evening's feast. I could feel Flint staring at me; he was eager to make conversation, as was I.

"So, Jep, do you still believe that Chenchi is the conspirator?" said Flint, smugly.

"What makes you imply that?" I replied, sharply.

"I have ears, besides the man has motive and as the rumours emerge that Gil was planning to betray the Baron, it would only be fitting that Chenchi would aid his previous mentor. But how does one progress this theory? Now that is the question," said Flint, standing to his feet.

"You are the detector," I replied.

Flint sniggered and pointed his finger, "Precisely, that is why I would expect any information passed on that, let's say, falls on your lap."

Nodding my head, I tore loose a stalk of grapes, before casually walking towards the door. Flint called out to me before I had chance to leave, offering me his assurances that I could put my trust in him. I wandered across the courtyard considering the idea of speaking with Fulten and seeking his advice on entrusting the detector with our plans to meet the Cavaliers of Stanford, however I concluded that Fulten tutored Flint and I would leave our preparations to his senior judgement.

The day felt delayed and I found myself wandering around the lock up, fidgety and without purpose. Fulten had remained distant and had not been seen, which caused me greater anxiety for our plans to attend evening prayer together. Keen to occupy my racing mind, I entered the combat chambers and began relieving my tension, attacking one of the wooden blocks.

Stopping to catch my breath, Hota joined me in the chambers. He strolled over picking up one of the wooden swords resting on the rack, before facing me and smirking. Without warning he leapt forward, forcing me to defend a medley of strikes. His combination was swift and precise; however, he struggled to land a triumphant blow. My neat defending caught him off guard, allowing me to deliver several accurate counterattacks. Clashing our swords together, we met evenly, both grinning at the equal outcome.

"You are faster, my friend," said Hota.

"You are slower," I replied.

Fulten coughed from the entrance of the room, keen to catch my attention. He was insistent that we make our way for evening prayer, leaving Hota in the combat chambers. Walking through the courtyard, my attempt at small talk was swiftly rejected by Fulten. His usual calm manner had been taken over by apprehension and nervousness, which I could only put down to our pending meeting.

The fading light had prompted the traders to begin packing up their stalls for the day. Catching my attention was the sound of hooves, clattering through the square. On seeing me, the rider diverted his horse and rode towards me. Steffen, the guard who I had confronted in my home village of Somerby after his inappropriate pestering of my sister, peered down at me in his usual snide and pompous tone.

"It was rather unfortunate, the circumstances that prevailed on this square last night," said Steffen, smugly.

"Would it be right to assume that the Baron received a rather misguided tale?" I replied with a snarl across my face.

"Baron Asher was merely informed of the Baroness's choice to lodge amongst the common folk during her visit to Somerby," Steffen said, snidely.

Gripping the reins to his horse, the stallion became startled, rearing up on its back legs. Flustered, Steffen managed to steady his horse, looking down at me in dismay.

Gruffly, I said, "I return to Somerby in winter and will very much look forward seeing you again."

Mortified, Steffen rode away from the market square. Fulten smiled, looking at me approvingly. "You truly are a Blue Sword."

The overflowing congregation allowed me and Fulten to creep in unnoticed and loiter at the back of the church. Father Arrend addressed the people with confidence and clarity; he was a natural speaker, delivering each sermon with precision and passion. Fulten stared at the priest savouring every word he had to offer. His shared love of faith was the reason Fulten had remained so gracious over the years, allowing his judgment to always be influenced by his devotion to God.

Fulten's magnitude made it quick for Father Arrend to notice our presence, however our attendance did not influence his demeanour. I scanned the pews in search of Carre; however, he was not in the church. His absence caused me concern, especially after his apprehension and reluctance to see me in the first place. Father Arrend brought evening prayer to an end, offering the townsfolk blessings, before wishing them farewell.

Standing by the doors, both me and Fulten wished the congregation well as they left the church. Father Arrend casually strolled around the front of the altar, blowing out the candles from the service. Once the last person had left, Arrend nodded his head, indicating for us to close the doors.

Waving, he called, "Do come closer, there is much for you to learn." Getting closer to the altar, Father Arrend smirked. "I was informed that you were coming alone, Jep."

"All due respect father, I trust Fulten with my life," I replied.

"You are wise to do so, young Sword," said Arrend, undeterred by Fulten's presence.

The apprehension was unbearable, and it was apparent that Father Arrend was in no hurry to reveal the reason behind our invitation. Speaking of the history surrounding the secret society, he eventually divulged the he was the head of the Cavaliers of Stanford and insisted on our integrity in keeping the members of his association a secret.

"Will you swear on the Lord?" he said, abruptly.

Fulten lowered his head before signing the cross on his forehead. "May God be my witness, you have my word, Father," said Fulten.

Father Arrend glanced at me, awaiting my reply. "Yes, Father, I will not speak of the Cavaliers outside these walls."

Father Arrend turned and faced the stairwell leading to the church tower. Calling out, he ordered that the person that remained hidden step forward. Carre appeared, anxiously glaring over at me and Fulten. Another figure emerged from the foot of the tower; limping, he wore a tatty brown robe. His long grey hair was matted and rested over his shoulder.

Fulten gasped before walking forward to meet the frail old man. "My prayers have been answered; you live, Isaak."

Astonished, I remained voiceless, staring at the Baroness's father who stood before me alive. Greeting Fulten with a handshake, my mentor guided Isaak over towards me. Carre still appeared rather apprehensive as he looked upon our every move.

"You must be Jep, the one who guided my daughter to Whiten. Your determination has given me the courage to return," said Isaak.

"Lady Ivy was the one who remined determined, sir," I replied nervously.

Teary eyed, Isaak stuttered. "My dear daughter, how she is tormented by the wickedness placed on her by that monstrous man."

Carre uneasily scanned the church, insisting that we moved Isaak to the lock up. My over eagerness to learn the truth prompted me to pay little attention to the farmer's caution as I continued to push the conversation with Isaak.

"Now you have returned, we must know the truth about the Baron and the threat he poses to the town," I said enthusiastically.

"The Baron offers little threat to his people; the man is rotten, but not a traitor to the crown. On the day of my daughter's wedding, I retired from the banquet hall, keen to pray for forgiveness, for I knew I had handed my precious little girl into the arms of the devil. It was during this time I overheard the voices of two men, with which I was familiar. They toasted on the eve of the Baron's death; they conspired to have him found dead, slain in his bedchamber - and I was to be the suspect," relayed Isaak.

Fulten interrupted. "It makes little sense to exploit you as his killer."

Issak, abruptly replied, "It makes perfect sense; I despised the man who had groomed my child into marriage."

Demanding to know the identity of the voices Isaak had overheard that night, my question was disturbed by the sound of the church doors slamming shut. Startled, Fulten gripped the hilt of his sword;

however, on seeing the uninvited intruders, I felt immediate relief at the two familiar faces that glared back at me.

Ricard, the Baron's guard, stood smirking at our gathering, pleased by what he saw. His son, my dear friend Hota, was by his side; however, he appeared withdrawn as he peered over at us, expressionless. My initial calmness at the arrival of Ricard and Hota was short lived on seeing that my fellow Sword and best friend was armed with a crossbow and making no attempt to greet me. Hota's chilling stare brought me to realise that I was no longer in the company of companions; I was in a standoff with enemies.

25

CONFESSIONS AT THE

ALTAR

Hota looked over to his father, awaiting instructions. His usual confident manner had been sapped by his admiration and fascination over his father supremacy. Upon seeing the subtle nod from Ricard, Hota raised up his crossbow, pointing the wishbone at our gathering. His sunken eyes caused my stomach to grind, braced to discover who the arrow was intended for.

Time slowed as Hota squeezed the trigger to his crossbow which snapped back into his arm, releasing its arrow. Seeing my mentor's head jolt back, I felt dread on glancing down at Fulten to see the steel arrow impaled into his chest. Dropping to his knees, Fulten slummed back onto the church floor, leaving me to observe the colour draining from his face. Leaping down beside him, I felt disoriented, staring at the blood that began to seep out from the wound Hota had inflicted.

Clutching at my mentor's head, waves of despair filled my body on seeing more blood leak from the corner of his mouth; spluttering, Fulten attempted to speak, but his struggling for breath had impeded his speech. Yelling, I begged for him to look at me; I was helpless, watching his life begin to dwindle away. Catching his breath, he rested the palm of his hand against my cheek.

"Watching you grow has satisfied my desire for fatherhood," gulped Fulten.

My tears fell on his face as I pleaded with him to not leave me; his head tilted back in my arm and I knew he was gone. Grasping his head into my chest, I rocked, sobbing hysterically. My grief rapidly subsided and wrath began to flood my veins. Gritting my teeth, I got up to my feet, snarling as I eyed up Hota.

Marching towards him, I roared, pulling my sword from its scabbard. Hota had already reloaded another arrow into his crossbow and now aimed the wishbone directly at me. Engulfed by hatred and vengeance, I dismissed my disadvantage and my likelihood of a quick death was halted by Ricard, who had now rested his fingers on top of his son's weapon, denying Hota's opportunity to end my life. Ricard stepped out, shielding his son, shouting as he ordered my composure.

Raising his arms, he yelled, "Wait, do not be foolish." Stopping, I stared back at Ricard with wide eyes, giving him the chance to explain his son's cruel actions. "Fulten's sacrifice is truly tragic, but do not allow his death to be in vain."

"Why? Why Fulten? Damn you," I cried.

Poised, Ricard spoke with purpose. "This town is plagued with corruption and filth, all galvanized by the Baron himself. Take you, for instance; when you arrived you were dismissed, humiliated, all because of the rags you wore. But, display the right crest and you become respected and feared. Ask yourself, for those who do not strive, who will respect them? Not our Baron."

"It was you who plotted treachery against the Baron?" I asked.

"Look around you, Jep; this entire town is on the brink of revolting. The slaughter at the Baron's festival, the humiliation of the lady Ivy in the square - the people deserve better," Ricard insisted.

"What about Jen, Elis and Isaak - did they deserve better?" I argued.

"Their deaths were necessary; they knew too much and you were meddling beyond your means. You left Hota little choice but to silence the girl," said Ricard.

Scowling at Hota, I muttered, "You murdered Jen?"

"Like my father said, you gave me little choice; I did warn you of her loose tongue," replied Hota dismissively.

Glancing back at Isaak, he stood watching our altercations, trembling at Ricard's revelation. Asking what is to be the Baronesses fathers' fate, Ricard swore to me that he would allow all members of the Cavaliers passage upon my agreement to join his rebellion.

Discontented, I shook my head. "It all makes sense, the ambush at the river, the bowman at Edgar farm - it was you who led the Shadow crooks."

"I am the Shadow crooks, Jep; like you they are forgotten men and women all endeavouring to succeed in this spoilt land," replied Ricard.

Hota glared at me, scowling at my dismissal of his father's aspirations.

Looking back to him, I said; "You aligned yourself with Chenchi in order to infiltrate the Swords."

Sniggering, Hota replied, "Your obsession with Chenchi is exhausting; he knows nothing of our ideas, the man is as pitifully committed to the Swords as you are."

Peering back at Ricard I insisted on knowing if there was truth in Pip's accusations over Gil's involvement to overturn the Baron.

"Gil was difficult to tame, however he believed in our foresight," replied Ricard.

Spitting to the ground, I made my feelings to their visions known. Ricard sighed and glanced back to his son disappointedly, shrugging his shoulders. Contemptuously, he flicked his fingers towards me, giving the sign for Hota to put an end to my challenge. Hota's stern frown showed how unremorseful and empty he truly was. Staring back at him in disgust, it was the first time I had faced death and felt nothing but numbness.

Hota's finger began to squeeze the trigger to his crossbow; however, a large clatter against the locked church doors announced further interruptions. Flint's voice called from the other side of the doors; privy to the altercation inside, he yelled, demanding admittance. His persistent and repetitive banging of his fist against the wooden door began to alarm and worry both Ricard and his son.

Sniggering, I mocked Hota on seeing his usual calm and poised manner overcome by disgruntlement. Ricard peered over to the three members of the Cavaliers, before cunningly grinning back at me.

"It appears we are too late; this young, rage driven Sword has viciously murdered three upstanding members of this grand community, along with his dear mentor." Chillingly he looked at his son. "We have no choice, Hota; we must strike him down, before he has chance to continue on this treacherous and wicked act of terror."

Hota smirked over to his father, idolising his plan to portray me as the traitor. I had no choice to but engage both Ricard and his son. Thrashing my sword upwards, Hota groaned as my sword sliced into his forearm, causing him to drop the crossbow amongst the pews. Ricard recklessly charged towards me, enraged with anger at my attack on his son. Stepping forward I raised my boot, kicking him hard into the stomach, forcing him to stumble back into the benches behind him.

Yelling, I called out to Flint, declaring that I was under attack. Ricard knew that he would face a more gruelling challenge against two Blue Swords. Briefly glancing over to Hota's wound, he commanded him to engage me in combat, whilst he reinforced the church doors. Without hesitation, Hota jumped to his feet, growling, pulling his sword loose.

Giving him little time to react, I sprinted forward and furiously hacked my sword down towards him. Struggling to hold back my attack, I could see the dread in his eyes as the wound on his arm had weakened his ability to defend each one of my vengeful blows. Ricard was quick to notice his son straining; he abandoned his attempt to barricade the doors and raced forward to aid Hota.

Deserting my attack, it was me who was now on the back foot, battling to defend Ricard's rapid and skilled combination of strikes. The precise and elegant manner in the way he handled his blade was far too creative for my own ability. Edging back down the aisle, Ricard was relentless in his assault. Father Arrend, Isaak and Carre had now disbursed from the altar, keen to avoid our enemy's sword. Struggling to hold off Ricard, I now noticed Hota was stalking me from behind his father.

Stumbling back against the steps leading up to the altar, I was grounded and moments away from death. Unbeknown to me, Carre had unlocked the church doors and Detector Flint was now tearing towards us, with his sword drawn. Coming to a halt, Flint glared down towards Fulten, noticing the arrow imbedded in his chest. Furiously, he looked at Hota to whom he was standing the closest to it.

Pointing his sword towards our dead tutor, he shouted; "Who slayed him?"

Before I was able to answer, Father Arrend called out to Flint, stuttering as he revealed Fulten's killer.

Ricard raised his sword, prepped to deliver my fatal blow. Flint reacted swiftly, yelling to Ricard and catching his attention, only to see his son now at the mercy of Flint's blade. Ricard looked on in horror, as the tip of Flint's sword now rested against his son's throat.

A composed Flint said, "Yield, or I will spill his blood."

Ricard briefly paused before leaping towards Father Arrend and pulling him into his body. Laying the steel of his sword against the priest's throat, we found ourselves in a further standoff. Father Arrend trembled, only to be hushed by Ricard, who had become flustered from the lack of control. Taking a moment to mull over his options, he sullenly looked over to his son.

"Take my son outside and lock the doors on your return," insisted Ricard.

"No father, I will not abandon you," pleaded Hota, desperately staring at Ricard.

"Silence!" shouted Ricard, "You will flee and unite with the Shadow crooks; my apprehending will not be for nothing."

Mumbling, Hota made a second plea to his father; however, Ricard dismissed his son's loyalty as weakness. Negotiating with Flint, Ricard swore to release the priest, should the detector return without blood on his sword. Flint had no choice but to oblige. Hota glared back at me, scowling, before being escorted out by the tip of Flint's blade.

Flint did as request and on returning, proceeded to lock the church doors. A disgruntled Hota banged against the wood several times before going silent.

Pushing Father Arrend aside, he smirked over to me and Flint. "Offspring; they never appreciate the love of a father."

Flint called over to Ricard on seeing him raising his sword. "You had no intention of being taken captive."

"This town is already overrun with too many Blue Swords; I must ensure that at least one of you will join your mentor," he replied, chillingly.

Flint glanced at me, uneased by Ricard's unwillingness to submit to our numerical advantage. Stepping closer to me, Flint insisted that we take the experienced guard together. Foolishly, I chose to ignore Flint's advice and allowed my anger to cloud my own judgment. Dashing forward, my uncontrolled thrust with my sword caused Ricard little trouble as he ducked away from my attack.

Having no time to swing his blade back at me due to Flint's pending attack, Ricard jabbed the hilt of his sword into my face, causing my nose to crunch. My watering eyes left me disorientated and stumbling back. Flint attempted to swipe at Ricard from the other side; however, the senior guard's ability made light work of blocking the detector's blow and allowed him to deliver an accurate counterattack.

Wiping my eyes, I attempted to regain composure, observing Flint and Ricard engaging one another in a medley of attacks. Carre yelled, urging me to participate and aid my struggling comrade. The black dots from my eyes hindered my vison and I remained dazed by the Shadow crook's blow.

Flint had been outmatched by Ricard's ability and was now battling to defend each of his opponent's strikes. His body was wedged against the arm of one of the church pews, leaving him desperately trying to fend off Ricard's relentless and savage assaults. Staggering forward I limped, bloodied, and disorientated to save my fellow Sword.

Panting and exhausted, Flint made one last attempt to hold up his sword. Ricard pulled back his blade, lining its tip down at Flint, prepping his finishing blow. Roaring, I drove my sword into Ricard's back, thrusting the steel forward, until it penetrated through his body and out of his chest. Pulling back my blood-soaked blade, I staggered back, observing Ricard gasping for breath as he turned his body to face me.

Frowning, Ricard gently shook his head at me in disbelief. Clutching at the open wound on his chest, the blood seeped between his fingertips.

"Coward's way to kill a man," he croaked.

Gurning, Ricard reached out to balance himself on the nearest pew. Unable to hold himself up, he crashed onto the ground. I glanced down at his corpse, scowling.

Flint sighed. "It was not a coward's way; it was a shrewd way. The man was ruthless."

Looking across to Fulten's body at the far end of the aisle, our victory was tinged by sadness. Father Arrend stood over my tutor; wiping away his own tears, he started to pray.

Flint rested his hand on my back. "We will honour him." Glancing back to Carre, Flint said, "You will attend the lock up and request their attendance."

Kneeling beside my fallen mentor, I gently stroked his forehead. The consequence of learning the truth had cost Fulten his life and had left me broken at the loss of a dear friend and father figure.

26

LIVING FOR THE

SWORD

Father Arrend and Isaak stood on the altar, talking amongst each other, bewildered by the evening's events. The wicked truth was not only had I lost my cherished mentor, but his life was snatched away by Hota, a man I valued as a friend and companion. Mulling over his treachery, I felt hatred and thirst for revenge. His escape had meant he had got away and was free to wander the land unpunished for the murders of Fulten and of Jen.

Lev rushed into the church, demanding to see Fulten. Glancing over at his covered body, Lev became teary eyed.

Pointing his finger at me, furiously he said: "Why didn't you inform us of your plans? You should never have come alone."

Flint approached Lev, gently replying. "Fulten insisted on Jep not exposing the plan; I feel your grief, but the blame only goes to the one that gutlessly executed him."

"Where is that double crossing whore's son, Hota? I will take his head," called Lev.

Fawkes entered the church in company with the governor; on seeing Lev's reaction my stomach knotted with apprehension at how they would react to Fulten's death. Fawkes paid no attention to anyone as he strutted up the aisle towards Fulten's corpse. Kneeling beside his fellow Sword, Fawkes gently touched Fulten's head.

Gazing down at his companion, he muttered: "Rest well, my friend."

The governor faced me; peering at the dried blood and disfigurement on my face, glancing around the church, he observed the aftermath of our clash with Hota and Ricard.

"This investigation has unearthed hell and taken many fine lives, yet the truth has been uncovered." Frowning, he addressed the room. "We have lost the most noble Sword ever to have displayed our crest; Fulten will look down upon us, proud of the circumstances of his death."

Before walking out, he insisted on returning Isaak to the Grand Hall himself and ordered us to remove Fulten's corpse.

Father Arrend called: "What of Ricard's body?"

The governor snarled, squinting down at the dead guard. "Dispose as you will, my advice is leave him for the crows."

Isaak came to a halt before leaving the church with the governor; turning to face me he smiled. "I am sorry that my predicament has caused you so much sorrow. Your bravery and determination will never be forgotten. Now I understand why my daughter has grown so fond of you."

Ignoring the governor's disapproving expression, I said: "Lady Ivy, she is a gracious Baroness."

Sniggering, Isaak replied. "I have learnt the rumours and I know my daughter. I wish you peace, Jep."

Once back at the lock up, I entered the stables to find Fawkes stood by Fulten's horse. On seeing me arrive, Fawkes glanced down at the ground behind him, before reminiscing about Fulten's love for his horse. I became insistent on apologising for not being capable of saving the beloved Blue Sword.

Sighing, Fawkes turned to face me. "You will honour his memory in how you serve. Besides, I am not the one to whom you owe an apology."

Fawkes nodded his head, pointing behind where I stood. Turning around, Chenchi was glaring at back me. Leaving us to speak, Fawkes walked away from the stables.

Sour faced, Chenchi offered me no sympathy, before relaying the governor's demand to speak with me.

"Will you ever forgive my accusations?" I asked.

Sniggering, Chenchi replied. "It was to be expected, coming from an uneducated peasant." We both chuckled at his poor attempt at humour. "Now that Hota is running with his pants down, I suppose I will have to tolerate you; also, my barracks are riddled with mice. I hate mice."

Watching Chenchi cross the courtyard, I felt relieved at his understanding and pleased at our consolidation. If I were to avenge the death of Fulten and Jen, I would need the formidable warrior by my side.

My summons from the governor was not unexpected. Standing outside the governor's chambers, I exhaled before knocking on his door. Being called in, Flint stood, leaning against the wall behind where the governor sat.

Eyeballing me with his ferocious stare, the governor rested back in his chair before summarising. "Flint has relayed your findings; so Hota planned treason against the Baron? All led by two of Asher's most valued assets. It seems your first investigation has turned out to be rather momentous. At least the Baron will remain hidden for some time, whilst he licks his wounds."

"What about Hota?" I asked.

Flint stood upright, placing his hands onto the governor's table. "Hota will be located and his head will roll for his crimes. As for you, Jep, I have requested you attend the city; I wish to enrol you as my student so that someday you may become a detector."

The governor rolled his eyes, unimpressed by Flint's prestigious invite. Glancing back at the governor, I paused, before declining the detector's offer.

"I am not ready, there is much to be learnt here and I wish to stay and help replenish our dwindling numbers."

It was the first time I had ever seen a hint of a smirk from the governor's mouth, which confirmed in my mind I had made the right decision.

It was dawn and the rain clattered down, leaking through the straw of my quarters; peering over to Hota's empty bed, I pictured his treacherous and murderous image, as I began to wonder what fate had in store for him. Preparing my uniform, I felt saddened at the thought of burying Fulten this day. Picturing his approving glance as he inspected my attire each morning caused my eyes to well up with tears.

Entering the parade room, all the Swords including Flint were already present. The mood matched the weather, grey and sombre. Little words were spoken, until Father Arrend arrived and informed us that Fulten was ready to be taken to the church. Walking out the front of the lock up, Fulten's body had been placed on a cart; he was surrounded by petals, with his sword resting across his chest. Flowers decorated the wagon giving off a vibrant and pleasant aroma. The procession was led by Father Arrend and accompanied by some volunteering townsfolk, who had wished to be involved in the proceedings.

Locals lined the square, lowering their heads as we passed. Walking behind the wagon with my companions, I did not take my eyes off my beloved tutor. Arriving at the church, no pews had been left unoccupied as the people of Stanford sat crammed inside, all keen to celebrate the life of their much-admired guardian.

Taking my seat at the front of the church, I peered down at the spot in the aisle where Fulten had fallen; the floor was now clear of the blood spilt from the previous day. Lady Ivy sat on the next bench along. Reunited with her father, she clutched onto Isaak's arm, her scarf covering the markings imposed on her by the Baron.

Father Arrend stood before the congregation, dressed in a glimmering white robe. Raising his hand, he silenced the musicians that played behind him on the altar. Opening the service with a prayer, he continued relaying a dedication to Fulten, before inviting the governor up to the pulpit.

Glaring around the room, the governor's reserved tone was perfect for masking his sorrow.

"We pay tribute to a Sword who fell whilst sheltering the people of Stanford from evil and treachery. Sword Fulten served with decency and empathy; his death comes as a great loss to us all." Pausing, the governor gulped before clearing his throat. "Not only have I lost a brother of our great crest, but I have lost a dear friend. May his memory flourish and his name not die, for the honourable Fulten truly did live for the Swords."

Whimpers could be heard from around the church; sobbing locals had become touched by the governor's sincere words. Fulten was a hero and a true inspiration to what it meant to be a Blue Sword. Leaving the church, I glanced over to Lady Ivy who was also shedding a tear for my fallen tutor. Noticing the Baron's absence, I was hardly surprised he was too ashamed to show his face.

Outside in the graveyard I watched as Fulten's body was lowered into the ground; I felt a further wave of sadness on seeing his lifeless body for the last time. His immaculately presented tunic and the petals that framed his body were truly fitting with his character. Muttering in prayer, I said my final farewell to Sword Fulten.

Back at the lock up, a feast had been prepared in Fulten's name. Donations of meat and ale had all been left by local traders, allowing them to pay their respects. The luxury food failed to lift our spirits as we ate in silence, all subdued in the gloomy atmosphere. Chenchi entered from the combat room. "Lady Ivy seeks an audience with you; she awaits you in the greeting room."

"Jep, if you are caught mounting the Baroness, do not think Fawkes will save you again," said Lev, lightening the mood and generating laughter from my fellow Swords. Even Sergeant Hock was able to crack a grin at Lev's much needed humour.

Pulling back the eroding iron door, I felt flustered on seeing the Baroness gazing back at me. It was even more appeasing to learn that she was alone. Ivy's beauty outshone the bruises left on her skin from the wicked Baron. Still dressed in an elegant black robe from Fulten's service, Ivy had removed her head scarf, allowing me to glance at her angelic features.

Gauging one another's mood, our intense looking at each other harboured the prolonged silence.

Ivy broke our stillness; "I wish to offer my gratitude and acknowledgement of your bravery in saving my father. I will mourn Fulten for many days to come. "

"Is that really why you are here, to thank me?" I replied, gently.

Ivy appeared uneasy as she cupped her hands together and began glancing around, unwilling to make eye contact with me. "I come because I want you to know, there isn't a moment that goes by where I don't see your face mirroring my affection for you. I deserve these markings, for I have committed the most horrendous of all crimes, that is to have fallen in love with you."

Moving closer towards me, Lady Ivy leaned her head up, pressing her lips on to my mouth. Unaffected by the potential of our intimacy being witnessed, we kissed, before Ivy gently pulled her head back, smiling and this time appearing unremorseful. Delicately, she placed her fingers onto my bottom lip.

"How cruel it will be to observe you and know that I have no right to you," Ivy stuttered.

Softly, I replied. "I will always be here for you, my lady."

Opening the door to the lock up, the Baroness called to her guard, indicating she was ready to be escorted back to the Grand Hall. Seeing her leave, I felt comfort in knowing that she was reunited with father, and I genuinely believed that our story was far from over.

Lev's earlier humour had clearly lifted the morale within the parade room; hearing jeers and laughter, I was keen to see what was causing all the commotion. Blair, the energetic young servant girl, stood in front of Chenchi, challenging him to a duel. Waving a wooden sword taken from the combat room, Blair playfully taunted the man mountain, keen to get him to engage her in combat. Chenchi frowned back at the girl, more enthused by sipping back the ale from his beaker than entertaining the boisterous child.

Fawkes sat back, grinning at Blair like a proud father. Seeing his unconditional love for the girl was warming. Lev was quick to turn his attention onto me.

"Stand fast, men, here comes our lustful wanderer. I fear the Baroness may not be contented by your swiftness," mocked Lev.

Fits of laughter broke out amongst the Swords, leaving Blair looking rather bewildered at Lev's satire.

Sergeant Hock removed his smirk on seeing the governor enter the room. Peering at the ale that lined the banquet table, the governor shook his head. Unravelling a scroll in his hand, he began to hammer a nail into the top of the document.

Glaring back at us, sternly he said, "I want the bastard in by winter."

Lev nodded his head at Fawkes, clearly already knowing the contents on the scroll. Approaching the wall, I began to read the writing.

Wanted, missing: HOTA GILBERT LEVERSON, Murder, Treason.

Chenchi was stood behind me, guzzling down his ale. I glanced back at him, keen to see his reaction to the sign.

Necking his drink, he belched and gripped my shoulder. "We best go find the turd," he said firmly.

"Together?" I replied.

Chenchi smirked. "Yeah, together, we will drag him back at the end of a rope."

Reconciling with Chenchi, he enhanced my eagerness to locate Hota. I would endeavour to avenge the deaths of Jen and my tutor, Fulten. Hota would be brought to justice, in the name of the Blue Swords.

ABOUT THE AUTHOR

James Horton left his hometown in rural Lincolnshire to join the police service in London at the age of nineteen. Serving as a police officer in several units, James has had his eyes opened to the highs and lows that comes with serving as a constable.

Suffering a stroke at the age of twenty-seven, James turned to historic action novels to help settle his mind and aid his recovery.

After his recovery, James decided to start writing his own novel, combining a career in the police and his passion of medieval stories. His first book, *BLUE SWORDS*, the first of *The Crimes and Crests Saga* has been based on true events, merged with a historic twist.

Available worldwide online and from all good bookstores

---

www.mtp.agency

www.facebook.com/mtp.agency

@mtp_agency

Michael Terence
Publishing